Nicholas Blincoe

Nicholas Blincoe is the author of three previous novels, including the modern classic *Acid Casuals* and the award-winning bestseller *Manchester Slingback*. He was born in Rochdale and after detours through welding, van driving and art college went to Warwick University where he completed a PhD in contemporary European philosophy. As we ~~~~~~~~~~~~~~~~ s a critic, screenwriter, journalist and ~~~~~~~~~~~~~~~~~~~ taken seriously as a model.

Also by Nicholas Blincoe

Acid Casuals
Jello Salad
Manchester Slingback

THE DOPE PRIEST

PRIEST

Nicholas Blincoe

SCEPTRE

Copyright © 1999 Nicholas Blincoe

First published in 1999 by Hodder and Stoughton
A division of Hodder Headline
A Sceptre Paperback

10 9 8 7 6 5 4 3 2 1

British Library C.I.P.
A CIP Catalogue record for this title
is available from the British Library

ISBN 0340 75045 6

Typeset by Palimpsest Book Production Limited,
Polmont, Stirlingshire
Printed and bound in Great Britain by
Mackays of Chatham PLC, Chatham, Kent

Hodder and Stoughton
A division of Hodder Headline
338 Euston Road
London NW1 3BH

For Leila Sansour

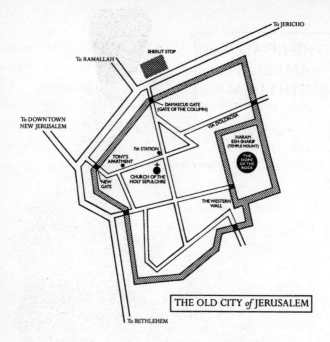

THE OLD CITY of JERUSALEM

To JERICHO

To RAMALLAH

SHERUT STOP

DAMASCUS GATE
(GATE OF THE COLUMN)

VIA DOLOROSA

To DOWNTOWN
NEW JERUSALEM

HARAM
ESH-SHARIF
(TEMPLE MOUNT)

7th STATION

THE
DOME
OF THE
ROCK

TONY'S
APARTMENT

NEW
GATE

CHURCH OF THE
HOLY SEPULCHRE

THE WESTERN
WALL

To BETHLEHEM

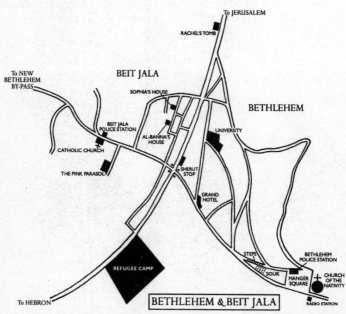

BETHLEHEM & BEIT JALA

To JERUSALEM

RACHEL'S TOMB

BEIT JALA

To NEW
BETHLEHEM
BY-PASS

SOPHIA'S HOUSE

BETHLEHEM

BEIT JALA
POLICE STATION

UNIVERSITY

AL-BANNA'S
HOUSE

CATHOLIC CHURCH

THE PINK PARASOL

SHERUT
STOP

GRAND
HOTEL

REFUGEE CAMP

STEPS

SOUK

BETHLEHEM
POLICE STATION

MANGER
SQUARE

CHURCH
OF THE
NATIVITY

To HEBRON

RADIO STATION

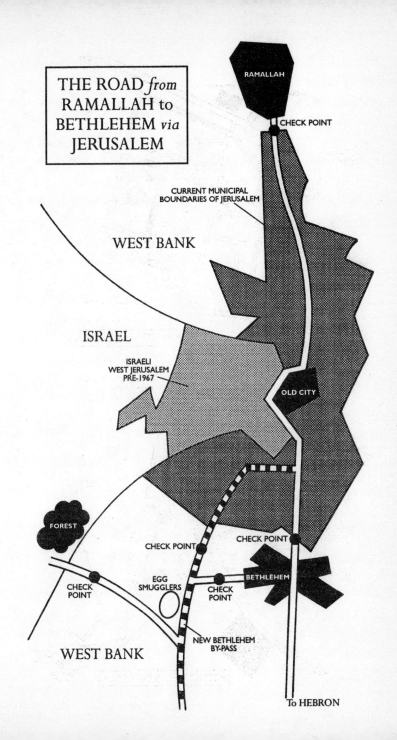

1

David was thinking, if he ever got another life, maybe he could make it as an urban perfume artist: aim for the liberation of London and deodorise it for the people. Today, the exhaust fumes were so thick and heavy he could taste the lead in his mouth. And still he'd managed to save one small corner of Mayfair, midway between two flower-beds in the gardens behind Farm Street Jesuit Church. He was taking it easy as he separated and savoured the different smells: the high and low floral notes and the final touch, the honey-wood scent of hashish from the joint between his fingers. David took another drag. Believe it: another reality, he could have been a *guerilla parfumeur*, like a kind of graffiti artist, only much much slower. Instead he chose to be an international dope-smuggling man, trying not to worry about the one half of his consignment that was sitting in a garage in Deptford, or the other half that was trapped in Lebanon and surrounded by the Israeli army.

Or that he was about to get married in less than forty minutes, but who was counting.

David's partner and friend, Tony Khouri, was crouched by his Mercedes in Carlos Place, twenty feet away on the other side of the park railings. He had one hand wrapped around his car phone, the other holding his grey top hat. David picked himself up off the grass, walked to the railings and shouted, 'Any luck?'

Tony didn't say a word. He just grunted, shouldered his way through the car door and slammed the phone back into its cradle. At a guess, there was still no progress in the Lebanon.

David waited for Tony to push through the park gates before he said, 'So what's the weather like in Beirut?'

'Raining.'

'Yeah?'

'Yeah. Mostly phosphorous shells with some cluster bombs.'

David tried to blow a smoke ring that said, *Touché*. He watched it drift away across the park towards the church, flimsy and blue but undeniably eloquent. He didn't bother asking any more questions; if there was any good news, Tony would tell him. It was now August and since the end of June they had been hoping that the remains of the Palestinian army would be allowed to ship out of Beirut. If they were, there ought to be a way to smuggle the remaining dope out with them. For the past six weeks, people had been telling them that an agreement was close but so far there was no agreed date. Anyway, Tony Khouri was upset by more than just the Beirut problem.

David said, 'You know, I don't mind keep apologising but you've got to stop sulking some time.'

'I'm not sulking, my friend. I never was sulking.'

'I told you I don't know how it happened. I was stoned, somehow I asked her brother to be my best man.'

'Yes, so? He's just a kid but it's fine with me. You didn't

spend the best part of ten years with him, through good and bad times. But so what? That's all I'm saying. Me and you, I thought we were brothers.' Tony shrugged, and not subtly. He had a way of doing it, rolling his huge shoulders and lifting his big slab hands to put every square pound of pressure into the gesture. 'But what I think, whatever you say, your future brother-in-law is suspect.'

'Come on, Tony. Are we still arguing about the colour of his hair and that fluorescent cummerbund he's wearing?'

'It's not just the clothes. There's also the make-up.'

David groaned. He'd already tried to explain the New Romantic thing to Tony and he wasn't going through it again. They both knew the real reason Tony was offended and it had nothing to do with teenage fashion. When Tony got married three years ago, he asked David to be his best man. Never mind that David was waiting on a deal at the time and, one thing leading to another, he missed the ceremony by three weeks. Tony expected the invitation to be reciprocated and passing him over now looked like a deliberate snub. David couldn't win – his only strategy was to keep distracting Tony, hope to take his mind off it. He scooped his top hat off the grass and spent a moment arranging it on his head, as though his only worry was finding just the right angle, then said: 'I tell you who does like dressing up.'

'What?' Tony gave him the heavy-lidded look, waiting as David stuck the joint back into his mouth. 'Who are we talking about here?'

'If I tell you, you have to promise not to get bigoted on me.' David kept the joint in his mouth, hoping to clamp down on his giggles. He counted a few beats, holding the smoke in his mouth. And exhaled. 'Okay. Okay. It's the priest, man.'

3

Tony popped a grin. That was it, he was laughing, saying: 'I'm no bigot, my friend. I grew up in Bethlehem, I've seen every kind of priest under the sun. I'm the one who could tell you stories.'

They were good friends, no point in being over-sensitive. It was just the occasion, the wedding and the other assorted factors. Sometimes it was hard keeping a perspective. Which was why David was on his sixth joint since breakfast.

'Here, Tony. You want a blast on this?'

He held the joint over, but Tony just shook his head.

'No. Your mother might see me.'

'What?'

'Your mother and father. They're gonna be here soon.'

'I know. I invited them.'

'I don't want to lose their respect. What do you think they'd think, they see me smoking drugs.'

'You just smuggled two tons of drugs into their country.'

Tony threw another shrug. 'They don't know about that, though, do they?'

David shook his head. No, they didn't. They knew he and Tony were business partners but they thought it was something to do with language schools. They loved that, the idea that he was both an intellectual and an entrepreneur. Though they did once ask why the language schools were all in the Lebanon. Ever since he served six months in prison on a dope charge, he was never wholly clear of suspicion with his folks.

There were two entrances to Farm Street Jesuit Church. The main one, on Farm Street, which had the big stained-glass window above an ornately carved archway. Then a smaller one at the back, opening on to the gardens by Carlos Place.

David knew it was time he headed for the front door and kept an eye out for the guests. He preferred to skulk out the back.

Tony nudged him. 'Your friend.'

He was pointing over to the Babbage kid, stepping out of the back door in a bright sash cummerbund. The sash was eye-catching, but even if David hadn't looked he could have guessed Tony was talking about his future brother-in-law, the way he put a twist on the word *friend*.

'Try and at least act cool, you towel-head motherfucker.'

Tony laughed. The first time they heard the term, *towel-head*, they were in Beirut. An American was getting worked up over something, probably the Iranian hostage situation because it would have been just about that time. Which just goes to prove that Americans can't distinguish between Persians and Arabs — or at least, this particular one couldn't. David and Tony were entertaining a group of Lebanese politicians over a drink in the bar of the Hilton or some other skyscraper hotel, when the guy stood up and just launched wholesale into a piece of John Wayne-style braggadocio. The whole room went silent, everyone turning to look at this bright-faced Yank. Then they began laughing.

Like Tony was laughing now, a big whoop. 'You crummy English dog.' And then he was waving at Marcus Babbage, 'Yoo-hoo, how you doing?' Using that same camp twist again.

Marcus was smiling too, but when David made to pass the joint over he started making a *Stop* sign with his hand, even mouthing the word. At first David thought it must be his parents, coming up a step behind him. But it was just Father Charles Standish.

Marcus turned to the priest, saying: 'Last-minute nerves, I'm afraid. Maybe we should leave him to suck up the fresh air.'

Father Standish said, 'It's the robes, dear boy. Strike the fear of God, as we say.' Then he turned his dentured smile on David. 'Plenty of time, Mr Ramsbottom. Plenty of time.'

The way the priest pronounced David's surname, he made it seem like a private joke between himself and Marcus Babbage. David turned sharply and caught Marcus choking back a giggle, as though *Babbage* was so suave it could never raise a laugh.

David said, 'I'm ready. Let's get moving.'

David flicked his joint to the ground and followed the priest down the marble-lined corridor and through to the main body of the church. David was thankful for one thing – after today he would never see Father Charles again. The man was maybe seventy-five but seemed both too tart and too brittle for that age. When David first met him, he assumed he was senile, listening as the priest tried to sell the Church's line on birth control. For instance, reason #1: the idea that the more children you had, the less devastated you would be by the untimely death of one. A hit-and-run incident, perhaps. Or, moving on to #2, because Vivaldi was the youngest of seventeen children, you could never predict which of your progeny might be a genius so it made sense just to keep on producing. Listening to him, even Annabella was surprised, and she was a genuine Catholic. In Father Charles's defence, he didn't seem absolutely convinced by either of the two arguments. He advanced them in a half-whisper and finished by fluttering his hand, as though he could waft the words away – there was no reason to linger over the logic. The hands, like his body, had a cold-pressed limpness. David had to say, the priest seemed much friskier since he'd met Marcus Babbage.

Father Charles teetered along, hanging left into the nave and then right for the aisle. He walked as though he was strutting on spike heels but hadn't quite got used to them. Though now David knew he was only being malicious. It wasn't the priest's fault that he needed instruction before he got the go-ahead for a Catholic wedding. It was the rules, David being C of E. At least, he wrote C of E in the relevant box whenever he filled in a form. There was a time when he had written *None*, only to stop while he was in prison in case it seemed too ostentatious or counter-culture. Likewise, he never wrote 'Buddhist' – anything which made him seem like a *head* , that was just begging for trouble. Ten years ago, when David went on his first trip abroad, he'd put Buddhist on a form and ended up being strip-searched by one of the customs cops.

Marcus caught up with him, halfway along the aisle. He asked, 'Are you ready to meet your people?'

'Who's here?'

'A crowd of grisly Northerners. I assumed they were your relatives and told them they were a week early – they climbed back aboard the charabanc.'

'Any of your family?'

'A sprinkling.'

Tony Khouri said, 'What about mine?'

Both David and Marcus turned to look at him.

Tony said, 'What's the problem? I've got some relatives in town. I'm supposed to abandon them because I'm at a stiffy English wedding?'

Marcus Babbage was right, the charabanc was in town. David could already see his Granny Taylor, stalking through the crowd to see if anyone had followed her big fashion idea. She was wearing a pastel-coloured powder-puff hat, worn so low that the pointed tips of her bifocals seemed to prod out of the fur. Her new dress seemed unremarkable, what David could see of it beneath her tartan poncho.

He caught up with her, folding her into his arms for a kiss. She lifted herself up and squeezed back. It always made him feel like a little kid. Exactly like a little kid because the prickle of her face powder in his nose always whisked him away on some kind of pre-school trip.

He asked, 'Have you seen Mum and Dad?'

She pointed across the crowd gathered around the church steps. 'Well, your dad's over there, sniffing round that Mrs Cabbage.'

David was about to say 'Babbage. The name is Babbage'. But she was already on to another subject. She threw a corner of her tartan poncho up and over her shoulder, exposing a handbag embroidered with gold beads and hung on a chain. She pulled out a thick roll of bank-notes, held them tight for a moment before pressing them on David. 'My wedding present.'

'Gran. No.' He was shaking his head. She should know he had money, he bragged about it often enough.

'Take it.'

He nodded, breaking into a smile as he bent down for another kiss. It wasn't worth the anxiety. If he found out she couldn't afford it, he could always smuggle it back into her house. That had to be within his capabilities. Easier than working out what to do with the two tons of Lebanese hashish already in London or the missing two tons, stranded in a war zone.

Someone slapped him on the back. His worst nightmare, it was his older sister.

'You know, you're pathetic, you are. Trying to get round Annabella's family by asking the brother to be your best man, and keeping him on board by keeping him stoned. You know there's a law against corrupting minors.'

'Come on, Karen. Marcus isn't exactly a child.'

'No. But Annabella is. And what are you: dirty thirty, ex-jailbird and all-round seedy guy.'

'Seedy? I'm rolling in dough. I'm about to marry a fucking aristocrat-type.'

'You throw cash around like a pools winner and you're marrying a nineteen-year-old. Very classy.'

'Please, Karen.'

'You want me to go? I'll go.'

He watched her turn and trot away, knowing she wouldn't go far after putting so much thought into her wedding-day outfit. The dominant motif was high-sheen, her jacket and matching pencil skirt came in a high-gloss satin that just radiated light. He could feel the damage on his retina, but he was especially light-sensitive. At least he had proof that all the dope he'd smoked was working. Everything was flaring up around him but so far nothing had ignited his blue touch-paper. He only hoped his calm lasted through the reception. He knew it would get worse, once his female relatives hit the Malibu. If any of them turned on Annabella, he could see the beginnings of a life-threatening tantrum . . .

Tony Khouri walked up. 'What's the matter?'

'My sister giving me a whoosh of paranoia. I tell you, this wedding, it's fucking with my antennae.' He'd been feeling unbalanced all day. And it was so out of character: that impending-doom vibe. The sooner this was over, the better. 'Come on, Tony. Let's grab our seats. I've got us ringside seats, front row.'

Farm Street Church wasn't big. It just about snuggled between the narrow street and the garden behind. But it was well proportioned and the interior was fairly restrained, at least by Catholic standards. It was done-out in the Victorian version of medieval chic, but inclined towards the Arts and Crafts-style rather than heavy-duty Gothic. More like *Liberty's* department store than Manchester Town Hall. Today it was filled with music and scent: a female soprano singing in the gallery and the ends of the pews dripping with white lilies. It could make you warm to Jesuits. Though the charm really belonged to another time – back when the priest was a bright young convert.

There was still no sign of Father Charles but that was okay, there was no sign of Annabella either. David didn't want to keep checking his watch, that was the best man's job. He looked anyway, she was already twenty minutes late. The choir were doing their best to fill the time, especially the soprano, but they were only the support. Everyone was waiting on the main act.

Tony was sat on the other side of Marcus. Now he leant over, slapping David on the knee. His voice echoing round the whole church as he said, 'It looks like she stood you up, my friend.'

David nodded, *yeah yeah yeah*. Just keep a lid on it, you loud-mouthed bastard. But he didn't have to say anything. He just shot Tony a sidelong look and that seemed to be enough.

Tony said, 'Sorry. I have an idea. What if I go and stand in the street and keep a lookout?'

'It doesn't mean she'll get here any faster.'

'No, but . . .' Tony shrugged. He wasn't going to lie. He used body language instead to suggest there might be a way to speed things along. And if there was, he would look into it, push and cajole, whatever it took.

David said, 'Go on, then. It'll make me feel better, probably.'

'That's what I'm saying.' Tony grinned and rolled to his feet. Rather than take the side route, around the edge of the church, he headed right back down the central aisle. David could even hear him booming out, 'Hello, Mrs Ramsbottom. That is a beautiful hat.'

David looked back over his shoulder to see Tony sweet-talking his mum. She was smiling all over her face, drinking in Tony's brown velvet eyes and firm, slightly bruised-looking lips. Like this was Omar Sharif's stockier younger brother. David found himself on the verge of groaning but managed to switch into a hum. He matched the tune the choir were singing, if not the words. They seemed to favour Italian songs.

Marcus Babbage was leaning forward. 'You're relaxed?'

David nodded. 'What can I do? The bride's supposed to keep us waiting.'

'I know. I know. So why am I so bloody nervous?'

'If you want, go have a look as well.'

Marcus turned his head towards the doors, as though he was weighing it up. David glanced across to the vestry. Father Charles was peering out, throwing one of those questioning looks. David tried to mime *No-Fucking-Clue* with his eyebrows. The old guy must have got it because he nodded and disappeared again.

Looking back over his shoulder, David tried to find Tony.

He was gone but Karen was there, running at full pelt in her tight skirt and white heels. There had to be some news. David knew it was bad even before she skidded up, tearing a clump of lilies off the side of the pew as she tried to stop.

'There's a roadblock.'

'What?'

'A roadblock.' She was gasping, but her eyes were direct, telling him he was about to get everyone into trouble.

'Is it the cops?'

Marcus Babbage was shaking his head like something had possessed it, he just wasn't quite sure what. 'Oh fuck, man. The fucking pigs.'

David was looking back up the aisle. He guessed Tony had already run, there was no point following him out of the front of the church. That left the back door and the gardens . . . but then what? He couldn't tunnel out of trouble. They would just pick him up on the other side of the gardens.

David slapped his head. 'Of course there's a roadblock. I forgot, they're shooting a big film in Grosvenor Square today. That's it.' He gave Marcus a grin before adding, 'Re-creating the riot outside the American embassy . . . you know, Vietnam.'

Marcus had been so tense he grabbed hold of the idea that this was only a film and seemed to deflate with relief.

Karen said, 'How do you know about this?' The implication: how do you know but no one else has even heard of it?

David said, 'Father Charles told me. In fact, maybe I'd better go have a word with him, see if he thinks Annabella's car will get through safely.'

He stood and smiled, looking over to his family, the left-hand section of the congregation. Then to Annabella's, on the right. Somehow the differences seemed to have been softened. There was the same mix of weird hats, a sprinkling of florid faces among the older men, the odd hair styles among the youngest kids. And all of them staring up at him, their eyes asking: *What's wrong?*

David widened his smile until it hurt and gave a relaxed wave. The choir was beginning 'Jerusalem', the first number to have English lyrics. David recognised the intro and got in on the same beat as the soprano, his voice even louder than hers.

'And did these feet . . .'

He had a strong voice, and if it was a little rough across the top, there was something beautiful about it a layer or two further down.

'In ainsh-er-hunt times . . .'

His only fault, he tended to over-croon and over-emote; always stuck in the lounge bar when he could be climbing for the stars. But he knew how to work a crowd.

'And did thee ho-ly lamm-a God . . .'

He threw in a bit of footwork, a sidestep and a twirl. Half the congregation were laughing, the rest were smirking. Everyone looked relieved, the groom was happy, everything was under control.

David waved again and pointed to his left. He was just going to have a word with the priest. *Back in five.*

He walked as steadily as he could towards the little door to the side of the altar and the narrow corridor beyond. If he carried straight on, he would end up inside the house where all the priests lived together. The door off to the side, that led to the vestry. As David put his hand on the door, he could hear the strangest sounds coming from the inside.

Father Charles was stood in front of a mirror. At a guess, he was doing voice exercises.

'La la la la – Hah hah hah hah – oh oh oh.'

The priest turned slightly as David's reflection passed across the mirror. Then he went down, clocked to the chin with a strong right. David took a breath, running a thumb over his knuckles to check that he hadn't broken one. He had hit the priest so hard. The way the old man crumpled, he could almost have turned to smoke and spirit, leaving his empty robes to fall like a pile of washing. For a moment, David was scared he'd killed the man.

David was almost through undressing Father Charles when his sister appeared at the door.

She said, 'I want you to promise: never get in touch with us ever again. As far as this family is concerned, you're dead.'

David didn't know what to say. He assumed she was acting on her own authority, she hadn't taken a poll. But he nodded, *Okay*, and kept hauling at the cassock as he tried to pull it over the top of Father Charles's head. The man didn't move but at least he was breathing.

'I mean it.'

He said, 'I know. I promise.'

David slipped his head and arms inside the cassock and looked in the mirror. He smoothed the creases and adjusted the slightly skewed collar. Once he hung the cross around his neck, he was done. The one last thing, he bent down to his discarded suit and pulled out the roll of cash his gran had given him. The priest was still lying on the floor, thin and unnatural in his nakedness.

David looked back up at his sister and said, 'See you, Karen.'

She closed her grip on the knob of the vestry door. For a moment it seemed she was going to try and close it, an attempt at a citizen's arrest. But then she stepped out of the way.

'Yeah. See you.'

David half skipped, half ran down the corridor, his black skirt billowing. He took the steps at the end three at a time and pushed through the next door. Now he was in a semi-open passage, lined with columns that ran parallel to the gardens. He tried to look without looking, to see if he could see any police cars in Carlos Place or, across the park, in South Audley Street. At first there was nothing, then he caught the nose of a car parked by the Connaught Hotel at the junction of Carlos Place and Mount Street. And when he bent his knees and tried to saunter at a crouch, he saw another between the gateposts by the public library on South Audley Street. He straightened up, took another five steps, and he was inside the priests' house.

He'd had no problem hitting Father Charles. It was payback for the four hours of theological instruction and no jury would condemn him. Now he was back inside the house, he recognised the room where the priest conducted his classes. It was the dim glint off the cheap melamine table that reminded him. There was something about modern ecclesiastical furniture, the failed attempt at homeliness, the dreariness. He remembered the various chaplaincies he'd seen in his life: the one at university or the others at the prisons he'd done his time in, since then.

He served six months in 1978: three on remand in London and three in Kent after he'd been found guilty. Not so long, perhaps, but definitely long enough. If he was caught this time, he could be looking at years. So *Adios* and *Thank you*. Marriage to Annabella Babbage might have been fun, but not if their total sex life was hands-under-the-table during visiting hours.

David snapped the catch on the front door and steadied himself. He almost jumped down into the street and had to remind himself he was a priest. He started to repeat, *Father David, Father David*.

'Father?'

There were another three police cars in Carlos Place besides the one parked by the Connaught Hotel. David turned sharp left, back into the gardens. He decided that was the route with the most options. He didn't pay any attention to the little voice behind him.

'Father?'

He kept his breath steady, taking slow strides towards the South Audley Street gates and trying to see exactly how many police cars were stationed there.

'Father. Can I speak to you, please.'

He felt the tugging on his cassock and turned around. There was a little girl stood there: really little – like ten or twelve years old. And with big dark eyes blinking up at him.

He said, 'What?'

'Father, I have sinned.'

'So?'

2

Sophia regretted telling Shadi Mansur the story. It happened fifteen years ago, she must have told him about it before now. She put a hand to her earphones and said, 'Shut up, just one second, please.'

'You're saying the priest gave you outdoor confession: alfresco, in the park?'

Sophia needed to keep track of what the newsreader was saying over in Studio Two: actually a glass-fronted closet built into the corner of her studio. It wasn't easy to concentrate with Shadi so hyperactive, giggling in the swivel chair and slapping his hands on the armrests, but there didn't seem to be any reason to worry. She could see Yusuf at his microphone, working his way through the lunch-time news. When he finished, her two-hour music show started.

Shadi said, 'So what happened? Did he hear your confession?'

'He tried to dissuade me. He said there was a big wedding in the church, it was impossible to use the boxes.'

'You couldn't come back later?'

'No. I was distraught, it had to be there and then. I

told him the confession box never matters in an emergency.'

'Is that right?' Shadi wasn't clear on the rules.

'Not in an emergency. In an emergency, nothing matters.'

Sophia remembered giving the priest the same argument. He shook his head at her, asking if she was sure. He didn't think the Church was so flexible.

She said, 'I had to chase him all the way across the park until he gave in. We sat on a park bench and I began crying because I had been so wicked. But then, all the time I was speaking, he kept doing that signal with his finger . . .'

Sophia spun a finger in the air.

'. . . you know.'

'Speed it up.'

'Yes. Or wrap it up. I don't think I ever saw anyone use the sign again until I started working with Yusuf.' She did the signal again, more slowly, describing an elegant long-sided O in the air.

Shadi focused on the slim length of her finger and the steep parabola of her mocha-brown fingernail. He said, 'So, he was a priest in a hurry.'

'I don't know. He was really annoying me. So I hit him.'

'You hit a priest?'

'I didn't like his attitude. I don't think I hurt him. I was only twelve years old.'

Shadi was laughing so hard, his whole face seemed to crinkle and redden; everything apart from the moon crater of scar tissue on his temple where, eight years ago, he had headed an Israeli smoke grenade and almost died. That bit of skin went pale. Shadi came from one of the few Muslim families in Bethlehem and he had mixed feelings about priests. He went to the Convent School with Sophia and, before the smoke grenade incident, he did almost two terms at Bethlehem University, which was run by the Catholic teaching order, the De La Salle Brothers. After he came out of hospital, he transferred to an American university and he and Sophia lost touch for a few years. She went to the Sorbonne on a history scholarship, he went to Detroit to do International Relations with the money the PLO gave him as compensation for his injuries.

Sophia said, 'I'm sure I told you about the priest before, Shadi.'

'No, honestly. I would have remembered.'

Shadi was supposed to be working. He came by to check the scripts that Yusuf Salman wrote for the news bulletins but, today, he got caught in a tailback at the security checkpoint and arrived late. Yusuf was already on-air. Shadi didn't seem particularly bothered, he was happy to stick around and chat with Sophia. She could not remember why she began telling him about her impromptu confession in the London park but at least she didn't need to explain the background details. Shadi knew all about the confessional. After school on a Saturday, he would sneak into the church and watch the other kids go through the regular Saturday confession. On one occasion he was discovered in the box himself, halfway through an elaborate list of sins.

Now he was drumming his fingers on the edge of her mixing desk, like an over-excited three-year-old. Saying, 'I wish I'd been there. Oh boy, I wish I'd been there.'

Sophia said, 'How am I doing for time?' She glanced at the clock. Time to panic. There were only thirty seconds before she was on-air.

'Okay, Shadi. That's it, time's up.'

Shadi looked idly around, as though he had no idea what was going on.

He said, 'What's the big rush?'

Yusuf was standing up in the newsroom closet, still talking into his microphone and simultaneously trying to signal to Sophia. She heard his voice in her headphones, saying, 'That's the news this lunch-time. You're listening to Bethlehem AM radio. Stay tuned to this station for Sophia Khouri playing *The Music You Want to Hear*.' At the same time he was trying to give her a silent count with his fingers – like 'ten seconds, nine seconds, eight seconds' – but he was only managing to tie his fingers in knots.

The eight-track cartridges of adverts and jingles were racked together on a shelf above her desk, the labels on the spines facing outwards. Sophia grabbed the cartridge with her show's theme tune and slotted it into the tape machine. She swooped up the volume, holding it for a moment before she cross-faded with her microphone.

'Good morning, Bethlehem. I'm Sophia Khouri and I hope you'll stay with me over the next two hours while we listen to *The Music You Want To Hear*.'

As she was speaking, she reached out to stab the *Play* button on the CD machine. There was a moment when she fumbled because Shadi had left his clump of car keys and his mobile phone on her desk, but she recovered. She nudged the volume up, finishing her introduction a beat ahead of the vocals: Khaled singing *Didi*. She didn't know if this was one of the tunes anyone wanted to hear because she hadn't yet gone through the request slips. It was a safe bet that Khaled would be there, though.

When she did start flicking through the requests, she was

surprised to find that eighty per cent were downbeat, very slow-tempo songs. She looked up, pushing a curve of black hair off her face as she asked Shadi what was up with everyone, why were they all so miserable?

Shadi said, 'Maybe the fact there are three funerals today . . .'

'Oh no.' She felt guilty but she was surprised, too. There were funerals every other day but three was getting a little extreme. She said, 'Whose?'

'One guy Hamas admit is theirs. He was trying to make a bomb, fell asleep and blew himself up.'

She knew about that one, she had even heard the explosion. She said, 'You wouldn't think building a bomb was so boring. Who are the others?'

'Dr Ayash the pharmacist had a heart attack . . . and then there's the lawyer.'

'Oh yes.' She knew about both of them, too. It was Dr Ayash's second heart attack, horrible for his family but not a surprise. The lawyer was an unnatural death – he died because he had sold a house in the old city of Jerusalem to an Israeli.

Yusuf Salman was clearing up his scripts, standing on the other side of the glass that fronted the music studio. The black tie that he always wore when he read the news was hanging loose around his neck. He once explained he wore it in case he was reading out a death notice and one of the deceased's relatives walked into the studio. Sophia told him, *Good thinking*, but still thought he wore the tie for the same reason an actor might change his hairstyle before he began a film, just to get into the part. In everyday speaking, Yusuf's voice was light and thin but, once he started on his twice-daily news reports, it sank a lot deeper.

She switched the channel on her microphone so that it came through the speakers in the corridor. 'So what's the latest, Yusuf?'

He pushed open the door and stepped into her studio, saying, 'You missed the news?' Making like he was deeply offended.

'It was Shadi. You know what he's like. Chat, chat, chat.'

Yusuf looked uncomfortable. There was no doubt that Shadi could be insanely talkative but Yusuf didn't want to be dragged into one of Sophia's teases. At school together they were all friends, but Yusuf stopped feeling comfortable around Shadi a long time back when Shadi got involved in politics. It grew worse once Shadi began working for the Minister of Social Affairs. The problem was, Yusuf's father was a lawyer specialising in land deals. Yusuf knew someone would eventually accuse him of dealing with the Israelis. It didn't help that no one liked his father. Yusuf wasn't sure what he could do about that; perhaps use the radio station to mount a professional PR campaign, call it *Abu Yusuf Aid*. It had a ring to it.

Shadi was saying, 'There was one problem, the third item you read out. It needs a rewrite.'

Sophia was amazed, 'You heard the news? How is that? You talked all the way through it.'

Shadi said, 'You don't think I've got big ears? I can listen to two things at once, it's no problem.'

Yusuf was scrabbling through the pages of his news script. 'The third item?'

'It's a sensitive issue.'

'What, the First National Palestinian Music Festival: that's sensitive?' Yusuf was holding the script up, shaking his head.

'You didn't hear? Suha Arafat couldn't make the opening ceremony.'

Yusuf looked again. 'I thought she was the guest of honour. It was on the press release.'

'There was a mix-up. She accepted the invitation, then her office messed up.' Shadi shrugged. 'The date clashed with her international commitments.'

Sophia laughed. 'What is it? She's shopping in Paris?'

For someone who liked laughing so much, Shadi almost managed to play it straight. He said, 'I understand she is in Paris.' But he couldn't stop the repressed grin from bouncing across his eyes. He gave in. 'She is unbelievable. She not only forgot about the festival, she forgot to tell Arafat about it. When he heard there was a National Palestinian Festival of Music and no one had invited him, he dragged all the organisers over to Gaza to explain themselves.'

'Oh God.'

'Imagine, Ramallah to Gaza, it took them all night, so they missed their own opening ceremony. Then they were made to wait in a line on a bench, no one speaking. Even Arafat, when he arrived he didn't say a word. He just walked slowly round the room until he was stood behind them. Then he crouched low and whispered: "You have no shame." One of the guys almost had a heart attack.'

'Oh god, oh god.' Sophia was biting her lip. She didn't know whether to laugh or whether to brace herself. She wasn't sure what was coming next. Maybe it was going to be very very bad.

Shadi said, 'Don't worry. They managed to explain. Though it wasn't easy: the reason they invited Suha in the first place was because they didn't want Arafat to give his usual three-hour speech — they had a full programme, time was tight, they couldn't fit him into the schedule. Of course, they couldn't say it quite like that.'

'But they managed to get away with it?'

'Well, they got a warning.'

Only Sophia and Shadi were laughing comfortably. In fact, Shadi was cracking up. He could laugh for up to ten minutes, they'd all seen him do it. And then he would end saying, 'But I love that guy, I really do.' Meaning Yasser Arafat.

Yusuf just stood there, his mouth twisted in a smile that didn't fit his face.

The radio station operated out of a couple of rooms above a gift shop, just off Manger Square. From the window of Sophia's studio there was nothing to see except a blank wall of the Church of the Nativity. But if you went up on the roof, there was a sweeping view to the south, taking in the refugee camp at Dheisheh and on towards Hebron, nearly twenty kilometres away. The roof was a good place for the radio mast, but Hebron was still way outside the station's reach. Bethlehem AM was a small outfit; Yusuf Salman was the only full-time member of staff and Sophia was one of three part-time DJs. The format to her show was straightforward. Every day, she played a dozen songs and read out the letters that came with them. That was it: *The Music You Want to Hear.*

When he had first sat down, Shadi had promised that he would go as soon as her show started. It just showed what his word was worth. Even after he finished dictating a new script to Yusuf, he stayed around, swivelling round in the chair they used for interviews, pumping Sophia for more details on the priest story. What was most annoying, he was talking over the ad for *Tony's Ford and Renault Dealership*. He might be able to listen to two things at once but she didn't have the same concentration.

She said, 'Shut up, Shadi. I want to hear my Uncle Tony's new advert.'

Tony Khouri always insisted on doing his own ads, reading from a script he also wrote. Yusuf had been the producer this time and said the recording session was a nightmare, from the beginning to the end.

Shadi said, 'I've been meaning to ask: why does he call it a "dealership"? Does he think that's the English word for car seller?'

'I don't know. Why don't you ask him?'

'He doesn't even sell Fords. In fact, he doesn't sell any new cars. So how can he be a dealership?'

Sophia didn't know. And now she'd missed the advert, although it was stupid to get annoyed. She could just play it for herself later, she had the cassette. She was the one who loaded it in the machine.

She knew the station wasn't making it on ad revenue. The problem was, the total population of the Bethlehem metropolitan area, the city itself including Beit Jala and Beit Sahur and the refugee camp, was only about forty-five thousand. To get a bigger audience, the transmitter also needed to be bigger. It would mean moving to somewhere with a stronger roof than the present building, but that wasn't the main consideration. The larger the audience, the more chance that someone less friendly than Shadi would turn up and begin taking an interest. As long as the station remained local, they had limited independence. The more listeners, the more likely that some big man from Hebron would climb on board, trying to use the station for political influence or to line their pockets. While the station was small and losing money, the only problem was keeping it going day to day.

According to Sophia's script, the next ad was for El Mariachi, the Mexican restaurant at the Grand Hotel. Sophia had made the ad herself. Now it was waiting in the mouth of the second cassette player, ready for its first airing. She smoothly cross-faded from her Uncle Tony to the sound of Spanish guitars.

Shadi said, 'The priest . . .'

'You can forget it, Shadi. I'm not telling you what I confessed.'

She wanted him to listen to her ad. But Shadi wasn't ready to give in yet.

'At least tell me the penalty.'

'Nothing. There wasn't one.'

'Nothing? He didn't give you any penalty at all?'

'No. It was weird. He just said, *That's it?*' Sophia gave the words a spin, just like the priest had done. 'He told me to get lost. It wasn't worth his time.'

'You couldn't have been much of a sinner.'

'I guess not. But I thought I was at the time.'

The El Mariachi guitars were getting wild now, coming to a crescendo that closed the ad with style. Sophia said, 'Look at that, it's over now. I thought you were going to listen to it, give me your comments.'

'I liked it.'

She didn't know if he was lying. Whether he had even heard any of it.

The radio was playing in the salon when Sophia returned home.

Yusuf Salman was reading the four o'clock bulletin, incorporating the approved script amendments. His deep newscaster voice sounding muffled through the kitchen wall. After each bullet point, Yusuf was echoed by two clearer male voices. One was her father. Sophia didn't recognise the second man.

Her mother placed two glasses on a tray. She told Sophia the visitor was *Abu Yusuf*: Yusuf's father.

'Yusuf who's on the radio?'

'Yes, his father.'

'What's the problem, the Salmans have a radio, he has to come round and listen to ours?'

Her mother made a disapproving click at the joke but didn't let loose with her tongue. Sophia was embarrassed, because she was close friends with Yusuf, but she found Edward Salman distinctly unappetising and so did her mother. It was about the only thing they agreed on. Sophia noticed that the windowsill had been cleared of pot plants, and when she opened a cupboard to get a drinking glass for herself she found a geranium hidden there. Her mother always hid her flowers when there was a visitor she suspected of having an evil eye.

Sophia listened again to the voices. She said, 'It's just the two of them?'

'They're waiting for your Uncle Tony.'

Her mother set out a tray with lemonade in a jug. Sophia took it through to the salon and found her father and Edward Salman sat either side of the radio, scooping watermelon seeds out of a blue-and-white bowl. Salman was pear-shaped and fleshy, Elias Khouri grey-skinned and frail, but his large womanly eyes were bright with interest. Both men ate the seeds automatically, leaning so hard into the radio it was as if Yusuf's voice had magnetic appeal. Sophia knew her father sat like that because he was deaf in one ear. Edward Salman seemed genuinely attracted to the sound of Yusuf's voice, fingering the loose fat under his chin and nodding as though he was hearing the wisdoms of the world.

Then Yusuf started on the item about the dead lawyer and Edward Salman started speaking hurriedly, easily overpowering the radio's plasticky breath.

'What is the matter with me, making you listen to Yusuf's chatter when I could be learning new things from you.'

Elias Khouri said, 'I doubt I know anything new.' Then, 'Thank you, Sophia, dear.'

Sophia put the tray down. 'How are you, Baba?'

Her father had seemed especially slow-moving that morning when she'd left him and headed for work.

'Fine,' he said now. 'You know me, slow as a donkey and twice as strong. How was work?'

'Good.' Sophia turned from one to the other as she poured out their lemonade.

Edward Salman said, 'How was my boy?'

'Okay. You remember Shadi? He came in and made Yusuf rewrite the story about Suha Arafat.'

Edward Salman stiffened. 'Shadi, huh? I hear that he's doing very well for himself. Me, I'm not sure about that boy.'

Her Uncle Tony arrived just as she was leaving the salon. She heard her mother first, the scraping of the bolts on the door and then the enthusiasm of her greeting. The way Samira Khouri treated Tony, he would have to be a film star for it to make sense. Tony rumbled a compliment at her and she couldn't even reply, she just giggled. Then he turned and Sophia heard the sound of his feet, like bags of wet sand slapping on the stone floor. He was a very fat man. In this heat, he generated so much wet steam it was difficult to bring him into focus, as though he was shimmering inside a mirage. Perhaps Samira treated Tony Khouri so fondly because he so often appeared in the kind of romantic soft blur used in Egyptian soap operas. Though Sophia could remember when her uncle was more dashing, if she thought back hard enough. The difficulty was remembering what he did exactly, back then. Those days were surrounded in their own haze, you would have to be psychic to piece the truth together. A psychic or perhaps a historian.

It took Tony two attempts to scissor his legs high enough to clear the plug cable to the radio and join his brother and Edward Salman.

'What's the news?' he asked.

Sophia told him, 'The body of a lawyer was found behind Zuzu's supermarket in Beit Jala.'

'God oh god oh god. Another one?'

It was Edward Salman who said *No*. 'The same one. The one found yesterday.'

'I thought . . .'

'Yes.' The lawyer closed the topic.

Elias pushed up from his chair with his knobbled and arthritic hands to meet his brother. They kissed three times, then Tony turned to Edward Salman for another three. They all addressed each other by the names of their eldest sons. First Abu Yusuf, then Abu Charlie after Tony's son who was studying in the States. And finally Abu Sophia. Sophia was Elias's only child.

Sophia waited to kiss her Uncle Tony and promised to get him more lemonade. He said he needed to replenish the oasis, patting his stomach.

The three men were meeting to discuss Elias's problem. As she stood at the sink, Sophia could look out from the kitchen window and see the problem for herself. It was a small piece of land that bordered their yard and separated them from the newly arrived al-Banna family. The land was set into a hillside and at the moment it was semi-derelict, the old terraces sagging into mini-landslides of yellow stone. At one time it had been planted with vines but now there were just a few olive trees dotted around. Elias Khouri used to tell people, he bought the land to build a house for his son and as he never had a son, now was a good time to sell it. Someone asked why he didn't build a house for his daughter. Sophia remembered his reply. He asked if they thought he could ever tell his daughter to live where she was told. The way he said it, he might have sounded like someone who was easily pushed around. He wasn't a weak man, though; just different to more typical Bethlehem men. Sophia knew he would never feel he had to compete with them, even if he wasn't disabled.

Her father was not telling the truth about the land, though. He wanted to sell it because he did want to tell her where to live. He wanted her to go back to France, or at least somewhere abroad. Her university fees may have been paid through the scholarship, but there were still living expenses. Elias had spent a lot of money on her. If he sold the land, he would have money again to spend on her.

He was talking about it when she returned with a clean glass and fresh lemonade. Both her Uncle Tony and Edward Salman agreed that she should get out of the country.

Tony said, 'You hear, Sophia? We want to see you on the world stage.'

'Doing what?'

'It doesn't matter.' He didn't have an idea. As she left the salon, he shouted out, 'There's nothing for you here except more Hebron shit – isn't that true?'

Tony had turned back to the table. Elias and Edward Salman were nodding at him: of course it was true.

The lawyer wanted to know exactly what happened when prospective buyers came to look at Elias's land.

'What happens?' Elias said. 'The family al-Banna happens. They start shouting and waving sticks, pick handles, old tyres, whatever they can find.'

'They admit they want the land for themselves?'

'They want it. They just don't think much of the asking price. They don't like it, they don't like its neighbourhood.'

Tony said, 'They're not in the same *zone*, even.' He let the single English word absorb some of the stress of the situation.

'They prefer to create *facts on the ground*.'

'Waving sticks,' said the lawyer.

'That, yes,' said Elias. 'But even, say, having a picnic out there, or fixing a swing to the cedar tree for the children. It's not as though I would object to that.'

'The thing with Hebronites, my professional opinion, is that they are so pushy, they have no shame. It dries my blood.'

Al-Banna, the old man and his family, were one of the first families to move from Hebron to Bethlehem after the Palestinian Authority took over the city at the end of 1995. What everyone suspected, they were a bridgehead for their clan, which was large and powerful even by Hebron standards.

Tony said, 'What can you do? We're all Palestinians. Why do they think they have stronger rights?'

Edward Salman said, 'If they don't want to pay the asking price, then good. Better to keep Bethlehem a Christian town.'

The lawyer preferred to speak to Tony, although Tony had no direct interest in his brother's land sale. He didn't mind, except that he had similar problems of his own. All handled by Salman and none any closer to a resolution.

Salman tapped the table. He was ready to sum up. 'The way I see it. We can either do this or we can do that. We can take the case to the court in Ramallah, who will take probably a year coming to a judgment. Or we can return to the clan council and try and persuade them to take a stronger line against the Hebronites.'

'So there's absolutely nothing we can do?'

'Well, you could be less negative.' He shrugged. 'What can I say? Think positive, dream about climbing aboard a plane and flying away for good.'

Elias threw up his hands, 'God oh god. There's a dream.'

Tony said, 'I'm almost tempted. If I could sell up, maybe I would join you.'

'You would sell everything?' Elias's voice was suddenly quiet and serious.

Tony nodded before he caught the rising fear in his brother's eyes. 'Except for the apartment in Jerusalem, of course.'

Edward Salman joined in. 'Of course. No one could get the price.'

'No.'

They sat quietly together for most of the next ten minutes. As Elias well knew, for an apartment in Jerusalem an Israeli would happily pay more than six or seven times what you could ask from a Palestinian. But then the police would be asking Tony's wife to identify the body, the next time one was found behind Zuzu's supermarket.

Samira Khouri closed the meeting when she came into the salon with three cups of coffee on a tin tray: the universally recognised signal to wrap up a visit and move on. Samira always worried that a long talk would drain her husband, and Elias looked grey, even in the bright afternoon sunshine. Edward Salman gulped his coffee back. When he stood, Tony got up too.

'Let's go together.'

The two of them waddled down the steps from the door to the garden. Their Mercedes cars were parked opposite the house, side by side by the wall of the Baptist Sunday school. As they passed through the gate, Tony opened up his hand and said, 'Try this.'

There was an almond lying there, plucked straight off the tree. Although the garden was small, Elias found room for a few fruit trees: orange, fig and olive and a couple of bushes of pomegranates. The almond tree had the best fruit. The other trees were there to look nice – you could always buy good fruit.

To the left was the piece of land that Elias was trying to sell. It didn't look much but its deeds were clear and it ought to have been easy to find a buyer.

Tony said, 'You see them?'

'The men standing by the low building?'

'That's al-Banna's sons, he's got five of them. Every one a thug.'

Edward Salman looked again. 'What are they doing with that building?'

'Chicken farming. If you walk over, you get within twenty-five metres, you can smell the chicken shit.'

'Chicken farming? This area isn't zoned for business.'

Tony perked up. 'You think you can get them on that? Illegal chicken farming?'

The lawyer paused, rubbed a hand over his chins. 'Actually – no. Not a chance.'

'I sometimes wonder: what's the point of lawyers in a country where no one obeys the law?'

That would give Salman something to think about, on the drive to his house. But not too much, because it was only a five-minute drive. Tony didn't want to overtax him, exhaust his finely tuned lawyer brain.

These days, Tony wanted to be law-abiding. He didn't feel he had the energy for any other kind of world. It wasn't like he was in his twenties, early thirties any more. He didn't have the energy to be an outlaw. His house was only five minutes away, too. He could easily walk, but it seemed much too far in this heat. He was forty-five, not so very old. But he was fat and he was tired and his blood pressure was ridiculously high and he was ridiculously stressed. Paying the college fees of two sons, that was forty thousand dollars a year even before he thought about paying their rent or their Visa bills. He had his used-car business but no one was buying cars, they preferred to drive their rusting heaps into the ground. Tony wasn't making money, he couldn't meet his overheads, his only asset was his land, most of which had no clear title. And even if he could clear the deeds, he knew he would never get the kind of price he needed, just to keep going.

Except for the apartment in Jerusalem which he could sell tomorrow for three million dollars. The offer was there on the table. Edward Salman believed it could go as high as four million. All he needed to do was meet the people involved, start the negotiations.

Tony and the lawyer stood at the gate, head to head. Tony whispered, 'So what do you advise?'

Salman looked around, whispered back: 'Take the money and move to America immediately.'

'And never come back?'

'You won't be able to.'

It wasn't as though Tony hadn't thought about it. Sometimes he went as far as imagining it; pulling up his roots entirely and going into exile. But he couldn't do it really, not in actuality.

The Khouris were one of the original ten families of Bethlehem. How many people could be as confident that their family had lived in one place for hundreds of years, perhaps even for ever? He wasn't claiming he was a good man, a great patriot, even particularly honourable. But he lived in Palestine when he could have moved. In the years when he had money, he built himself a bloody big house, started a business and employed Muslims from the refugee camp. It was thanks to people like him that some kind of minimal economy had kept Palestine ticking over all these years.

What was it that Sylvester Stallone said in the *Rambo* video? 'I just want my country to love me as much as I love it.'

Well, maybe that was going a bit far. And if Tony felt tears pricking at his eyes, it was mostly self-pity. He couldn't fool himself. He looked back at Elias's house. Sophia was sitting out on the balcony, eating seeds. He waved, she waved back and then turned away again. It was okay for youngsters, for her or for his own sons. But Tony could not think about leaving. No matter how much shit there was in the water, it was still his small pool and he was a big fish at home.

He said, 'Stall them for now. I've finally got in touch with the friend I was telling you about. I think there might be a way to sell the Jerusalem apartment and stay in the country.'

3

David caught the smell of the aircraft fuel turning to vapour above the hot concrete and clicked into airport survival mode. After fifteen years on the run, he barely even had to think about it. He had his customised strategies; for instance, he never said he was here on business. There were times when he'd tried, but he never managed to look like a businessman, not even one of those that describe themselves as *creatives*. Not even one of those who claim to write *code* and turn out mean Nintendo games. So each time he got the feeling it was time to move on, his line was always the same: 'Me? I'm a holiday-maker.'

The Israeli official nodded and dropped her head, slim hands flicking through the pages of his passport. David was left staring through the security glass at the polished shine of her hair.

Her eyes flickered up again, just briefly, and he took it as a question. He said, 'Ireland.' Almost adding: not all of it – just a mouth-watering sliver. But another of his tailor-made strategies was never be a smartarse. And never, never ever, try to do an Irish accent. See also Rule #2.

He refocused his gaze, pulling back from the woman's hair

until he was staring only at the surface of the window into her booth. This was another part of his technique, a way of emptying his eyes of everything until his face hardened into a blank, inscrutable mask, the expression associated with prison hard men and the women who work the name-tag tables at conference hotels. David was never any good at the look, despite the number of tricks he used to help himself with it. Now, instead of staring at the blunt surface of the glass, he was staring deep into the reflection until he could make out the individual faces in the crowd spreading out around him, waiting for their turn at the passport booth. And when he reined in a little, tightening the depth, he began examining his own reflection. What he saw was a man in his mid-forties. Which was okay: he was in that mid-range. Then, a face that was as tanned and lined as a Dallas housewife, a Greek sailor, an ageing rock star or a modern-day Humphrey Bogart. Take your pick. All in all, he preferred the Humphrey Bogart comparison, although his hair style tended to veer off towards the ageing rock star. Today it was trimmed neater than usual and since he no longer wore a moustache, no one was going to mistake him for the geezer who played bass guitar in Black Sabbath: Geezer Butler. That had happened to him three times one week, when he was trying to live in Toronto.

'Give this ticket to the people at the gate, Mr Preston.'

When the woman handed David his passport, there was a white ticket sticking out of the top. The ticket had to be a signal to the security people on the gate behind her booth; a well-used signal – it was bent and grubby. David noticed other passengers had blue tickets folded into their passports. These were the passengers who looked most at home in Tel Aviv airport, who exuded the most confidence at being home.

David said, 'Thank you.' He sloped off.

This was his first time in Israel. Also his first time on a two-leg transatlantic haul where both halves had been strictly no-smoking. When that was topped by a twenty-minute wait in a no-smoking customs queue, it was understandable that he was uncomfortable. He had smoked his last cigarette six hours ago in a transit lounge in Amsterdam. His last joint . . . maybe twenty-four hours ago.

David followed the exit sign that took him round the back of the girl's booth to the gate where the next level of security were standing. He tried to hand over the white ticket alone but the man took the whole passport.

'Go collect your bags.'

He pointed over to the carousel but held on to David's passport.

'When you have your bags, come back here.'

David was going to ask if he could smoke yet, but he looked up and found the sign: *Smoking is not cool.* As he pressed himself into the crowd waiting for their bags, he already had the cigarette between his lips. Another second, the cigarette was glowing and his Zippo was snapped back shut, tucked into the pocket of his jeans. Airport security were already taking an interest in him, if he was caught smoking they weren't going to get any more interested. And anyway, he'd seen two women light up on the far side of the carousel. Both women wore tight leggings and slash-neck T-shirts. David didn't look less cool than them – though he admitted, it was always going to be a subjective call.

David had bought the tartan suitcase especially for this journey. The tartan reminded him of the poncho his grandmother was wearing on the last day he saw her, which was also the last day he saw Tony Khouri. A combination like that, you would think it would set up sufficient friction in his memory: that something would stick. But David found himself standing alone in the baggage hall, the last man left, watching this garish suitcase begin the second of its solo laps around the carousel. And even then, the flash of recognition only came as two security guards started pointing at it.

An hour later, David was sat on his airport trolley, his hand resting on his found bag, waiting for the security people to come out of their huddle. He could see them through the open door of their office. They were all young; the oldest was about twenty-sixish, the rest were way junior. And they all had a similar manner, a style that was both efficiently curt and somehow annoyingly dithery. Maybe they were trained to act like that. Even now, looking at them, he wasn't sure they were talking about him. From their body postures, the way they stood, they could easily be talking about a basketball match, a Spielberg film, the price of Ecstasy, something like that. But David was the last remaining passenger off flight KLM 205 to be dealt with. Of the others, the posh-looking gold-draped woman, the two kids with the fluff moustaches, the man who looked like a gypsy and the boy/girl backpacker couple, he was the only one that was still around, still raising *questions*. He could kick himself. He knew he had looked a fool, jogging beside his bag and trying to read the label before it disappeared back behind the rubber fringes.

David's eyes were on the office door and the huddle of security people when he heard a voice behind him. He turned. The man was small with a healthy sallow complexion and hair that looked like an English lawyer's wig, except that it was brunette and was minus the fancy plait at the back. There was nothing fancy about this guy. He was holding David's Irish passport in his hand.

'David Preston.'

David nodded.

'Where will you be staying during your visit to Israel?' The man spoke in the exact same way as the other security people; the term was *brusque*. David knew his short-term memory wasn't the best but he was sure this man wasn't a part of the security team that had been dealing with him so far. He was older, for one thing, maybe close to forty years old. Then there was something about his manner. David did not know where the man had come from, how he had managed to appear behind him, or how he came to be holding his passport.

'Where will I be staying? At the Grand Hotel. Bethlehem.'

'Do you have a reservation?'

David said, for the fourth or fifth time, 'Yes.'

It was true, he did have the reservation. In their last exchange, Tony Khouri had given him the address of the hotel and told him to book ahead. Then he had apologised again for not being able to put him up at his own house. Things were difficult, he said. All Tony and David's conversations took place via the Web, in a discussion group entitled 'Rattan Forum: Producers, Importers, Designers'. David was proud of the site. It belonged to him although he paid a kid in San Francisco to run it. He was surprised how many other people used its chat rooms, some of them even rattan producers.

David wrote back to Tony, suggesting that if things were so difficult, perhaps it would be better if they didn't meet at the airport. Tony wavered but decided that would be going too far. He believed that meeting people at airports was a profound responsibility, it was the thing that separated man from the monkeys.

The new security man flicked through David's passport. He didn't look up as he asked, 'Is this a holiday for you?'

'You could call it a holiday. I call it a pilgrimage. I've reached that time of life. I thought I should check my head and visit the Holy Land.'

David didn't know why he was laying it on so thick. But until he understood the man's real interest, he was switching strategy. The impression he was going for was relaxed, amiable, more than slightly loony.

'So who am I speaking to? None of you guys wear name tags.' He squinted at the man's lapel, as though he was trying to find something to read. 'You're all so secretive. I guess that's a security thing.'

He was sure the guy was heavy-duty. He was getting all the vibes: this wasn't airport security, more like state security.

The man looked up, snapping the Irish passport shut and holding it out. He said, 'Ben Naim. My name is Sammy Ben Naim.'

David, surprised to get an answer, took the passport and said, 'Pleased to meet you, Sam.'

'Sammy.' The man said it precisely, the same stress on both syllables. But the threat was there, even as he smiled. 'I prefer Sammy, if you don't mind. Enjoy your stay in Israel, Mr Preston. Try not to act like a sheep's behind.'

David jolted upright. 'What was that?'

'Goodbye, Mr Preston.'

The secret service guy turned. David was left staring at his back. But he knew what he had heard, the phrase 'sheep's behind'. If this Sammy Ben Naim was trying to tell David he had been made, he wasn't especially subtle. It was more like infant-school stuff: Ramsbottom, sheep's arse. *Sheep's behind* was a little too polite for Manchester infants.

David opened his passport. There was an Israeli stamp inside it, which would be a problem travelling to some countries. Not that David was likely to have any urgent business in a place like Syria or Iran, but it was a shame to limit a valuable passport. The Irish passport was genuine, not a fake and not stolen. At one time they had been easier to get hold of than they were now.

David turned his trolley and started towards the exit. Before he walked into the customs corridor, he eased a look over his shoulder. As Sammy Ben Naim marched into the security office, the huddle broke up. So he was clearly someone senior. David was thinking, I'll give you sheep's behind, you frizz-head motherfucker. Then thinking he had to calm down. His edginess was out of character.

Sammy Ben Naim walked over to the CCTV screens. He said, 'Okay, let's see what he does now.'

He watched David wheel his trolley into the arrival zone, gradually slowing like a man walking across a carpet of honey. There was no one waiting for him, so perhaps he was going to have to make his own way to Bethlehem. But instead of heading directly for the *sherut*, he began meandering again, wheeling in and out of the clumps of teenagers that liked to sit around the airport. The first group he approached, he spoke to a girl in an Indian print dress, sat on the dirty floor while one of her friends beaded and braided her hair. Whatever David said to her, he startled the girl. She jerked back so hard a bead flew off and skittered dumbly across the rubber tiles.

Sammy turned to one of the young women from the airport security team and said, 'What's that? He tried to hit on her?'

About half the security team were gathered around the CCTV screens, standing in a respectful semicircle at Sammy Ben Naim's back. The one Sammy spoke to shrugged, she couldn't say whether this character was hitting on teenage girls or not. It didn't matter, Sammy had it figured out now. He said, 'Ah. She thought he was a cop.'

Already, on-screen, David was calming the group down. It was his smile, his open hand gesture combined with whatever he was saying. They were no longer either scared or distrustful. The beaded girl mouthed something to him, which he repeated a couple of times.

Sammy was impressed. 'Now he's learning Hebrew.'

The girl was laughing now. She turned to a male friend who reached in a shirt pocket and tossed something over. David caught it with another nod and smile. For a moment, Sammy couldn't tell what it was and then saw David pull out a flap of paper. It was a packet of Rizlas. It seemed that David was prepared to just take a couple but the girl waved him away, telling him to take the whole packet and welcome.

Someone from the airport team said, 'That was it? That was what he wanted?'

Sammy nodded. 'It's what they call reefer madness, *adoni*.'

Someone else spoke, joking: 'After having you on his case, Commander, he probably needs to chill out.'

All Sammy had wanted to do was take an early look at David, an opportunity to assess his style. Now he was wondering, Is that it? His gimmick? He wins everyone's sympathy because he comes over as a lovable stoner? Sammy could feel the change of mood as the airport staff warmed to the guy. Sammy didn't say anything, though. Strictly speaking, he was on their turf, they were lending him assistance. He didn't want to alienate them.

Sammy continued watching as David walked out of the airport building. Another camera picked him up as he stood outside, on the wide paved section where the *sherut* drivers rounded up their customers. David was crouched down, making as though he was tying his shoelaces. Sammy guessed he kept his dope stash in his sock. There was no way to get a close-up and confirm.

A girl from the airport team said, 'Will you follow him?'

'Why? I know where he's staying. The Grand Hotel, wasn't it?'

She said, 'It's what he wrote on his landing card. He might have given a false address.'

Sammy didn't even pretend he was listening. He was looking at his watch and deciding on his best strategy.

'Suppose he's lying? Saying he's staying in Bethlehem when he's not.'

'Why would he do that?'

Now she was confused. How would she know? Sammy had not told them if his guy was a spy, a terrorist, a smuggler . . .

'If you don't mind, Commander, what is your interest in him?'

'I'm going to help him with a property deal.'

She didn't know whether or not to laugh. 'That needs Shin Bet?'

Sammy kept his voice flat. 'Who says I'm Shin Bet? I'm a housing officer.'

* * *

It was steaming. Before David moved to America – to the continent of America – he spent time in southern Africa. Even there, it never seemed to get quite so choky. David palmed the plastic envelope of grass he had taken from his sock and pulled a fresh skin from the Rizla packet. Looking to his left, he could see the fins of the jets swimming above a prefab concrete fence. In this weather he might as well be standing directly behind their engines at take-off, at least he would feel a breeze. David moved back into the fringe of shadow by the airport building. As he rolled a joint, he looked around for Tony. He still couldn't see him.

David flared up his Zippo and was just savouring that first smoky mouthful when the joint was yanked from his lips. He found himself looking at a hugely fat man, sweating in a safari suit and insulting him in English as he rubbed the joint to dust between his enormous fingers.

'Are you crazy? Tell me, either you're crazy or you're a fool.'

'Tony?' David was so amazed, he didn't even notice the remains of his joint blowing out of the man's open hand.

'What's the matter with you? Has living in America softened your brain?'

'Christ, Tony. Have you put on a little weight?'

They were stood face to face. Tony took David by his arms and pulled him one step forward. David had been living in Anglo communities for so long, the cheek-kissing no longer came naturally to him. But it was so good to see Tony after all these years.

'You're looking fit, David.'

'And you. I mean, the weight, you wear it well.'

As they reached the multistorey carpark, Tony was still apologising for the rough handling, snatching the joint out of his mouth. 'I just want to emphasise, this is not the best place to be caught smoking hash. The most security-conscious airport in the most security-mad country in the world. Think about it.' Tony was huffing. It wasn't the heat or the steps up to Level Six of the carpark. He stopped on the half-landing just below his level. 'I'm sorry to make a big deal out of this, David. You have to understand, I've got a lot on my mind. I'm scared to death about this whole deal. Not to mention, I had a nightmare just getting to the airport today.'

'Come on, man. It's me. I was being stupid.' David was all the way contrite, he was in the wrong. He said, 'Fifteen years. Can you believe it?'

Tony was finally smiling. 'I couldn't believe it. When my son told me he got an e-mail from someone called David Preston . . .'

'You knew it was me?'

'Are you kidding? I knew right away.'

They were at university in Manchester together, the class of '74. When David relayed a message to every Khouri with a listed e-mail address, he was betting that Tony would remember the Lancashire place names: Ramsbottom was a small town, a few miles from Preston.

He and Tony grinned at each other. 'So — what was your nightmare, man?'

'Oh, yeah. Transport problems.' Tony padded up the last few steps and pushed open the door. 'I couldn't get into Israel without hiring a chauffeur.'

Tony pointed ahead. David stared at the ten-seater minibus. 'That's ours?'

There was a dull-looking fat man in the driver's seat. When Tony hauled back on the sliding door at the side and threw David's case inside, the man didn't even bother to look around. Tony hissed, 'We should be okay with him. The guy doesn't speak English.'

He didn't look like he spoke any language. He was mumbling along to the radio, his unshaven chin bobbing up and down on his neck. David said, 'Where did you find him?'

'It wasn't easy. He's from East Jerusalem. I think he might be the city idiot. But he doesn't know me and I don't know him. I'm just trying to be discreet. Have all the angles covered, you know.'

As they climbed aboard, Tony shouted at the man to turn up his radio. He cranked it up a notch and asked a question. You needed to lip-read to tell what he was saying but Tony just shook his head and gestured *higher* with his hand. The radio was up to industrial levels before Tony was satisfied.

They sat mumbling together in the very back seat. While they were still within the security perimeter of the airport, they kept to small talk. David kept it moving along, saying: 'It was a stroke of luck, man. I remembered your kid was called Charlie so when I found a Charlie Khouri, I was like, bingo.' David couldn't remember exactly where he had tracked him to, one of the northern US universities, either Milwaukee or Michigan: he remembered it was included in the e-mail address. 'Charlie must be what . . . close on twenty by now?'

They were driving down an avenue of palm trees, ending with a checkpoint. Tony kept his eyes ahead, running through the data on his two sons; the one in America doing law, the one in the United Kingdom studying engineering. David nodded.

Yeah, it sounded good. As they cleared the security barrier, David said he didn't have any children, he never thought about remarrying either. In fact, he was never married in the first place, but Tony knew all about that. What with being on Interpol's most wanted list, it didn't quite work out. At the time, he had been too scared to speak to his fiancée in case her phone was bugged.

'What do you reckon, could me and Annabella have had a future together?'

David sneaked a sideways look at Tony and watched his old friend give a slight, almost imperceptible shake of the head. So there was something they could agree upon, even if Tony wasn't saying it up front. David thought, maybe it was time to quit doing the polite thing. They should touch on the big issues.

He said, 'Did you ever do any business since Beirut?'

Tony shot a look at the driver, at least at the back of the man's neck, before whispering, 'Business?'

David grunted, *uh-huh*. You know the kind of stuff. He saw him shake his head again. This time the gesture was firmer, except for the muscle that was flickering beneath the skin on his jaw line. David wasn't sure how far to push it.

After the bust at the wedding, they had made their separate ways to Beirut. Tony arrived first. David had trouble getting in. By this time the Israeli army controlled the whole country. When David finally bought himself some plausible journalistic credentials and slipped into Beirut, their shipment was still missing and Tony didn't have any leads. All he knew was that their contact had stashed it: apparently, somewhere safe. The problem was, this man had also disappeared. It was another week before they heard the dope was hidden in the Palestinian refugee camp at Sabra.

David said, 'Do you think anyone ever found it?'

Tony shot him a sharp look. 'What are you saying?'

David shook his head. Tony had misunderstood him. He wasn't suggesting Tony knew anything. He was just asking him to speculate on the matter. Tony was still whispering, so David whispered back: 'I don't care about the dope. I said, then, I was out of the business. I've stayed out. These days, my only interest in the stuff is pleasure. I'm through trying to make money from it.'

Even when they knew where the consignment was hidden, they couldn't get to it. The Israeli soldiers weren't letting anyone out of Beirut. They weren't letting anyone out of the camps either. It was another couple of days before Tony and David found out why.

Tony said, 'I can speculate. I speculate that no one ever found the dope because there was no one left alive to find it.'

David said, 'Come on, Tony. I'm sorry I brought it up. I was there, too.'

They went to Sabra together. It was the day after the massacre. They were warned not to go but David had his journalist card. Tony pretended he was his hired driver. They made it through to the camp before the last of the bodies had been taken away. They didn't stay longer than five minutes, they just turned around and went back to the city. The next day, David left Beirut. That was the last time he saw Tony.

'I was only trying to say, I've not been working these last fifteen years,' David said. 'I'm broke, all my savings gone. This deal's come at just the right time.'

Tony said, 'I'm sorry. I'm broke too.'

'And the best thing, it's only real estate. When you came back to me with this deal, I was ready to get down on my knees, I was so grateful. I was thinking, the estate agents out here have got to be crooks – you trust a smuggler to sell your house.'

David wasn't so stupid. He knew the Palestinians had a law against selling out to the Israelis. The Israelis, too, had all kinds of laws designed to stop the sale of property to non-Jews. But in their case, the laws worked. It was flat-out impossible for a non-approved person to buy a home; if they ever managed to move in, the army would march in and move them right out again. The Palestinians had more trouble enforcing their laws, which was why they relied on death squads. David knew this much from US newspapers, which he didn't believe were necessarily impartial observers of Palestinian/Israeli issues. But he got similar information from his conversation with Tony over the internet, so he couldn't claim he was unaware of the risks. But the main thing on his mind, as of this moment, was the lack of a good smoke. He wondered whether Tony would let him light up a spliff, but when he asked Tony turned on him, telling him to be serious.

David smiled. 'You thought I was being serious?'

He lit a cigarette instead. This had to be the longest he had gone without marijuana for twenty-seven years, including the time he spent in prison in the late seventies. He was not enjoying the experience, abstinence was doing nothing for him. Travelling never used to be like this, the constant strain, the non-availability of designated smoking areas. The hassle . . .

'Oh shit, Tony. There's one other thing . . . This guy in the airport, I think he knew who I was.'

They were driving down a steep and twisting valley road,

their driver keeping pace with the high-speed traffic as he hit the bottom of the curve, banked, and headed up the other side. Tony had a fat hand on the seat ahead of him, trying to hold himself steady. His voice came out reasonably even.

'Who was the guy?'

'An Israeli official, he said he was called Sammy something?'

'He gave you his name?'

'That was odd, wasn't it?'

Tony sucked at his teeth. He didn't know what to make of it. 'What did he say?'

'He just made a joke. He said, don't be a sheep's behind.'

David knew that Tony would get the reference. When they had first met Tony had made a similar joke: not immediately, he had at least waited until the end of freshers' week, when they were already friends. Tony had to admit he didn't know how significant it was, an Israeli apparently making the same joke.

He said, 'We have to look at it calmly. What did he do? Did he try to stop you? He was on his own. He can't see you as the dangerous terrorist type, a trained killer . . .'

'Oh, please.'

'Well, anyway. You asked me. I say, you're in. Let's not go looking for worries.'

David decided to chew it over himself. He looked back to the road, the expanse of gritty landscape with the new towns clinging to the skyline. The motorway seemed to be following the lines of an old terrace, like a contour line drawn around the hill. The minibus clung to the curve, and as they rounded the hill David realised this was Jerusalem. The airport, he knew, was on the outskirts of Tel Aviv, so he had just travelled from one side of the country to the other in forty-five minutes. Downtown Jerusalem was a modern city, with all the usual accoutrements. They passed a bus station, sunk into a kind of underpass by the side of the road, a few hotels, a whole lot of traffic lights. The only difference was that the city was mostly made out of a distinctive dull yellow stone.

Then he got his first sight of the old Jerusalem. The bus cruised through yet another set of lights, crested another hill and suddenly David saw it – the City with its walls and watchtowers and flying bridges that spanned the grassed-in moat. The stone looked brutish now, throwing back the white heat of the sun. It had something of the look of an English or Welsh castle, but David had never seen any castle on this scale. The road swept down, following the line of the walls as they grew steeper and higher. David's neck was tilted and stretched enough to interest a chiropractor before the minibus ducked through a narrow pass and headed away, cutting off the Old City behind a rocky hill.

After another ten-minute ride on a six-lane carriageway they slowed into a traffic jam. The radio had spazzed-out into a crackle and their driver was retuning. He hammered the buttons on his dash until he caught an Arabic station, an up-tempo song, the voice cracked with emotion that could have been joy, could have been pain. David couldn't tell what the man was singing, but his Arabic had always been useless, even when he did most of his business with Arabs. And then he was only familiar with Palestinian and Lebanese dialects. The singer sounded more Mahgreb than Mediterranean. But it reminded David of songs he'd heard before, and soon he was nodding along with his head as the bus crawled along in the diesel slipstream of an old wagon.

Tony said, 'It's time we separated.'

The line of traffic ended at a checkpoint fifty yards down the road. Again, David was surprised they'd reached it so fast, just a few miles out of central Jerusalem. There seemed to be no distance in this country, everything began and ended on top of itself. Looking ahead, he saw that the road had been narrowed with traffic cones and lined with plastic blocks like enormous Lego bricks and by sandbags.

Tony said, 'Get a taxi on the other side of the checkpoint. I'll swing back to Jerusalem and get rid of the driver. When I get back, I'll find a way to contact you at the hotel.'

David picked up his suitcase, gave Tony a wave and slammed the doors. He took the footpath through the checkpoint. No one paid him any attention. The teenage soldier boys were stood in the road, where they checked the passes of some drivers, waved others through. David patted his inside pocket, pleased to feel the hard cover of his Irish passport, even more pleased that the soldiers were not interested.

The other side of the checkpoint was like an automobile graveyard, beaten-up old cars parked two and three deep on either side of the road. David guessed these were the cars of Palestinians who worked over the border in Israel and weren't allowed to take their cars with them. Now there was a constant stream of foot traffic passing through the checkpoint and re-entering Bethlehem. A real mix, trudging along: women in long black dresses with embroidered pinafore fronts, some carrying boxes or plastic baskets on the tops of their heads; a few women in veils and a few others in jeans and shirts; men dressed in Western clothes, jumble-sale suits on the older and poorer men, jeans and sweatshirts for the boys; again, a few in Arab smocks, sheets and pillowcases. He knew he was back among Arabs. And if it didn't look like much so far, he wasn't worrying. He'd always enjoyed himself in the past.

He picked up a cab immediately, a Mercedes heavily modified in the style he remembered from the Lebanon all those years ago – a long-wheelbase model with the original seats ripped out and replaced with benches. It was a nine-seater, but the driver obviously decided David could afford the whole fare. David didn't mind.

David said, '*Marhaba*' – Hello – and settled back. For some reason, the driver had tied a peacock feather to the Mercedes ident at the end of the bonnet. David watched the feather whip around in the dusty breeze and focused on the joint he was going to roll, once he got to the hotel.

The radio was playing, picking up the same song he'd heard in Tony's car. As the music tailed away, it was replaced by a woman's voice. David liked it, the way it glittered with knowing laughter, only minimally suppressed. Every so often, it sparked with incongruous English phrases – *drive time* – and, three beats further on, the phrase *shiny happy people like all we Palestinians*. There was a definite ironic slant on that last line. Then the R.E.M. song came out of the radio in a tinny blast of mono. David sang along. His voice was better than Michael Stipe's, and almost as clear.

They were driving down a shallow hill now, the taxi taking long carves across the road to avoid potholes. Ahead, David could see another traffic jam. He wondered how the wheels of stationary cars could churn so much dust off the road. He was still mouthing along with the radio, although the air was getting so thick it was filling his throat. Even his nose seemed to be inflamed, his eyes pricking. The people on the street were feeling it too. They were running, holding scarves or handkerchiefs to their faces.

It was only when the smoking canister came flying through his open window that David realised he was caught in a tear-gas attack. He tore off his jacket and tried to pinch his mouth and nose shut under the material, at the same time struggling for the door handle. His eyes were already so swollen, burning dry, he could see only coloured stripes of red and yellow.

Someone hauled open the door from the outside and David rolled for the sidewalk, across a bed of broken stones, until he ended in the gutter. Above him, young men and teenagers were rushing around, stifling their coughs with their kaffiyehs, eyes bloodshot but bright and watery as they peered into the smoke. As though this was almost an everyday thing, they could handle a gas attack. David gulped and flapped like a fish on bone-dry land.

4

Sophia turned down the third tequila. Yusuf sank his, still trying to remember if it was salt, tequila, lemon or salt, lemon, tequila. On the table in front of them a pot of refried beans bubbled on top of a lamp of methylated spirits.

Yusuf said, 'You made adverts for this place but you've never eaten their food?'

Sophia pulled her mouth into a crinkly line, using her imitation of her friends' American college voices as she said, 'Go figure.'

Maybe it seemed strange, she was the last person in Bethlehem to eat at the new Mexican restaurant in the Grand Hotel. But she knew they would insist on giving her a free meal as a *thank you* for the radio ads. And even though they would say they understood when she invoiced them for the advert and, every subsequent week, for the airtime, she could see it hotting up into an embarrassment. Maybe it was her, maybe she was being over-sensitive. But the hotel would definitely remember the times they gave her a complimentary meal, each time she stopped by the lobby and dropped off their bill.

The way the *maître d'hôtel* kept bouncing back with the

tequila, asking if they would like to go one more time, it was clear that it was a present from him to them, business to business. Yusuf was drinking it down, laughing as he said 'When in Mexico.' Sophia didn't think there was anything wrong with running an economy on favour-for-favour lines, she just thought that while the radio station was struggling, it would be better to insist on cash.

Yusuf finished his salt-and-lemon act, but the *maître d'* still stood by, cradling the bottle of tequila. Sophia guessed he had something on his mind.

He said, 'I was wondering, what's happened to your programme?'

'You don't like it?'

'You call it *The Music You Don't Want to Hear*? What's the point of that?'

She had begun her new show yesterday and already she had got a lot of feedback. She explained, 'It's alternative.'

'Okay. I understand. But I think the music people want to hear is better than the music they don't want to hear. It's my opinion.'

He meant, it's my opinion as a businessman and an advertiser; even though he might prefer not to pay for the adverts. He was the eldest of the sons from the family that owned the hotel and he had money on his mind.

Sophia said, 'The old show's still on. Still in the exact same slot.'

'Yes, but with Yusuf.'

Now Yusuf was ready to butt in. So far he had kept quiet. 'What do you mean, saying *Yusuf* like it's leaving a bad taste?'

'No offence, Yusuf. But you sound like you're reading the

news. Like: *I'm playing your favourite tune, and another two people died of heart attacks.*'

It wasn't as though Yusuf had wanted to take over Sophia's show. But now he had, he felt he deserved a bit more support. 'I've been doing it for two days. What is your problem – you can't show any patience? How would you feel if people came in here the second day you opened and said what's the matter with your waitress?'

'What is the matter with the waitress?'

Sophia stood and said, 'Excuse me.'

If she went to the bathroom now, she knew the situation would be calm again when she got back. Yusuf would back-pedal and the other guy would step back, too. In a place that was always so tense, you couldn't afford to let the smallest things turn into minor explosions. The problem, of course, was that every time you suppressed something, it was just another thing left simmering.

As Sophia crossed the foyer, she heard an Englishman talking to one of the *maître d*'s brothers. She glanced over and saw a man who was perhaps forty-five years old, dressed in a pair of loose blue cotton trousers and a white shirt that was designed to be untucked, outsize and flowing. There was nothing so unusual about him, but after another two steps she paused, suddenly convinced she recognised him. She looked back. He was leaning on the reception desk, arms crossed, asking if they were sure: there were no messages for Room 210?

Washing her hands, she was still trying to place the man. She ran through the possibilities: a visiting professor, an author she once saw lecturing at university, or a regular at a bar – an Englishman at home in Paris. Perhaps she only knew his face from photographs – he might be a minor celebrity. On her way back into the restaurant, she paused in the doorway and looked left and right. The man was sat on his own in the corner by a window. He had a bottle of Black Label on his table rather than tequila, and he was reading the menu.

As she took her seat, Yusuf was toasting the hotel – he and the *maître d'* had made up their quarrel. Sophia nodded her head towards the man and whispered, 'Who's he?'

The *maître d'* looked and said, 'Him? An Irishman, he's been here two days. When he got here, he had to be carried to his room. A smoke grenade landed in his taxi as he passed Rachel's Tomb and he was half blind and suffocated.'

'In a taxi? That could be serious.'

He shrugged. 'We got Dr Alawi to examine him. He told him not to worry, he would be on his feet again, eventually.'

They all turned together, but quickly. The man certainly looked confused, sat on his own, picking up the menu and then putting it down again. Up and down, up and down, as though the whole concept of a menu was a new one to him. Sophia began to doubt that he was an academic, though it might be that the tear gas had affected him more than Dr Alawi had suspected.

She said, 'Do you think we should ask him over?'

If David ever told anyone his life story, they would at least figure he was a world-class traveller; better, an airport athlete. But these last few years, it seemed he was beginning to slide. This was his fifth day in Bethlehem and, most of the time, he was flat on his back – first with the effects of the CS gas which blended with his jet-lag and kept him pressed to the bed-sheets. Then, last night, he had barely slept at all. And whether he was wide awake or drowsy he found it difficult to concentrate on the most everyday things. When he went looking for a pharmacist, for instance, he found it easily enough. He knew the sign, the martini glass with a snake wrapped around it, framed by the red crescent that was the Arab version of the international first aid symbol. But instead of buying the various necessaries and hygiene aids he needed, he only filled the doctor's prescription for anti-nausea tablets and bought a tube of toothpaste. He didn't even remember the toothbrush. Not to mention talcum powder to dust the inside of his shorts and ease the humid testicle problem, plasters to help his feet go bare inside their sandals and a pack of *Tums* for indigestion relief. There were probably a few other things as well. Next time he would make a list.

What he'd seen of Bethlehem, it was a thronging place but not very attractive. Though it could be a different story, once he recovered his equilibrium. He hadn't seen the tourist spots yet. Up to now, he'd barely gone twenty yards from his hotel. And then he'd immediately turned around and gone back to his room for a siesta. It wasn't that he was worried about getting mixed up in another riot. The man at the hotel desk explained that recently the tear-gassing had become a regular late afternoon date between the local youths and the soldiers at Rachel's Tomb. He assured David that he was in no danger. David nodded and explained he was just tired. When he got his head, body and soul together he would have a good look around. There was no hurry. For now, he mostly wanted to sleep.

David had tried to have a siesta that afternoon. When he gave up, it was already dark outside. He cleaned his teeth using a blob of stripy paste squeezed on his finger. It didn't help the furry feeling in his mouth. He gargled a mouthful of water from the tap, even though he hadn't yet asked if the local water was drinkable. His only health precaution, he tried not to keep it swilling around in there too long. Then he sat on the bed and searched for the fiftieth time for the lump of dope that had gone missing between the airport and the hotel. He didn't expect to find it. He was pretty sure it fell out of his sock when he was rolling around the street and choking on CS gas. The dope had to be lying in a gutter somewhere, perhaps stuck to the bottom of someone's shoe like gum. All he had was the Rizla packet, given to him by the neo-hippie chick at the airport.

He wondered exactly when he had become a bad traveller. Through southern Africa, a short spell in Australia and a few years travelling in Central America before deciding to live in first San Francisco and, later, a string of Canadian cities, he seemed to get slower and slower. Not that getting slower was a problem; for one thing, he was getting older and, for another, he was nearly always stoned. Maybe it was a side effect of being so straight that, today, he was so sure he was losing his zest. But knowing the reason didn't make it any prettier.

He had put on a clean shirt and trousers, both in linen, hoping the creases looked stylish rather than straight-from-the-case. Then he had dampened his hair and gone downstairs to eat. On the way, he had checked to see if Tony had left him a message. When he was told there was nothing for him, he had shuffled on into the restaurant, feeling abandoned.

For some reason, despite the fact it seemed so incongruous in the middle of the Holy Land, he was glad the hotel restaurant was Mexican. If he made up his mind to have fajitas, the only difficult decision would be choosing his starter dish. He found he wasn't capable of concentrating on anything as prose-heavy as a menu. The waiter was a major distraction: he looked so much like the man at the desk. He came over, once, twice – the second time with a bottle of Black Label whisky – a third time and still David hadn't chosen his starter. The fourth time, he was about to wave him away again when the waiter said, 'No.'

'The party on the other table, they wondered if you'd care to join them?'

David looked up to see a man and a woman, both somewhere in their mid- to late twenties. He really only had eyes for the woman, though. He was feeling so inert, it was a shock to see anyone who was so alive. Her eyes were dark and full of electricity. If he could plug into them, perhaps they would recharge the lithium cells of his soul. He didn't know how he had failed to notice her before. Maybe she hadn't been sitting there when he had entered the restaurant. If she had been, he was genuinely scared for himself – for his eyesight or his sanity or worse.

He stood up so quickly his chair pinged backwards across the polished tile floor and smacked against the wall. He left it. Their invitation had come so abruptly from nowhere he was scared it was a misunderstanding. If it was, he didn't want to know. He wanted to skip ahead to the moment after this moment and make sure that, when he had his knees underneath their table, it would be too embarrassing for anyone to explain that they were only saying hello, they never meant for him to colonise their airspace.

'My name's David Preston.'

He led with his right hand, offering it to the man. His left hand was hooked under the back of the free, third chair. As they shook, he swung the chair into place next to the woman. He preferred to think ahead: if he lost the initiative the man might switch seats and David would be the one pushed to the end of the table. He wanted to make sure he was sandwiched between them, fractionally closer to the woman so he could keep turning towards her. The only thing he was worried about, he might look too needy, even desperate.

He wondered, this business of losing his zest, perhaps it was simply that he was becoming lonely. Not that he was ever lost for company for long. He still had the same smooth talent for rubbing along with people, whoever they were, wherever he happened to be. But he was beginning to get scared that one day it would end. The problem with being transient, you grew more and more faded compared to normal people; in the end, they either stopped seeing you or, worse, just looked right through. That was a nightmare.

No, literally. That *was* a nightmare. One that he had on his second day, squeezed out by the weight of his jet-lag.

David turned away from the man, knowing that he had already failed to memorise his name. At that moment, the nightmare came back to him. He had woken up convinced that loneliness led to fading, there had been a big health scare, spurred on by a report in the newspaper: for some reason, the *Vancouver Sun*. David spent the five minutes after waking staring at the lines on his hand, waiting for his life line and wealth line to come back into definition and his love line to return to a thick plait of pointless dead ends. David didn't usually remember dreams but this one came back with the touch of the strangers' hands. Particularly the dry, warm hand of the woman.

'Sophia. Sophia, Sophia.'

He hoped, saying it three times, he would never forget her name. He really didn't think he would. Though it was no guarantee, he'd forgotten more important things in the past.

Then he said, 'Have we met before?'

He couldn't be sure that he wasn't spinning her a line – just that for some reason he didn't think so. And inside, he was going *remember remember remember*. But he tried to keep his smile as steady as he could. There was no point in panicking, that never helped.

She actually looked slightly uncomfortable. 'I don't think so.'

'No?' There was something about the way she was acting, David couldn't read the signal. So he said, 'Not *before*, huh? Maybe I met you after?' He had no idea what he was talking about. His only concern, just to keep the smile in place. Reminding himself of what he'd heard about synchronised swimmers, the pain they go through – and still they come up smiling.

It turned out that talking nonsense was a sound move. Her companion had started laughing, slapping David on the back as he said, 'Before/After? How would you know?' All David could think was that he must be making sense on some other plane. Or the guy was very drunk. David took a chance and asked if he minded repeating his name. The man reintroduced himself as Yusuf, David reshook his hand with enthusiasm. Somehow, he already knew that Yusuf and the very beautiful Sophia were friends and nothing closer.

David turned back to her. 'No, honestly. I can't place it and I'm really embarrassed about that, but I do know you.'

'I doubt it.' She was smiling. You might call it coy, if the word didn't suggest something a bit weak. She wasn't at all weak-looking.

He was reaching and reaching, up on his tiptoes in his memory store. Then he had it.

'Your voice.'

'My voice? No. It's impossible.'

He could have sworn she was blushing and that only made him more positive. 'Absolutely. Now all I have to remember, where did I hear that voice before?'

'No, really.'

She was absolutely blushing. More than that, there was a warning to her tone. Normally, if David sensed he was tripping along an off-limits area, he would have pulled back. But this had got under his skin. He knew it was her voice alone. If he had ever seen her face before, his memory was much much worse than he ever thought. No one could forget her face. He said, 'Please. Come on.'

He was snapping his fingers, looking to her friend Yusuf for help.

Yusuf was laughing. 'Are you kidding? She is famous for her voice.'

She said, 'Leave it.'

Yusuf said, 'She is the voice of the music no one wants to hear.'

For a second, it was like someone had hit the Pause button inside David's skull. He froze in a total blank. Then it clicked. She was the voice on the radio.

'You're the drive-time DJ. I caught your show just before I was gassed.'

Sophia knew he was the priest from the park. She couldn't

explain the feeling of panic when she thought that David – *Father David?* – might remember her too. After all, there was the sanctity of the confessional. Even though it took place in a park rather than in a box. But she still could not remember the confession without a twinge – it was an embarrassing situation. And this man, this incognito priest, what did she know about him? He might be retired or resigned or anything. He might just have a big mouth – the kind who gets a little drunk and lets it all come tumbling out: *Whoops, I shouldn't have said that, should I?* So when he mentioned the radio show and his accident with the Israeli smoke grenade, she moved the conversation along by asking him for the full story.

David was surprised that everyone had heard about his struggle and his injuries. But he enjoyed the sympathy and gave them a long and elaborate version of the events, only breaking off to reassess the hors d'oeuvres. In his view, guacamole dips, humus, olives and falafel were an incongruous mix. Yusuf had to explain, it might be a Mexican restaurant but there was no reason to go mad – better have some normal food as well.

It was closing in on midnight when Yusuf accepted the waitress's offer of a third round of coffees. David excused himself, he needed to use the loo.

Sophia waited until he was through the door before she said, 'Did you know that he's a priest?'

Yusuf didn't know. Not that he was surprised, Bethlehem was always full of visiting priests. But not all of them were gassed on entry. He whistled, jokingly saying, *Uh-oh*. It was only after a pause that he asked Sophia why a priest was paying for a hotel room when he could stay with the Franciscans at the Church of the Nativity or with the Brothers at the university or with any of the other Latin orders around the town.

She had already thought that one through. 'I think maybe he is having a crisis.'

Yusuf chewed at his lip: it could be that. He called over to the *maître d'*, who agreed, it was possible, but he wasn't going to make a definitive judgment without talking to his brother. They were asking the waitress what she thought when David's head appeared above the steps to the bathroom. Sophia had to tell them to shut up: if the poor guy was in crisis, all this gossip and speculation wasn't going to help.

David shambled in, his hand on his chair before he paused and looked around at the red faces.

'What's up? Have you kids been fighting?'

Sophia said, 'That's it. I want to move on somewhere. What do you think?' As she spoke, she remembered Shadi talking about a new place. He had been asking her to visit for weeks. Maybe tonight should be the night. She said, 'I was thinking of *The Pink Parasol* only Yusuf is not so keen.'

David asked what the problem was. 'Is it some kind of low class place?'

'No one ever called it sanitary.' The way he shivered, you got the idea there was a real chance of infection.

'So what's the attraction?'

'Nothing I can think of,' Yusuf said. 'Unless you want to smoke.'

'Well, now . . .' David could already feel his mouth peeling back into a grin, just the anticipation of smoking a little genuine Middle Eastern hashish, untouched by any of the additives used to bulk out the weight. 'We could just pop along and have a goodnight toke.'

'You want to go? Really?'

It was Sophia, asking if he was serious. He was absolutely serious.

The underground carpark beneath the Grand Hotel looked as though it had been dug out by hand. Yusuf's car bounced over the rough spread floor, the chassis scraping against a misjudged ramp. As they pulled out into the street, Yusuf turned back to David's story.

'After you were gassed, who helped carry you from the car to the hotel?'

David was sat in the back. As he answered, he leant forward, waving a hand towards the windscreen, as though the streets were still full of smoke and shouting. Saying, 'Oh my God. There were police, there were rioting teenagers, everyone. Probably monks too, I don't know. I was blinded . . .' Then something made him pause, a thought disturbance. He said, 'Yusuf? Did you say you were the radio news guy?'

'That's me. First with the news, on the hour, every two hours or thereabouts.'

David couldn't believe he had been so stupid. 'You aren't going to put this in one of your news bulletins, are you?'

'Absolutely I am.'

The sound gushing against David's ears, it was the sound of a premonition, fifteen years of freedom ending with the slam of a gaol door. He said, 'I'd prefer you didn't do that. I'm trying to keep a low profile.'

They were pulling up on a side street, by a window lit with fairy lights and coloured with smoke. Sophia turned and smiled at him as she was climbing out of the car. She said, 'You are joking. You are already notorious.'

Yusuf fiddled with the door locks while Sophia ran for the bar. David lingered on the pavement. He said, 'Come on,

Yusuf. I'm old news, right? Who's interested in something that happened five days ago?'

Yusuf walked round the car, nodding. David pushed the bar door open for him, one arm almost cradling him as he whispered, 'So you'll leave me out of the bulletins . . .'

'You're right,' Yusuf said. 'But there's the religious angle. A priest comes to Bethlehem and, in the first five minutes, an Israeli soldier tosses a smoke grenade into his car.'

'Huh?' David didn't get it. 'Where does the priest fit in?'

Sophia saw Shadi across the room, sat with fifteen of his cousins. The moment that he saw her, though, he picked up the shared hubble-bubble pipe and started walking over to her table. He was careful with the pipe, making sure the smouldering embers in the bowl didn't get disturbed. As he sat down, he said, 'Who's the guy at the door, standing with his mouth open like that?'

Sophia looked back. David was only a metre behind Yusuf, but he seemed to be caught in a freeze-frame, pasted into the doorway. Yusuf sauntered onwards, only slightly unsynched, looking mildly goofy. If Sophia had to guess, she would say that he had mentioned that they knew David was a priest. She wondered if she should confess that she was the one who had given him away. Would she then have to admit how she had known he was a priest? Because she wasn't going to do that – not a chance.

David broke out of the frame and caught up with Yusuf. 'You're going to say I'm a priest? Is that what they call black propaganda?'

Yusuf looked puzzled, 'Propaganda?'

'To make the Israelis look bad?'

'I'm not going to make them look good. But you are a priest, aren't you? I mean, that's what we've heard.'

Yusuf looked to Sophia for confirmation. She said, 'It's what everyone's saying. The man who was gassed was a priest.'

As she spoke, she turned to David so he got the benefit of the shrug and the innocent smile that she used as she tried to throw her lines away. David noticed that when she smiled, her top lip turned slightly inside out, thickening into a pout. It was just physiological, it didn't mean for certain that she was especially sexy. But you couldn't help thinking. After a smile like that, David really did not want her to think he was a priest.

'Do I look like a priest?' He used his eyebrows as he spoke, trying to inject some mischief into the question; some devilment. It didn't seem to have much effect on Sophia, nor on Yusuf.

What could they say? He didn't *not* look like a priest. One thing you learnt if you grew up in the Holy Land. Priests and nuns came in all kinds of packages.

David decided, this was a fucked-up moment. The only thing he could do was play it *Zen-style*. There was always another possibility; and in this case, it was right to hand. Their friend had this huge water pipe, all fired up and ready to go. David lifted his fingers in a blessing over the pipe and said, 'Hallelulah for small mercies.'

Shadi passed over the hose flex with the mouthpiece on the end and David took a hit. The smoke filled his mouth like nothing he had ever tasted before. He felt his neck constrict. He began spluttering even before he worked out what was so unusual, so utterly revolting, about the mixture smoking in the bowl.

It was tobacco flavoured with chocolate.

Nicholas Blincoe

Shadi unclipped David's fingers from the smoking hose. David let him, just carried on coughing the cloying taste of choco-tobacco from his mouth. He should have noticed before, by the smell, there was not even the slightest hint of hashish in the smoky clouds above the bar tables. He could smell raspberry tobacco, strawberry tobacco and tobacco tobacco besides the chocolate, all of it making his head spin.

Yusuf caught Sophia's eye. She knew exactly what he was thinking as he looked at David gulping and sweating opposite them: *Definitely one of those priests in crisis.*

5

Sophia was on the old steps by the souk when she saw David the priest, or ex-priest, or whatever his exact status was. The steps were slimy with vegetable debris. Sophia had to pick her way between the streams of sluiced water running from the market stalls downhill to Manger Square. David was ten metres below her, his shaggy-cut head bobbing against the flow of the crowd. He didn't see her. He was too engaged with the street life around him. It seemed that the man could pass nothing without taking a close look. He had a chaotic style; zigzagging to his left and then to his right as he went from window to window and around the different street stalls: the shops with the spice bins outside, the boys roasting chickpeas in huge brass roasting pans and shovelling them into paper bags with a scoop. She guessed those things must seem exotic to him. But he even looked in the shoe shops, the hardware stores, all the pharmacies.

Sophia had a paper bag in one hand, her father's medicine, and her box of CDs in the other. She twisted the box upwards to check her watch. It was twenty minutes to her radio show; she had time to stop and chat. But as she started downhill, she ran into her Uncle Tony, coming out of the money-changer's at the foot of the steps with a thin wad of dollars and a thicker roll of shekels. He tucked the money into his breast pocket and waved her down.

'Sophia, what's the hurry?' It seemed that even looking at someone in a hurry made Tony breathless. 'You have to run in this weather? Are you late for the music no one wants to hear?'

'Not yet.' She pointed to David, bent over the selection of sweets at the sweet shop on the corner. 'I thought I'd say hello to the crazy priest.'

Tony looked, blinking twice to refocus. Then his mouth dropped open; as though the remains of his chin just slipped away and there was no longer anything to stop his face sliding down into his shoulders. 'That's him? That's the priest everyone's talking about?'

Sophia said, 'You should have seen him in the bar. He caught a mouthful of smoke and started coughing. He pulled a face like in a horror film. We thought he must never have seen a hubble-bubble pipe before. Then he started saying, you know, *damn and blast*. Asking if this was a joke. Then, when he recovered, he started moving round the bar, chatting to everyone.'

'He was trying to buy hashish.'

'You've heard?'

'I think everyone has.' Tony stared across the heads of the boys at the sweetcorn stall. David towered over them, even though his head was lowered, looking into the basin of hot water with the corn cobs cooking inside. 'I just didn't expect him to look like that. Did he say he was a priest?'

Sophia nodded. 'Yes. He finally admitted it.'

'Shall we go and say something? You could introduce me.'

They watched him mouth something to the boy selling the corn: a polite *shockran*, thank you, in Arabic heavily accented with English. Then he turned the corner by the mosque and shuffled into Manger Square. The square held the Church of the Nativity and the police station and pretty much nothing else but gift shops. Sophia didn't know if David needed a few souvenirs. He seemed to need something, moving in a slow daze. She didn't know what he was thinking, perhaps preparing his mind before he prayed at the church. Maybe that was why he was moving so slow, being so indiscriminate about the shops he looked over. If he was in crisis, maybe he was scared of what he would feel when he got to Christ's grotto and so he was retarding the moment. Sophia shrugged. It was possible. Who knew what went through priests' minds, especially when they *doubted*. Although another reason he was going so slow could be that he had a hangover from last night's tequila.

When she called out, he stretched round to pinpoint her voice. There were so many people on the streets, talking or just hanging around, he didn't see her until Tony steered her out of the crowd.

'David. How are you?' And as she turned, 'This is my uncle, Tony Khouri. Father David.'

Now it was the priest's mouth that dropped open, and though he still had enough chin to hold his face together, he really did not look too good. He seemed to be trying to bend his mouth into a smile but it ended as a frozen pout, as though he was kissing someone bigger and pushier than himself and had died of embarrassment.

She asked, 'Are you all right?'

He shook his head and said, 'The bar last night. You know. I made a fool of myself.'

So it was embarrassment. She said, 'I suppose you don't let your hair down so much.'

Her own head was slightly tender. She wasn't going to make a big noise about it, she just mentioned it. She stood there and watched him rub his hand round and round across his face as though he was trying to rub out his features. She had no idea how to help him. He looked so lost and confused.

She said, 'Do you want an aspirin?'

He mumbled something, it was hard to hear over the sound of his palm rasping on his two-day beard. Then he pulled his hand away and said, 'Maybe. Right now, I'm feeling a little too nauseous. Plus, I didn't sleep very well. Are there any flus going around?'

Sophia didn't know. She looked to Tony and he shook his head.

'Perhaps something you've eaten?'

'That's another thing. I don't have any appetite.'

Tony said, 'Welcome to Palestine, home of the health problem. We definitely have too much stress.' He held out a hand for David to shake. 'You notice the number of pharmacies in the city. There's an old law saying that no pharmacy can open within fifty yards of another. So now we have one exactly every fifty yards, anywhere you walk.'

David took hold of Tony's big, meaty hand. Its solidity, its breadth, helped keep him upright. He had got over the surprise of finding that Sophia and Tony were related. But he still couldn't believe the weight Tony had put on.

Sophia asked, 'Are you going to the Church of the Nativity today?'

'I don't know. Is it far?'

She told him it was hard to miss and pointed. The church covered one side of the square.

'The fortress-looking thing? Right. Is it any good?'

Tony butted in, 'It's a world-famous tourist attraction. Why don't I show you round?'

David nodded, *Great*. He was only sorry that Sophia had to slip out. She told them it was time for her radio show and pointed to a street to the side of the church. 'The radio station is over there, above the gift shop.'

He watched as Sophia threaded a way through the cars – Manger Square was basically a large, ugly carpark, currently in the process of being resurfaced. Tony explained it was part of the preparations for the millennium. David said, really, they were laying fresh tarmac? Bethlehem 2000 was going to be some party.

Ahead of them, a group of tourists were stepping off a coach. Their tour guide was waiting, ready to point them in the direction of the church. David let Tony steer him in the same direction. Like Tony said, the church was an international attraction, and David detected a Slavic language, possibly Slovak, as the group passed by. Next they were swamped by a group of Scandinavians, all staring straight ahead – they were going to the Church, there were going to be no deviations. It seemed to David that no one saw anything of Bethlehem but the Church of the Nativity. It was a shame. He found plenty elsewhere in the town to interest him. Admittedly, he had to work at it, take his time and really examine everything he saw.

He really hadn't got much sleep the previous night. Perhaps his problem was that he had slept too much the first three days when he had been recovering from the gas attack. Now he had the opposite problem, and even drinking too much wasn't helping with the insomnia. The past two nights he had lain in the dark of his room, fingering his way round his anxiety; almost hoping that he did have flu because the alternative was that he had caught a dose of depression. The anxiety lasted until he set out for a night-time stroll. He skirted round the packs of dogs and the military patrols, sniffing out the breeze that was coming off the desert. When dawn came, he was facing east on the road that led up to the plateau of Manger Square. During the day, the landscape around Bethlehem looked like an overworked quarry. It was only when it was filtered through the sunrise that it lost the dull yellow colour of cheap cement and became heart-stoppingly beautiful. David caught the glow and forgot how out-of-body he was feeling. Or at least, almost got the feeling of dislocation to work for him. Then didn't. He loved a good dawn, he just didn't think they had a spiritual significance any more.

He turned to Tony and said, 'You should have met me earlier. We could have rolled a number, breathed in the colours.'

'I don't think so,' said Tony. 'And whatever you do, please don't try and buy hashish again.'

'I know that now.' He rolled his eyes. 'So what else have you heard about me?'

'Let's see. The last five days, you were involved in an accident with a smoke grenade, you were treated by Dr Alawi, you like to wander around at night.' Tony counted off a few items on the stubs of his fingers. There was just one more thing: '. . . oh, and you're a priest. How did that one start?'

'You can't guess.' David waited a moment, knowing he was being unfair on Tony. He had only just worked it out himself. He started describing the stubborn twelve-year-old who nearly got him arrested, all those years ago.

'That was Sophia?' Tony couldn't believe it, though he knew the dates fitted. Sophia was in London that day, staying in a Bayswater hotel with the rest of her family, wondering why her Uncle Tony had decided to leave the country so abruptly. He said, 'It doesn't sound like Sophia. She was never religious, even at that age.'

'She was that day, she was rabid: like the rugrat version of Joan of Arc.'

They were walking in the gap between two parked coaches: a squeeze but at least it was free of tourist crowds. When Tony pulled up suddenly, David was slow to see the problem because Tony filled all the available space. It was a bad place to stop. The midday sun was beating off the shiny metal of the coachwork and mixing with the heat of the engines and the diesel fumes steaming off the blacktop. Then David saw the khaki green of the paramilitary vehicles.

'What's the problem?'

Tony said, 'Wait, something's happening.' He signalled for David to turn around. They edged back up the space between the coaches and circled round the far side of the square, behind the wire barrier that fenced off the part being resurfaced. David kept glancing over to the army-style vehicles. They were parked outside a squat stone building.

'What is it?'

'You don't see? They're bringing the prisoner out of the police station.'

The squat building had to be the police station. The trucks and Jeeps were police vehicles. David couldn't see any prisoner and was about to ask Tony when he realised the guy had to be in the central truck, the one surrounded by moustached young men, holding automatic weapons.

When they reached the Church of the Nativity, Tony stepped over a low chain on to a white marble piazza that surrounded the church. David hung back, staying on the carpark side while he tried to work out what the prisoner could have done. He had to be Palestinian Public Enemy #1, if he really justified that amount of fire-power.

The truck windows were fitted with grilles. Behind them, David saw the outline of a bald, fattish man. Then one of the policemen banged on the side of the truck and the prisoner turned. He had a face that sagged with helplessness.

Tony was halfway across the piazza, merging with the thick crowd of tourists queuing for entry to the church. He turned around, saw David and hissed at him. He flapped a hand at thigh level. A discreet gesture, it read: *Get your ass over here.*

David stepped over the chain and got in line. He asked, 'What's that guy done?'

'What's he done? Exactly what we want to do.'

'Someone else who wants to sell out to the Israelis?'

Tony nodded. 'They kept him locked in the police station, it must be seven days now. I guess now they decided it's time they moved him. I'm only surprised he's still alive.'

'You think they're going to, you know . . .' David tried to think of a euphemism. 'Maybe lose him in the desert?'

Tony shrugged. David remembered, in the old days, the biggest thing about Tony was his shrug. Now, even with all the extra weight, it was a kind of half-deflated gesture. 'I don't know. It might be nothing. The police station is moving soon, that building will be demolished to make way for a new visitors' centre. Maybe they're moving him to a new prison . . . maybe he'll never reach it.'

The piazza was full of tourists, patiently cooking in the midday heat. Tony pointed over their heads, towards the narrow entrance into the Church of the Nativity. 'Well, we can pray for him. Or ourselves.'

David said, 'I'll light a candle for the guy. If everyone's convinced I'm a priest, I might as well see if I've got any of the fringe benefits.'

Tony had been thinking about that. 'You know, we could stick with the priest story. That way, I could invite you round to my house and no one would think it was suspicious. All they would see, I'm just being naturally courteous, that's all.'

'A priest? Me? Come on, Tony. You want to do serious for a moment?'

'I am serious. It will work.' The problem was, the lawyer was moving more slowly than Tony had expected. He explained, 'We're working on a legal way to sign my Jerusalem property over to you. The idea is you'll be the one selling the place and I won't get shot as a traitor and collaborator.'

'But there's a hold-up?'

'It's legal intricacies, technicalities. I don't know. But we could be waiting for another two weeks, maybe more. If people see me with you every day, they are going to start wondering who you are. But if you pretend to be a priest . . .'

'When the shit hits, you can claim that you were fooled as much as anyone: this international criminal, who would have thought he'd pose as a priest?'

Tony nodded. 'That's it. That's what I was thinking.'

David stared ahead. He had no idea how a priest would act: his only role models were Cesare Borgia on the old BBC television series and the priest at his wedding. Maybe he could do Pat O'Brien in *Angels with Dirty Faces*, that was a more promising example. Once he got inside the church, he might see a few more types. But he and Tony had been waiting almost ten minutes and they still had half the queue ahead of them. David asked if there was another entrance. Tony pointed to a door just a few yards away. There was no queue.

'That's the entrance to the Catholic chapel. This is the way into the Orthodox chapel, where Jesus was born.'

David decided to stand it out; he'd better learn to suffer for his faith. Another ten minutes later, he realised why the line moved at such a crawl. The entrance was three feet high and only wide enough for one person at a time. And as people were using it to both come and go, traffic was slow.

But finally he was through the door, inside a cool chamber of wooden columns and worn stone. The air was heavy with incense and methylated spirits, perfume clouds and soft lamplight. As Tony prodded him forward, he found himself in a larger, bare chapel with a stone floor and a ceiling blackened with lamp and candle smoke. At the far end, a raised stage was hung about with brass chains and swinging incense burners, also brass. The backdrop was a huge carved piece of ecclesiastical furniture that could have been an altar if it had stopped halfway, instead of rising past the roof beams.

It looked like a Welsh dresser designed by Byzantine wood carvers and filled with portraits of the saints. David recognised the Orthodox style. He knew, if they owned the rights on the site of Christ's actual manger, they would have decorated it as though it was the birthplace of the Little Lord Elvis.

He pointed to the next queue, curving around the edge of the Byzantine screen. 'Is that it, Jesus's birth site?'

Tony nodded. 'Do you want to go down?'

The queue began at a narrow curve of steps that descended into the cave-like cellars of the church. David peered down. Quietly, he started singing, 'Away in a manger, no crib for a bed, the little Lord Jesus lay down his sweet head.'

'Please don't do that.' Tony was beginning to blush.

'Why? You don't think I've got a good voice?' David took it up a notch; a tweak of the volume control and a sliver of an Elvis croon. 'The stars inna bright sky, lookin' down where he lay.'

'What's up with you?'

'I'm just making a joyful noise.'

There were people looking now, the Orthodox priests with their biker beards and ponytails were muttering among themselves. Tourists were turning away from their guides, looking over their shoulders to pinpoint the voice.

'Stop it, David.'

'The little Lordah Jesus, ah-ah-sleep onna hay.' He dropped his voice to a whisper as he asked, 'I think I'm cracking up. You really want me to play a priest?'

'It's the best way. Please don't ruin the story already.'

There was a Latin nun staring now. Tony recognised her, a big and clumsy Swiss woman who taught at the local convent school. He flashed her a grimace-grin.

David said, 'I'm only pointing out I'm under stress. I need to find a way to ease the tensions.'

'Is that what this is about?' Tony asked. 'You want me to score dope for you?'

'The cattle ah lowin', the baby ah-ah-wakes.' David threw out his arms and filled his lungs. 'The Little Lord Jesus, no cry-yin' he makes.'

'I swear, they'll lock you up. They'll kill me.'

'Just an ounce. If I have another night without sleep, I'm going to lose it.'

'There is no hashish in Bethlehem.'

'A-WAY IN A MANGER.'

'Enough.' Tony pulled David round, out of the line of sight of the staring nun. He held him tight, standing almost nose to nose, as he said: 'Listen to me. This is a small town, everyone knows everyone and everyone is conservative. There are no drugs.'

'Come on, you are Arabs.'

'What the hell does that mean? We spend our time wallowing in hash smoke and eating Turkish delight? Get real, David. We're shell-shocked, we live under occupation, we've just come through the intifada. We lead narrow lives. Remember, ninety per cent of us are Muslims. This isn't an oriental fantasy. We behave ourselves.'

'Lebanon was full of dope.'

'To fund a six-sided war. And half that dope was coming from Afghanistan anyway, funding their own war, with CIA help.'

David knew that. He was beginning to feel uncomfortable listening to Tony's tirade: made worse because Tony's voice didn't rise above a whisper and there were tears in his eyes.

'You know, there's a taxi driver in town who likes to smoke a little dope. Everyone believes he's a drug addict and they think he's going to die. That's what it's like here. No one takes drugs, no one understands drugs. There is no drug culture. You want to get stoned, then you go to Jerusalem. And don't get any stupid ideas about hanging round the casbah like an American hippie tourist. Go to West Jerusalem and buy it off a Jewish kid.'

David was nodding, trying to show that he understood. The truth was, he didn't know why Tony was getting so emotional. He was shaking so hard, he was drawing more attention than David had managed with his singing. There was an outsize nun staring at the two of them. It looked as though she was about to come over and find out what was wrong.

David wasn't thinking on a conscious level, he knew he had to act so he relied on spontaneous instinct. He placed a hand on Tony's head and started muttering prayers. They were actually Buddhist prayers, or half-remembered scraps of a Buddhist prayer. But David kept his voice so low, no one could hear anything. They just saw one man praying over another, a hand resting in blessing on the other's troubled brow.

Tony's mouth was open. It was probably shock, but from a distance it might have looked like an expression of beatification.

Yusuf was waiting on an interview. The guy had to come from Ramallah and it looked as though he wasn't going to make it. Sophia was sat with Shadi in the main studio. There was still another ten minutes before her show began.

Shadi said, 'Who is he waiting for? Someone from the music festival?'

Sophia nodded. 'One of the organisers. He said he wanted to check that we had the revised details of the programme. Yusuf said, so e-mail them, don't come in person. But he said it was no problem.'

'He said that? He's going to drive all the way to Bethlehem on the desert road and he told you it was no problem? You know what it's about, don't you?'

Sophia guessed that the man wanted to make a statement about Suha Arafat. Her shopping trip must be over by now, perhaps she would squeeze in a visit to the festival's closing ceremony. Sophia was about to ask Shadi for the gossip when the door of the radio station opened and their old teacher, Sister Hilda, walked in. Sophia said, 'Don't look round, Shadi.'

'What is it?' He was already turning, he couldn't resist. When he saw Sister Hilda, it took the spirit right out of him.

Sister Hilda had barely changed since Sophia and Shadi were in her class, studying the basics of French literature. She was actually Swiss, built on German lines with Italian colouring. What was French in her was less obvious, because it was so badly blended. You looked at her large brown eyes, trapped under the chain link of her thick dark eyebrows, you saw someone caught in their own conspiracies and brooding that they had to conspire alone. Her problem was that she was a shy woman who controlled her condition with a strict regimen of pettiness and spite. It mostly worked, until a sudden passion erupted and the shyness returned in blushes and stutters.

'What does she want?' Shadi hissed out of the side of his mouth, ventriloquist-style, so Sister Hilda wouldn't see his lips move. The nun was still paused in the doorway, clutching tight to her Pan Am flight bag. She wouldn't move until she was sure of her surroundings.

Sophia said, 'Probably to use the tape-copying machine.'

Sister Hilda was satisfied, there were no surprises in the radio station. She pushed open the door into Sophia's studio and said, 'Little Shadi, dear. When did I last see you?'

He could probably give her the exact date but he said, 'I don't know. A couple of years?'

'At least that, dear. I know you weren't such a big man then.'

Sophia decided she wasn't going to mess around. She would sacrifice Shadi if she had to. She said, 'I'm sorry, my programme starts in a moment. Would you mind chatting in the corridor.'

Sister Hilda had her head down, she was rummaging in her Pan Am bag. When she looked up, she was holding a cassette.

'I'm here to copy this,' she said.' Shadi, you can keep me company at the machine.'

Sister Hilda hadn't been able to believe her luck when she had first seen the tape-copying machine. That was six months ago, and since then the nun had come in once every ten days. The cassettes were part of an informal library that had been circulating among the nuns since Sophia was at school. They were recordings of religious singing, usually the singing of priests. Sister Hilda organised concerts at the school and if a visiting priest was known to have a good voice, he would be persuaded to make a recording with the choir. Sister Hilda owned microphones and an old four-track machine. Since Sophia had started work at the radio station, she had discovered that the recordings weren't just a Bethlehem craze. Sister Hilda belonged to an international swap group.

Shadi went off with the nun, looking dazed. Sister Hilda herded him ahead of her, patting him on the back as she went. The pats were heavy-handed. Sister Hilda was a strong woman. She batted him towards the store cupboard first, to pick up a box of Maxell tapes before taking him over to the duplicating tape machine.

Sophia managed to forget about Sister Hilda over the next hour. Her show was going well; from what she heard, people did want to hear her music after all. They might be lying to her face and complaining behind her back but at least she was enjoying herself, tracking through her record collection. Today, she began with an Edith Piaf song, *Le gitane et la fille*, and then Nina Simone's *Black Is The Colour of My True Love's Hair* and, so as not to alter the tempo, another Simone song: *Four Women*. When Sophia finally did pick up the pace, it was with an MC Solaar track that reminded her of university in Paris and one by Fairuz's son Ziad Rahabani. The next record she chose was by Air, long enough to stretch over a coffee break and give her time to smoke a cigarette. When Sophia saw Sister Hilda standing by the machine she was shocked: the nun had to be making hundreds of copies using the station's limited supply of tapes. It was a moment longer before she realised the nun's lips were moving. She was talking to someone. If it was still Shadi, Sophia couldn't see him. He was obscured by the open door of the store cupboard.

She was quite close when she realised it was Father David. He was looking panic-stricken, but he was nodding and saying *yes, yes*. When Sister Hilda spoke English she always used

German stresses, which seemed to give the words a kind of precision, not always an accuracy. She was speaking so rapidly she was difficult to follow. There was also a breathlessness about her. And a blush. David looked torn. Sophia could tell that he didn't know if he should try to catch what she was saying or if he should run away. He probably didn't want to believe what was obvious: Sister Hilda had fallen for him.

Sophia decided, she would save him.

'You're here for your interview?' She smiled brightly as she took his arm.

When his eyes swung on to her, they were so full of anxiety and helplessness, they bulged. 'What?'

'I thought you were going to be late but you're right on time.' She tightened her grip on his arm and tugged him. Sister Hilda thought she had him glued to the spot but he came away with a soft sticky sound and followed Sophia back to her studio.

A few minutes later, he could speak. 'Thank you.'

She looked up and nodded. He was welcome. Then she put her head back down to her pile of CDs and shuffled the cases into the playing order. She was poised on the cross-fader, ready to bring up another French house track.

David said, 'There's only the two of you working here?'

Sophia nodded. 'Basically, yes. Just me and Yusuf, although there are a few volunteers.'

'How do you cope?'

'We manage. A lot of songs are so long, you can put one on and then go off and do something else. There's one that's over an hour long but it's so popular we play it almost every day. *The Coffee Cup Reader.*' There was a cup of coffee on the mixing desk. Sophia turned it over into the saucer, twisted it round twice and turned it back to look at the pattern of grounds in the bottom.

When she smiled and showed David, he asked, 'Is that good?'

'Of course it is. Do you want me to read yours?'

He would have to get a cup of coffee first. But Sophia told him it didn't matter. She could guess part of it. Sister Hilda wanted to know if he could sing; and if he could, could she tape him?

He was surprised; although she didn't have the whole story. 'The problem is, she already knows I can sing. She heard me earlier, singing in the church. She told me I have a unique gift. She wants me to sing at an event she's organising, something to do with a music festival.'

Sophia whistled. He was in trouble. She told him, 'Sister Hilda's like a little kid. She's notorious for her crushes on priests that can sing.'

Sophia thought she could tell herself it was David's own fault. If he hadn't started singing, he wouldn't be in this trouble. But she knew she was really the one to blame. Sister Hilda would have known who David was, she might even have been stalking him, waiting for the moment he opened his mouth. All Sophia could do was apologise for being so indiscreet. The only person she had told was Yusuf, but it was no surprise that everyone now knew David's story.

She said, 'But please, please don't tell anyone about my confession. Not that you would, of course.'

She shot a guilty look at David. She shouldn't even have suggested that he might spill her story. He might be in crisis, but he probably still kept the priest's code.

David shook his head. There was nothing to tell. He didn't say that he couldn't remember anything of her confession. He only wished he could.

6

Four a.m. David kicked off the loose bed-sheet and swung a leg onto the floor. As the cool marble met his feet, he tried to spread his toes and flatten his arch so the maximum amount of sole connected with the stone. He often claimed to know the secrets of foot massage. The line he used was something like: *I only have to touch those sole spots and I'll connect directly to your life source. It's a Veda thing, baby.* He doubted that anyone had ever believed him – maybe just the one girl in Austin, Texas, but she also gave him credit for curing her flu so she wasn't likely to complain. He wished he knew the genuine trick because he was certain now that he had a case of Palestinian flu. He could not sleep. It was crazy lying there any longer, staring at the ceiling of his hotel room, desperate for a nice fat joint.

Ten minutes later, David was in the lobby of his hotel, trying to slope past the dozing concierge without disturbing him. It didn't work, the man was half asleep but still insisted on coming out from behind his desk and shaking David's hand, calling him Father and wishing him the best of the day. David nodded his head in a vague suggestion of a blessing. Then he was away, through the door on to the barely lit streets.

At this time in the morning there were nothing but dogs, cops and soldiers on the streets. A couple of Palestinian policemen were kicking around the street corner at the entrance to the hotel's carpark. Then, at the junction for the main Jerusalem–Hebron road, an Israeli armoured convoy crawled by on its regular patrol. The Israelis were shadowed by an old truck flying the Palestinian flag. David lit a cigarette and followed it with his eyes as it passed through the traffic lights. There were a few Palestinian soldiers inside, kept from sleeping by the hard jolts of the potholes through the truck's suspension. Another three or four Palestinian military types were sitting on a wall across the road, just by the stop for the Hebron bus. David gave them a sidelong glance through his cigarette smoke but looked away without being able to guess whether they were police or soldiers. They had their own distinct uniform, different to either the Bethlehem police or the men in the truck. He had to say, the Palestinian Authority were keen on getting their boys kitted out, as though it was their number-one priority. They just hadn't decided on the final *look* yet.

No one, neither the Israeli nor the Palestinian patrols, paid him any attention. It was just that seeing so much heavy *presence*, he couldn't help but get paranoid. The lack of sleep was definitely doing something to his head. It felt as though the inside of his skull was coated with metallic paint: every thought seemed to ping around without sticking, just setting his teeth on edge. He was too aware of being a thinking being; yet he seemed to have no control over his thoughts, leaving them to ricochet around his mind. All the years he'd spent moving, he couldn't remember suffering quite so much insomnia before. He could hardly blame the strange bed in his hotel. He travelled so much, it was the *unstrange* beds that felt strange to him . . . another line he'd used more than once, drinking late in hotel bars. Asking the woman who might be there, sitting beside him, could she grasp the paradox? The bar at the Grand Hotel closed around midnight, so there was no alternative to these night walks.

David took a look at his watch, calculating that if he looped around the whole town, he would be back in Manger Square in time for the dawn. He could pray for the mother of all sunrises to come and burn the shadows away. The way he was feeling, he might as well be a priest in crisis. It was how he felt.

He reached Sophia's house an hour past dawn. He knew it was hers. She was standing out in the yard pulling at the shirt of an old man who was standing on a kitchen chair and looking over his wall into the neighbouring olive grove. It had to be her father, Elias. The man looked frail – he was a small man anyway, but he seemed to have picked up a slow puncture. He was now almost completely deflated. And yet he was giving an impression of vigour, standing on his chair, red in the face, shouting at the four burly-looking men on the far side of the wall. You only needed one glance to know these men were related, a father and his three sons. They even spoke in the same tones, their harshness contrasting with Elias's mispitched voice, a sign that the old man was partially deaf. Still Elias matched the neighbours, harangue for harangue. The neighbours' main advantage was height: the wall was high but they stood on a hillock of broken rocks, Elias only had a kitchen chair. They were all taller than him anyway. David thought that Sophia had the right idea. She should get Daddy off his chair and back into the house. This was a situation that could turn ugly.

David ran over. 'What's the problem?'

Sophia may have been surprised to see him, but she just turned to her father, calling him Baba as she pulled him around to look at David. 'This is Father David.'

David was thinking, four of them and three of us, these wouldn't be good odds under any circumstances. He could go for the two oldest boys, but he was going to get a real hammering. No doubt about it. If Sophia didn't think of something, they were in shtuck.

He should never have doubted Sophia: she had diplomatic skills to spare. David became the excuse she used to make her father step down and return indoors. But even when she had his chair safely tucked back under the kitchen table, Elias Khouri couldn't help bobbing back to the window to see if the neighbours were still out there. They were: the four men ignoring the steadily climbing sun. It was a symbolic occupation, they were keeping the pressure up.

Sophia's mother laid out food: bread, a bowl of olive oil and a bowl of ground thyme decorated with a few sesame seeds. This was *za'atar*, a traditional breakfast dish David had learnt to eat years ago: you dipped the bread in the olive oil and then swiped it through the ground thyme. Today, it was just an appetiser. Sophia's mother was back at the cooker, frying goat's cheese in a cast-iron skillet, shouting over her shoulder.

Sophia said, 'She wants to know if you've eaten.'

'No. I mean no. But thank you.' David wasn't hungry. 'I was just walking by, I don't want to be in anyone's way.'

'You're not in anyone's way.' Sophia was going to keep him there, reminding her father of his obligations as a host.

Every time Elias went to the window, Sophia was a pace behind him. David didn't know what they were saying but he could tell she was still using him to exert leverage on her father because after a few more sorties to the window he came and sat down at the table opposite David and apologised.

'We are having neighbour trouble, Father. I'm sorry. It's so silly, really.' Elias was pushing at the swollen knuckles of one hand with the thumb of the other. 'They know I am going to court today so this is their last chance to deflect me. They don't know me very well, though. I will not soften.'

Sophia said, 'They don't want to soften you, Baba. They want to exhaust you. If you carry on like this, you won't be healthy enough to make it to Ramallah.'

'I'll make it.'

Sophia started telling David about the Ramallah road. She paused a moment, letting a series of images flick through her mind until she had the appropriate one. David had to think of a rollercoaster ride.

He nodded.

'Well, imagine a two-hour drive, all the way you're travelling through a desert.'

'It's a bad road?'

'Bad? It's evil. My last trip, I had to take the *sherut*. Nine people in a taxi and no air-conditioning, I thought I was going to die. I'm serious. We had a window open but then the man in front of me was sick, his vomit blew back over me . . .'

Elias Khouri had been standing at the window again, but as Sophia's story grew lurid, he turned sharply. 'Sophia. Please.'

She just continued, 'This foul-smelling spray, it filled the whole of the taxi and the driver doesn't even stop . . .'

'No, Sophia. Not at breakfast.' Elias was standing over her now, a look of pained embarrassment on his face.

'I've finished, Baba. I was just saying, all the drivers keep a pile of sick bags on the dashboard . . .'

'Sophia. Enough.' He turned from Sophia to David. 'I'm so sorry, Father. I don't know what she's doing. If she thinks she is amusing you, I don't know.'

David knew. She wasn't trying to spoil everyone's breakfast. She only wanted to distract her father and was using his own sense of propriety against him. David tried to help, keeping the conversation going. He said, 'Two hours to get to Ramallah? Why's that? It's only an hour to Tel Aviv.'

Sophia said, 'It's half an hour to Ramallah on the direct route, through Jerusalem, but the Jews won't let us use that road. Instead, we have to go the long way round, through the Valley of Death.'

'Are you serious, the Valley of Death? Like in the Bible.'

Sophia nodded. 'Maybe you should try it. It's probably easier to cope with the journey if you think of it as religious sightseeing.'

David shrugged, wondering what he was supposed to say. Maybe it was an appropriate time to make the sign of the cross. Presumably a real priest ought to have a feeling for these things. There was a pause, and David let the conversation slip. It was all his fault. In that moment, Elias was up again, across the kitchen and banging on the window with his fists. David couldn't catch what the old man was shouting but he knew that the situation had taken a new, more serious turn. He leapt up to see.

There was a metal door in the Khouris' yard wall. The neighbours had it open now, and were poised on the threshold.

Elias Khouri continued shouting the same phrase and David was beginning to get the gist: 'Get off my land.' The sound of the words translated themselves. Then the old man was off, scuttling like one of the garden lizards as he made for the outside door.

Mrs Khouri was screaming, she didn't want her husband out there in another confrontation. She tried to grab at him with a hand but she caught air, nothing else. David followed him to the door.

There was hardly any shade in the land between Sophia's house and the al-Bannas'. The scattered olive trees were thin and wispy. On the far side of the land, there was a broad-branched tree that threw a pendulum of shadow on to the ground. Someone had set up a swing for the youngest children but there was no one there now. It was just old man al-Banna standing in the gap in the wall, his boys at his shoulder and his nose ten centimetres from Elias's nose. David stood behind him, trying to ease him out of the way as he simultaneously fixed the al-Bannas with a wide-angle look: the face of a man who was steeling himself for something, whatever was necessary.

Sophia was looking out from the kitchen, trying to make her mother take hold of the telephone. She was telling her to call Uncle Tony, but her mother's hands seemed to have turned to jelly. She would not take hold, she just kept up a thin, soft wail and there was nothing Sophia could do but wait for the sound to work its way out.

'Please, Mama. Please, not now.'

She eventually took up the phone and Sophia ran out of the house. By the time she got to the face-off in the yard, David had managed to push his way between her father and the al-Banna family. Now he was hauling on the handle of the steel door, trying to shut the four men out. Sophia was pleased to see that her father was going along with David, that he was showing sense enough not to follow the al-Bannas as they escalated the issues. But still he couldn't resist leaping at David's shoulder, shouting, 'You think you can intimidate me? You can think again. I'll be in that court this afternoon. I'll be there. Me and my lawyer.'

Old man al-Banna had his foot in the doorway, stopping the door from closing. David was trying to push it out of the way with his own foot. Trying to do everything short of stamping down. He didn't want the situation to flare up. The sun was high now, hot enough to fuel tempers. It was certainly heating up the tin roof of the al-Bannas' chicken shed. The smell of chicken shit was wafting on warm thermals, over the problem land to Elias Khouri's house.

Sophia squeezed in beside David, folding her hand around his wrist as she helped him pull the door closed. She told al-Banna, 'You cross that line, we'll call the police.'

Al-Banna said, 'I already called my cousin. You know him? The chief of Bethlehem police.'

He was holding a big, old-fashioned cellphone in his hand, waggling it about beneath her nose for emphasis. Sophia suddenly saw the way it was going. It didn't matter that her father was still jumping around, promising that he would soon be in the court in Ramallah. They knew he wasn't going to make it. Long before then, he would be sitting in a cell in Bethlehem police station.

Her father was saying, 'Go and get your Uncle Tony.'

'Mama's calling him, Baba. He'll be here.'

She could already hear the slip and grind of the tyres on

the dusty road. The Bethlehem police come to answer their cousin's call.

She said, 'The police, Baba. Get back in the house. The priest is here, we'll hold them off.'

Her father was looking towards the road. Two police cars were pulling up at the school opposite. She saw the tremor of a tiny muscle working at the corner of her father's eye, the only sign that he was scared.

'Go inside, Baba.'

'No.'

A policeman in a dark beret was striding across the road, pausing at their gate as he waited for his colleagues to catch up.

'Please. Go inside,' she said again. 'Please, Baba.'

Elias Khouri had spent fifteen months in prison between 1973 and 1974. It was an Israeli prison where the Jewish-Iraqi guards worked out their frustrations with their new homeland on the flesh of their prisoners. Sophia knew her father was a brave man. This was nothing to do with bravery. He had a physical reaction to the word prison, to the thought of it even. The touch of the metal door stayed with him, the sound of the bolts as they turned against metal and slid into stone. He jolted at the sound of footsteps: whether they sounded like the dead steps on the ground-floor corridors or the echo on the upper walkways. And then all the other noises, the sound of a cabbage falling on to the kitchen floor like the dull thud a stick makes as it's swung against a mattress, when you are underneath the mattress. The blow does internal damage to the liver or the kidneys, but there are never any bruises on the skin.

Samira Khouri had picked up information like this from odd remarks that Elias had made, over the years, but also from

101

watching him and from listening as he slept beside her. She pieced together the few words that slipped out of his dreams and shared them with Sophia in whispers in the garden. Sophia picked almonds off their tree, her mother held the basket and they talked. The thing they never spoke about was how basic their information was. All they had were the elements of a movie, sound and pictures. They didn't want to even think about it, though it was always there, pressing against the little knowledge they had.

But why did they think about the beatings? The guards had done much worse, left worse scars without ever using a stick. Elias was deaf in his left ear after an infection caused by regular drenchings in urine. His arthritis came from being chained naked, in a crouched potion, and being hosed with cold water. The arthritis affected both his knees and his hands. The hands were the most visible. Elias was always pressing at his knuckles, as though he was trying to defuse the joints or spread the pain. Sophia always looked away whenever he did it. She preferred not to think about it. Not that it worked. One day she was shopping in the big Israeli supermarket in Jerusalem. She picked up a root of ginger and gagged as she recognised the shape of her father's knuckles in the swollen root.

Now Elias Khouri had the fist from one hand buried in the other, swivelling it round like a broken ball joint as he kept his eyes on the policemen. They swaggered into the garden, stepping across the polished stone lintel that separated the Khouris' land from the sidewalk as though it wasn't there.

Sophia knew it was too late now. Her father wouldn't go inside. She couldn't even plead with him to leave her to answer their questions. The policemen would not speak to her at all if there was a man around to talk to.

One of the policeman was a captain. Sophia didn't recognise him, but was not surprised. She knew he would be a Hebronite. He moved ahead of his men, beginning to exert his authority but doing it in an easy, open-handed, smiling way. Before he kissed old man al-Banna and each of his three sons, he made an encompassing gesture that included Elias Khouri and was presumably intended to create the feel of a charmed circle of geniality.

Elias Khouri clearly did know the captain: he greeted him by name as he stiffly accepted his embrace and kisses. Then he turned and pointed to David, saying, 'This is a visiting English priest, Father David.'

David understood enough of the introduction to put out his hand. The police captain shook it, warmly but briefly. Then it was business.

The al-Banna men backed off to allow the policeman to concentrate on Elias Khouri, expressing regrets about the whole problem. Sophia clung on to her father's arm. The policeman wasn't exactly trying to haul him away. Instead, he held out his hand to rest two fingers on the tip of Elias's elbow, preparing himself to sweet-talk him into coming quietly.

The policeman said, 'You understand that I have to have a statement.'

'Of what?'

'Of events. As far as your version goes, Abu Sophia.'

'My version? My version is these men are standing on my land.'

'Well, they are standing in disputed territory.'

'Disputed? The only people disputing anything are these hooligans. Everyone else knows that this land is mine.'

Elias Khouri was raising his voice. The policeman absorbed it, waited for the pause and then stepped in closer.

He said, 'I have seen signed papers.'

'Signed by whom? As a witness to what?'

'That this land belongs to the family al-Banna.'

'Of course they have that. If they write it themselves they can have a hundred pieces of papers. They can produce documentation enough to paper the land. If they write and sign these documents themselves they could cover the whole of Bethlehem, Beit Sahur and Beit Jala.' Elias Khouri was shaking, his head turned so that he was looking over the policeman's shoulder at old man al-Banna.

Al-Banna smiled back.

The policeman said, 'Thank you. Thank you. God willing there will be a resolution. We will find one. And now you will come to my station and give me your account of this matter.'

Elias was growing pale. He held his hands clasped at his navel. Sophia was still holding his arm in support and she felt the sinews tighten beneath her father's loose skin. Below the surface, he was completely tense, he could not be more tightly wound.

Sophia was not going to let her father go to Bethlehem police station. She said, 'You want my father's account of this matter? Go to Ramallah this afternoon – he's going to give it to a judge.'

The police captain glanced quickly at her. There was a flicker of disapproval mixed with disbelief, he was not sure why she had even bothered speaking. Then he looked away again, his own hand tightening on Elias's other arm. If they weren't careful, Sophia and the policeman might pull her father apart, just snap him in two.

Sophia was getting desperate.

David saw it. The last ten minutes, he had been watching her, registering every wave of fear and courage as they passed in cycles across her face. He wasn't sure what had made him so sensitive. He was feeling anxious himself, and this after a lifetime's experience dealing with policeman, customs guards, army personnel, prison guards. You only had to glance over his curriculum vitae. So he could easily imagine what she was feeling. But this wasn't imagination. He was feeling *for* her. And he could either flap around at the wall, choking for her, or he could do something.

He stepped forward and started babbling in English. 'Hold on, Officer. Sir. Sorry. It's my flock, my call. Mr Khouri's not going anywhere. I don't know if you're into the Church. The Catholics, like me. But you have to respect my beliefs.'

The policeman paused. He looked baffled but only barely troubled. The expression of a mildly stoned jazz fan, hearing a left-field squeak and deciding it might be deliberate, it may be a bum note, but deciding it wasn't worth figuring it out.

David had to face it, he seemed to have lost his easy way with the authorities. He felt a wave of vulnerability. It could be lack of practice, or a post-viral hiccough, but if he was no longer capable of dealing with these situations, it left him wide open to attack. When he heard a shout coming from the roadway, he jumped. He was so edgy. It didn't help when he saw the flash of another uniform, jogging towards the Khouris' garden. His first thought was that they were reinforcements, though he didn't know if they were coming for Elias or for him. Then he saw Tony and realised this was the cavalry, come at the last split second.

The Bethlehem police captain was still holding on to Elias

Khouri. He had to physically twist the old man around as he turned and tried to source the new disturbance. Tony was making most of the noise, shouting encouragement to his family between gulps of air. He looked as though he had run across town, he was so out of breath, but he kept on shouting as he kept pace with the uniformed older man. The man looked fit, a powerful man in his mid-fifties: another police chief.

The Bethlehem captain let go of Elias's arm and strode for the gate. He looked confident – although he was making quick beckoning gestures with his hands, signalling his men to get into position behind him. They moved into formation, forming a flying V at his shoulders.

Tony had dropped a pace behind his police chief and had stopped shouting. His man had enough presence for both of them. When he paused in the centre of the yard, he did it to let the other policeman make the first move.

The Bethlehem captain said, 'This is covered.'

Tony had to admire the way his chief kept his voice steady, saying: 'Yes. It's covered by me. This is Beit Jala. The road marks the boundary.'

'No. The roadside is the boundary, that includes the land alongside the road.' The Bethlehem chief was trying to sound certain but it was clear he didn't really know. It wasn't something he had ever bothered to think about.

The two chiefs were no more than a foot and a half apart. Almost chest to chest. In the strong sunlight you could see that their uniforms were different shades of green-blue. No question about it, they were not cut from the same cloth. But the real difference between the two men was religious. That was the subtext: one Muslim, one Christian.

Sophia had moved forward to catch hold of her father,

almost as though she expected him to keel over. David could understand. He was feeling giddy with relief himself. He could almost have fainted. As Tony sidled in beside him, he whispered, 'Not a moment too fucking late, you bastard.'

Tony hushed him, a warning to stay in character.

David hissed, 'Who is your guy?'

'Chief of the Beit Jala police force.'

'It looks like he's winning.'

'No. Today we've got a stand-off. Call it a draw, but we'll lose in the end.'

The captain of the Bethlehem police was shouting, 'Listen to me. Beit Jala is part of the municipality of Bethlehem.'

The Beit Jala policeman never once lifted his voice. He said, 'But civil cases are local police business. My jurisdiction.'

Tony said, 'You'd better get out of here before they start wondering about your angle. Meet me in Jerusalem this afternoon.'

'Meet where? I don't know Jerusalem.'

7

David picked up the *sherut* for Jerusalem at the crossroads. It was a minibus rather than a stretched Mercedes. The only free seat was at the back, on the same side as the sliding door. David took a moment to find it, the minibus was so dark. Every window had curtains drawn against the morning sun. Half a mile up the road, when the minibus was stopped at the Israeli checkpoint, a soldier hauled back the door and the unfriendly light flooded in. David was thinking, so okay, now he got the point. He'd be given just enough time to recover after the stand-off in the Khouris' garden, before a new scenario came along to bust his psyche. There was a pattern, he would have to get used to it.

The soldier leant into the minibus. He held out a hand as he made guttural clicks with his mouth, approximating a language rather than speaking one. Though David, like everyone else in the *sherut*, could tell he wanted their passports or travel documents. Another soldier stood to his side, a hand on the Uzi that hung like a gunmetal handbag from his shoulder. Resting not pointing. If the soldiers gave off an aura, it was more an air of petulance than real threat. They were only kids, after all. Not that it made David feel any easier – he knew petulant kids could cause as much mayhem as anyone on the planet.

David waited with his passport pegged between finger and thumb. Again, he had that teeth-setting edge of nerves. Why it was happening now, he didn't know. The closest thing to contraband was the map of Jerusalem in his jacket pocket, marked with an X where he was going to meet Tony. The Israeli army weren't going to get excited about that. He took a breath, trying to chill. To help focus, he concentrated on the felt-tip graffiti the soldiers had scrawled across their flak jackets. None of it was in Western script, but David took a guess that the slogans and logos were a mix of politics, personal statements and rock 'n' roll. The one checking the documents had a telephone number written across his arm in a girlish hand. David put that under the heading of romance. He nodded at the soldier as he held out his passport. The soldier nodded back, only glancing at the cover before waving a hand to show he had seen enough. He was more interested in the old woman sat next but one to David on the back seat. She had the same orange-sheafed photocard the other Palestinians had but not the square of white paper folded inside it. The piece of paper had to be crucial because the soldier gave a few more guttural clicks, his signal that she had to get off the bus. She picked up her bags full of aubergines and tomatoes and quietly climbed out of the minibus.

The soldier was going to slam the door shut again when there was a shout in French. Then the nun David had met yesterday was in the doorway, hoisting her skirts just enough to make the hop into the minibus.

'Good morning, Father,' She spoke in English now, her lips peaked into a smile.

David said, 'Hello. Sister Hilda, isn't it?'

Her eyes were cow-like. As she nodded, she cast them downwards in the style of a heavier and darker Princess Diana.

Sister Hilda spoke English with lilting Germanic vowels and hardly any rasp. David didn't know if she was softening her voice for his benefit. He had the impression that she had known he was on the minibus. Perhaps she saw him from a distance; he was the last passenger to get in the *sherut* before it drove off. David had an unholy vision of the nun legging up the road, skirts in hand and powerful Swiss mountain feet pummelling the road to catch up with him.

She asked, 'Are you bound for the cathedral, Father?'

'Er, yes, there and elsewhere. The whole tourist trip.'

'I can be your guide, Father.'

The minibus was beginning to move. Sister Hilda struggled towards the spare seat at the back, muttering *Pardon* as she swung against a fragile-seeming woman in black. The seat next to David was taken by a teenage boy in denim. Sister Hilda began to worm her way into the gap between the boy and David, pushing the boy out to the end of the seat. By the time the minibus cleared the checkpoint, she and David were squashed tight together.

Tony had insisted that they make their way to Jerusalem separately. They would rendezvous at his apartment in the Old City before going on to lunch with the lawyer, Edward Salman. It seemed that Salman had finally figured out a way to make David the legal owner of Tony's chunk of real estate. Standing in the street outside Sophia's house, David had said

111

that sounded like a reason to celebrate. Tony had ripped a page out a Jerusalem guidebook and marked the apartment's location with an X. He had refused to write anything else. He had actually wanted David to memorise and destroy it. David said, 'Right.' What he'd actually meant was *Yeah, right — how much memory do you think I've got after a lifetime of dope smoking?*

The map had stayed in the top pocket of his shirt, the same pocket he used for his passport. Now, as he slipped his passport back in place, his hand grazed the paper. He wouldn't need it for an hour or more, it was still only 10.40. David was hoping to scout around a little first, buy himself some dope from someone on Jaffa Street. It was how many days since his last smoke? He rustled his fingers in the dark of the minibus, a quick calculation, then found his hand suddenly swaddled by a larger, softer hand.

Sister Hilda said, 'I still feel an excitement, knowing I live so close to Jerusalem.' The excitement showed in a tremor that ran through her hand and into his. 'Where our saviour put his feet, I put my feet also. Do you know?'

David disengaged his hand. 'Yes.'

The minibus reached the corner before the King David Hotel and paused, its engine idling by a gate cut into the city walls. A couple of boy passengers hauled on the sliding door and in the time it took for it to shunt open and closed, David saw the entrance to a school on the other side of the gate. He wondered if he had missed his chance. Maybe he should have leapt out ahead of the boys and legged it to safety. He had a feeling this gate and that school both figured on Tony's map. But so long as the map was tucked inside his pocket, he wouldn't know.

He asked Sister Hilda, 'Do you visit Jerusalem regularly, or is this a special trip?'

A bubble of spit appeared dead centre on her lips. He wondered if she was on medication – frothing at the mouth was a symptom of some antidepressants. But the fleck disappeared as she spoke.

'Today I made a snap decision. I saw you board the *sherut* and thought, this way I kill two birds with one stone. I act as your guide and I also explain about the musical festival and the possibility that you sing for us.'

At least it hadn't been his usual aimless paranoia. She really had followed him on to the minibus. He could see she was the tenacious type, she wasn't going to be easy to lose.

The minibus was running downhill. It took a right at the traffic lights and stopped between a taxi rank and a makeshift market, set up outside the city walls on a modern piazza. As the minibus emptied, David realised most of the passengers were carrying bags of garden produce. Today had to be vegetable market day. Around half the Arabs mingling between the *sherut* stop and the city walls were dressed in traditional clothes, and this half were mostly women. They wore the full-length cotton dress of the Bethlehem area, black except for an embroidered breastplate of entwined red flowers. In contrast, the men wore Western clothes: only a handful in robes with cloths on their head.

David stood on the pavement, looking at an enormous gate with the Dome of the Rock mosque rising over the battlement walls. The one thing on his mind, how to get to West Jerusalem and score.

He said, 'Well . . .'

Sister Hilda hauled on his arm. 'This way.'

Nicholas Blincoe

The blue plate said Damascus Gate in English. David didn't know what it said in Arabic or Hebrew but he caught Sister Hilda saying *'The Gate of the Colon'* as she led him through its shadows and out again to watch the city throb into life. The sunshine still had an early morning brightness, waking up the yellow stone and stirring up the city. David couldn't begin to absorb the amount of activity; too much was happening in too small a space. Looking from the gate, down a marble-paved hill, he felt he was catching the moment when someone touched the volume dial. The noise began medium-low but swivelled through the numbers until it hit ten. It stayed that loud the whole time he spent in the city: the next hour trying to break free of Sister Hilda.

That soundscape, in full effect, detail by detail. There was the two-tone pitch of hagglers: traders and shoppers, the toing and the froing as they shouted, resorting to praise and abuse. The oriental music that set the negotiations to the strings of an oud and soulful wails. Make that scales of wails, as the singers hit every possible note. The music spilled out of the transistor radios hanging from nails on shops walls and out of the ghetto-blasters pushed under the shopkeepers' stools. All the shouts and the music intermingled with the rumble of the city's infrastructure, bare steel wheels from hand-barrows on the marble paving slabs and the hum of the different engines and motors; from the industrial fridges at the butcher shops, to the mini-tractors that hauled the eight-by-three-foot flatbed trailers along the narrow streets of the souk. The tractors were piled high with produce, deliveries, household items, ready-boxed brand-name deals.

David and the nun were trapped in a busy street as two tractors came from opposite directions, forcing the crowd ahead of them. The tractors looked like diesel-chewing toys; like customised lawnmowers. But the way the drivers handled them, they seemed to think they were truckers on the big rigs. They sat up in their cabs, behind polythene sheeting, whooping and waving as they signalled their right of way. David could see the street was too narrow, he doubted there would have been enough room even if the traders hadn't maximised their shop space by spreading out on to the pavement. He couldn't see a way out, so went for the fatalistic approach and let the crowd carry him forward. As the two tractors met, they slid nose to nose before locking wheel arches and jamming. David was squeezed between two tables of stationery, outside a bookshop. Sister Hilda was opposite him, outside a butcher's shop, pressed against a display cabinet of roasted chickens. She was flat to the glass door, the chickens revolving behind her head, rising and falling in a haze of golden juices, like a poultry-based piece of religious iconography.

She mouthed, 'Father David, are you safe?' Maybe she actually spoke out loud, it was impossible to tell.

David only nodded. Even that was lost, their view broken as one of the drivers erupted between them to snarl fresh insults at his fellow trucker. The flatbed trailer behind his tractor was piled high with aubergines. The other tractor was a wilder affair, crates of live chickens rattling their beaks against the crates' wooden slats.

When David next heard Sister Hilda's voice, it could have been coming from above or below, heaven or hell, it was just disembodied instructions. He wasn't even sure it was her. Her accent seemed to have taken a French turn. She made 'stay there' sound like *'ʒay ʒare'*; perhaps even *'caesar'*. She kept repeating it until she came back into view; as she spoke, she jabbed her hand in his direction, palm down.

David looked up and down the street. Now would be the time to escape but he was wedged tight. The tractors had stalled and their wheel arches were as tightly hooked up as ever. He didn't see how anyone was going to get them free.

When the young men came out of the stores and began jostling for position, David wondered if it was some kind of gang war. Maybe vegetable versus poultry traders. But then he saw the flatbed full of aubergines bounce and lift. The driver didn't seem to mind. He sat high in his cab, holding the other driver with a proud stare and a rigid moustache, while behind him the teams of traders kept bouncing his trailer until the two tractors were unhooked.

The driver turned the ignition and set off again, in the same direction. David didn't know if it was machismo: the tractors were just going to get locked again. But they didn't. The men who had freed the tractor stayed on hand, slapping the trailer bed as they shouted instructions, all the time bouncing the trailer around to make minuscule adjustments to its course. There was another team doing exactly the same thing behind the tractor with the chicken trailer.

The tractors began to ease past each other; the clearance space wasn't measurable, it was too small. But they pushed on at an insect crawl and everyone waiting in the street held in their stomachs and flattened themselves to walls. It was the chicken tractor on David's side of the street, and as the trailer drew alongside him he imagined the beaks bristling against him, tapping out little chickie Morse codes.

Perhaps even drawing blood.

He felt a crawling panic. He was under pressure, he had barely slept, he was being persecuted by a nun. And now the chickens were coming for him. Things had got serious. He had seen *The Birds*.

David scrambled across the corner of the trailer, thinking that if he could climb on top of it, he could hop from the coupling chain to the cab and on, over the head of the driver to the street beyond. As he leapt forward, his foot caught a crate and sent the tightly packed chickens sailing across the street in an arc of white feathers and wood splinters. A hand on his shoulder tried to pull him down but he had found his feet now. He was astride the trailer, one step from freedom. He tried to leapfrog the tractor driver by planting his hands on top of the man's head. As he pushed away, the driver went sprawling forward on to the tractor's engine casing. David didn't get much farther. He landed flat among the aubergines, feeling them squelch under him.

He heard Sister Hilda screaming, 'Father, Father.'

He was breathless, winded by the fall. There were hands on his hands, pulling him in four directions. He wrapped his fingers into the grooves between the paving stones and held tight. Beneath him, ripe aubergines oozed against his skin like soft, bitter sponges. Above him, the shadow cast by Sister Hilda's body fell like an iron curtain, a one-woman security cordon protecting him from the crush of the souk. A rasp had now entered her voice, giving it an edge as she shouted at the tractor drivers and their crews, telling them to get back.

When the rasping stopped, it happened so suddenly it was as though something had snapped inside the nun. There was a crack, like the breaking of bread-sticks taken from the freezer. Her voice broke into sobs.

David lifted his head from the paving slab. Sister Hilda was pointing to the wall.

'The same place our Saviour fell over, when he carried his cross.'

He twisted his head. On the wall, a plaque with the information, this was the Seventh Station of the Cross.

David tried to show shock and confusion, coloured by holy inspiration. When he spoke, he kept his voice low. 'Take me to the church and leave me there. I need solitude. I need to pray.'

She nodded as though she understood.

An hour later, David was limping alone through the Old City. He knew he was in a trough, his biorhythms felt like they had been programmed by Bill Ward, the drummer of Black Sabbath. They were so slow and heavy, they were an internal drag on his whole system. When he was in the streets of the souk, the music had been light enough and fast enough to stave off the metal vibe. Now he was wandering in the dim back streets, he was lost among hewn rock and castellations and walls that were more than two yards thick. He looked up at the sky and all he could see was heavy-duty chicken wire. The wire seemed to be protection from something; there were lumps of masonry and pieces of iron lying on it, as though someone up above had it in for pedestrians.

David took another look at the guidebook page that Tony had given him as a map. When he escaped Sister Hilda, he was in the Church of the Holy Sepulchre. He burnt up so much energy, waiting to make his break, he didn't have the wit to keep from getting lost. It took him more than an hour to reach the De La Salle school at New Gate, which he only found by walking round the edge of the Old City, keeping the walls to his left. The map labelled this the Christian Quarter. Following the route, he only had to take a right, then a left to reach Tony's apartment. Tracing the same street down a half-inch, he saw he would reach the Seventh Station on Souk Khan el-Zeit Street. Since his collapse, David had walked through the entire city. The streets were getting slightly busier again. He walked past two attractive-looking cafés before he dropped down a short flight of steps and found a door with an old rod-and-lever bell-pull.

David could hear feet echoing on stone steps, flat-footed and punctuated with heavy grunts. When Tony opened the door he said, 'Where the hell have you been?'

'Don't ask. I tell you, I've been crucified.'

He limped after Tony, up the steps to a spacious apartment on the top floor. He barely looked around, he just savoured the peace. But as he drifted around from room to room, something began to seem odd. There was something unplanned about the layout, something arbitrary. He asked Tony, who rapped a hand against the nearest wall and said, 'The apartment stretches across two old buildings. The whole city is like that, like rabbit-warrens.'

All across the city, lower and upper storeys didn't necessarily match because neighbours would buy or sell single rooms to each other as their families expanded or contracted. Tony explained, all you had to do, throw up a wall or knock one down and you'd changed the look of your apartment.

He dropped his voice to a whisper as he said, 'What do you think? The house that could make us rich or get us killed.'

David said, 'Make me rich, get you killed.'

'Yeah.' Tony didn't want to be reminded. But he shrugged and smiled. 'Don't worry. I'm going to find some risks for you.'

David looked out of a window. Below, he could see the cafés he had passed on the street. He said, 'Is this a good area?'

'Everything's good here. There's only so much space in a walled city.'

There was an arch between one room and the next. From the look of the stone this was where the apartment had been extended into the neighbouring house. 'What do the deeds look like, if they have to explain how a bit got chipped off here, another bit got added there?'

'All Palestinian real estate is complex – we've got subtle minds. At least in Jerusalem there are proper records. In Bethlehem, it's a nightmare. After the Israelis blew up our land office in '67, we had to start going to Turkey to search the old Ottoman files. The problem was, the Turks stopped being helpful and anyway, the files only go as far as the First World War. Every deal that took place after has to be pieced together from the separate title deeds. Now, when you're trying to buy land, you never know if you're speaking to the most recent owner or if you're being taken for a ride. Then you buy a plot in good faith, only everyone forgot about this small corner with an olive tree that was given to someone's dead uncle. What can you do? The current owner turns out to be his wife's nephew who studied optometry at the university in Belgrade before moving to Peru.'

'That happens?'

'Are you kidding? That's the best-case scenario. You see why the lawyers are always in work. They are the only ones having any fun.'

'Well, let's hope yours is a fun guy.' David took another look around and saw a flight of wooden steps leading off the corner of one of the two rooms. 'Is there another floor?'

'One room only, it's built on the roof. Do you want to take a look?'

David hauled himself up the steps. There was a sliding trapdoor at the top and he had to crouch awkwardly as he hauled it back. When he straightened, creaking, he found himself in a dim cell, lit by a narrow window.

'How is it?' Tony was at the foot of the steps, resting his bulk against the handrail, unable to decide if he wanted to go through the effort of hauling himself up there.

'Hold on.' David had found a door. He turned the key and the room was suddenly overexposed, turning into white light. 'Christ. That's better.'

Tony shouted, 'Don't go out on the roof.'

'What?' David couldn't hear. He stepped out from the shadow of the pillbox room to the edge of the flat roof, saying: 'This is the most incredible view.'

The sightline skimmed across the uneven crazy paving of the city rooftops in an almost straight line that took in the Church of the Holy Sepulchre, the glare of the Dome of the Rock and, beyond, the Mount of Olives. David felt it refresh him. He could see himself maybe dragging a deckchair out here. Imagine chilling in the heat, smoking, obviously. He would meditate on the view, do a little homespun synthesising of all the holy sites.

David yelled, 'This is not bad. I'd pay for this. Not three mil or whatever you're asking. But serious change.'

He looked back over his shoulder. Tony was standing in the doorway, gasping in the stone frame. His face was tomato red, the red of a beef tomato at the moment it is thrown away. He was gesturing furiously, flapping his big hands.

'Get inside.'

The gesture got shorter. Tony was breathless and unsteady. His other hand was clutching at the door frame.

David said, 'What's the problem?'

'Anyone who sees you, they're going to assume you're a Jew looking over the property before you buy it.'

Tony frowned. David followed his eyes and took another look at the rough edges of the cityscape. Behind the eye-catching spires and minaret towers, there was something strange happening out there. Not only the way medieval flourishes combined with everyday signs of life: washing lines, solar panels, satellite dishes, cellphone masts that looked like menorahs and genuine representations of menorahs that looked like TV aerials. The real surprise was the number of people out there, picking their way over the city, moving from roof to roof using steel bridges. A man silhouetted against the white of a church tower, bird-legged in his black knickerbockers and nylon pop socks. He balanced on a parapet before stepping out into space. His hat bobbed below the roof line like a furry Frisbee, until the man reappeared on top of the next building.

Two buildings to the left, an elderly man picked his way around a vaulted roof with his woman following behind. The warm city air had inflated her raincoat and filled out her wig, making her look cartoonish. As though Walt Disney had decided, if she stepped off the walkway, she should be able to float above the city like a bluish balloon, ridden by a fluffy mohair mouse. Ahead of these two, a squad of black-hatted youngsters paraded across a roof, before dropping down in single file, through a trapdoor and into a building. The building was mounted with a huge but spindly menorah, so big the steel rods must have been welded together on the roof.

'Who are all these people?'

'Those are the people who are doing the buying,' said Tony. 'Either them or the people who pay them to live here.'

'They live on the roofs?'

'It's aerial colonisation, so come inside before someone thinks you're one of them.'

They were climbing back down the wooden steps when they heard the doorbell ring. They paused, Tony a few rungs higher, frozen in fright. David realised the comic potential. The pair of them caught like that, Tony's huge weight bulging out into a fat arse and balanced on the tip of David's nose.

'What's that?'

'I can't see anything, you're sat on me, you fat bastard.'

Tony hauled himself up, three inches. David looked to his right and saw a brass bell, fitted on the end of a curved spring. The spring was whipping backwards and forwards, sending the bell dancing.

'Who's that?'

David shook his head. 'The fuck do I know? You're the local.'

Tony said, 'Okay. You keep back.'

Their feet were back on the floor. David let Tony push ahead of him, leaving him to stare down the stone steps to the apartment door. The bell kept ringing.

'So who might it be?'

Tony shivered, he didn't want to think. Israeli soldiers,

keeping rooftop activity under surveillance. Armed offi-
cers of the Israeli state housing department, checking on
the terms of the land leases. Gun-toting representatives of
Jewish charities, scouting for houses to take over. Local
vigilantes, trying to keep the houses out of Jewish hands.
Israeli secret servicemen looking to turn a few collaborators.
Palestinian secret policemen, ready to smuggle collaborators
into Palestinian-controlled areas for torture and imprison-
ment. Palestinian Authority assassins, ready to save the time
and effort of dealing with collaborators. Representatives
of the Islamic court gathering evidence of illegal trading.
Even local gangsters, looking to muscle into any illegal
situations.

Tony took a step towards the door. 'Who is it?'

The bell kept ringing.

David said, 'Do you think they heard you?'

'Perhaps not.' He took another step and raised his voice.
'Who's there?'

A faint voice. 'Hallo!'

Tony said, 'Sophia?'

Coming from the other side of the door: 'Uncle Tony?
I've been ringing the bell for fifteen minutes.'

He slapped down the steps and opened the door, using his
body as an impenetrable shield. 'What are you doing here,
Sophia?'

'I need a lift to Ramallah.'

Tony had a horrible thought. His brother had to be
sick. He said, 'What's wrong with Elias? Why isn't he
going?'

'Those bastards next door, they upset him so much . . .'

'But he is all right.'

Sophia said, 'He's going to be all right. But we decided it was better if I speak to the lawyer this time. Then Baba said you were going too.'

Tony didn't know what to say. Anyway he was too late.

Sophia was peering over his shoulder. 'What's Father David doing here with you?'

8

Before Sammy Ben Naim went to meet his Arab contact, he looked through the files, not that he needed to refresh his memory. The guy was called Edward Yusuf Salman, otherwise known as Abu Yusuf. Sammy had always called him Dr Salman, keeping it respectful and professional. Now they were sitting side by side, driver and passenger, in the carpark behind a row of old shops on Jaffa Road, West Jerusalem. The car belonged to the Israeli government, but only in the most indirect way. If the car was ever stolen and recovered, the police would key the registration number into their computers and come up with the owner's name, one Eli Baruch of Haifa. Who didn't exist. Or if he did, it was a coincidence. Mostly, Sammy used the car as his personal vehicle.

Sammy said, 'Why's everything going so slow?'

'Partly that Khouri's nervous. But mostly, it's been difficult for other reasons. I have other work, you know, legitimate cases. And if I have to go to court in Ramallah it takes all day.'

Sammy thought the guy was laying it on a bit. Right

from the beginning of their association, Sammy arranged for Salman to have special travel documents. He could drive direct to Ramallah. He didn't have to take the long way, through the mountains in the desert like every other Palestinian.

Sammy just nodded and said, 'But you're ready now?'

'Ready. In fact, I'm already late. Tony is meeting his friend now and I'm supposed to be there to explain our strategy.'

Salman was fidgeting, clearly anxious to get moving. It was a public carpark, he might be recognised by a neighbour and then have to explain who he was with. Why he was sitting in an Israeli car with the yellow licence plate. Sammy sympathised, the guy was right to be worried. But he was so annoying. The way he kept reaching up to adjust the sun visor, pretending to adjust it to exactly the right angle but really trying to obscure his face with his raised arm. Sammy slipped up, losing his calm for a second. He told the guy to stop it.

'You're going to break it, keep pulling at it like that.'

'You're slapping my wrists? Fantastic. I think I've been doing this long enough to know the dangers. Who are you? For all I know, you're some office junior. How much do you care about my safety?'

'I'm sorry for offending you, Dr Salman. Your personal safety is extremely important to us.' Sammy fixed him with a level look: an I'll-level-with-you look.

Back when Sammy joined the housing department, they used to run a pack of tame Lebanese middlemen. Each time a property came on the market, they would trot one of these guys out. Guys who would arrive with a briefcase full of cash – saying they would do anything to get a pied à terre in al-Quds, the Holy City. *Let me make you an offer you can't refuse.* But even then the Palestinians were growing wise to that strategy.

The past fifteen years, the department had been relying more and more heavily on local men like Edward Salman. When Sammy checked the file, he remembered reading a note that said Salman was relatively laid-back. If that used to be true, it wasn't now. The guy was incredibly tense, you wouldn't believe. But maybe he was being unfair. Salman was probably relaxed enough, considering he was risking his life.

Sammy didn't like to say, but the department considered the Khouri property important. He wasn't about to make Salman any more nervous, knowing this was the beginning of a whole new initiative. He might begin thinking the risks were too high this time.

Sammy said, 'I suppose you heard, the guy who was arrested in Bethlehem has been moved from the station in Manger Square.'

Edward Salman glanced sideways. He caught Sammy's eye but didn't bother answering. Of course he knew the man had been moved. The whole of Bethlehem knew, half of them saw him being loaded into the police van. There was no word, yet, where he had been taken.

Sammy said, 'Stupid question, huh? But we want you to know, he's on his way out. And God forbid they ever work out how you make your money. Your safety will be our first concern.'

Sammy looked for any sign that Salman appreciated the guarantee. He couldn't see one. Salman had every reason to be worried. There was nothing the other man had done that he hadn't also done.

Sammy moved on, saying: 'What do you know about the Englishman?'

'He's a friend of Tony Khouri's, it's all I know.'

'You don't know why he agreed to take the job, or how Khouri got to know him?'

Salman shook his head. 'I assume he's doing it for money. What do you think?' He paused. 'Otherwise, all I know is that his name is David Preston and he met Tony at university. I don't know that Tony is so sure he can trust this man but that's not my concern. All I have to do is convince a court that it's legal to sign a house in Jerusalem over to someone who's not Palestinian.'

'Well, it's not, is it.'

'It's not legal to sell it. But it could be surrendered, say the property was security on a loan. Which is the angle I'll be taking.'

'And once the house belongs to this David Preston, he can sell it?'

'To your man, yes.'

Sammy said, 'My man is a woman. But you're going to meet her.'

He turned the ignition, the engine started and with it the radio also. As he pulled out into the main street, Edward Salman sunk so low in his seat that all anyone would be able to see was the top of his head. If he really wanted to hide, he could slap a yarmulka on top. Sammy always kept one in the glove compartment of his car, ready for those emergency head-covering situations. He kept the hair grip tucked into the spine of his leather wallet. It was a fiddly little thing, he wouldn't want to lose it. The reason he thought of it now, Salman had a bald spot on his crown just about the size of a yarmulka. He always noticed men's bald spots. The reason was, his father had the weirdest one in the world – a highly shined spot in the centre of his big bushy hair. The edges were so regular, so smoothly round, that you would swear it was created by a barber and not a few coded notches on a piece of DNA. And whenever his father wore a yarmulka, it always looked like a specially designed Papa-cover. It fitted so perfectly that Sammy was genuinely surprised when he realised that not every man with a yarmulka also had this unmonkly tonsure. That it was a happy accident, it applied to his father alone. Sammy was four when he made the discovery.

Simon Ben Naim was an Algerian Jew who became Israeli, at least in part, because at the last minute he decided he didn't want to become French. Another ground-shaking event in Sammy's early life, the day it was explained that the reason his father spoke such uneven Hebrew was because both French and Arabic came more naturally to him. Which did not mean that his love of Israel was not *profond* – it was. By the time Sammy had got his head around the yarmulka, the Arabic and the French, it was 1967 and Simon was in uniform, a forty-year-old volunteer heading off towards the Jordan river to secure land the regular army had already won.

Maybe it wasn't so *profond* to draw parallels with Sammy's current situation. But there were a few. He was almost forty years old and he was working in the service of his country, continuing to secure the land they won in 1967. Sammy pulled up outside a smart, large town house, built at the end of the last century. There was an almond tree in the centre of its garden, its leaves filling the gaps in the ornate wrought-iron fence that topped the wall. And, in the garden, a group of Hasidim mulling things over, their heads together and their hats almost touching.

Edward Salman looked up, saw the black hats and made a strangled noise. He said, 'I'm not going in there. If anyone saw me with a head-banger, I might as well put a gun to my own head.'

Head-banger: because of the way Jews moved their heads as they prayed. The Palestinians used the word to describe the Hasidim, although it could be applied to all the Jews who prayed at the wall, apparently butting their heads against the bricks. It wouldn't apply to Sammy, he was not a believer.

He said, 'Relax. I told you, we're meeting a woman. Also, another guy but he isn't one of them either.' Sammy looked over at Edward Salman, who didn't seem at all convinced. 'Okay, you stay here, I'll bring them out. We're going to get something to eat anyway.'

Sammy stepped out of the car, walked to the gate. The meeting beneath the almond tree was breaking up, the black hats peeling away to reveal, at the centre, a small middle-aged man dressed in a T-shirt and army-coloured slacks, both freshly pressed. As Sammy walked forward, the man saw him and waved.

'Shalom, shalom, Sammy.'

'Shaul, *Shalom*. Where's Mrs Grodman?'

Shaul Dayan gave a comic rock of his head, smiling through his neatly cropped beard. Sammy looked to Shaul's left. There was an old woman sat on an aluminium-framed picnic chair. She looked more frail than Sammy expected, only about five foot tall, even with her hair frizzed up in a white-blue perm that looked like a static electric shock. She wasn't Hasidic, she probably wasn't even Orthodox, wearing her own hair like that. Sammy knew the Hasidim wouldn't be comfortable dealing with her. But her foundation was pledging twenty million dollars a year, covenanted for five years, towards land purchases. They could at least stand a little closer to her.

Sammy walked over to Mrs Grodman and held out his hand as he introduced himself in English. She stood before he could ask her not to, then when she gripped his hand, he realised he had misread her. She wasn't so frail. She was straight-faced, she looked businesslike. But Sammy felt a crackle run through her hand: maybe the static electricty that was keeping her hair on end. She was definitely excited by the whole situation.

She said, 'So tell me, what's your role, Mr Ben Naim?'

It was Shaul who fielded the question. 'He facilitates, Mrs Grodman. He makes sure your charity gets all the help it needs to do its good work.'

'Facilitates? That's some word, Mr Dayan.' She turned to Sammy. 'I may be the new kid here but I'm wondering how many Mr Fixers this deal needs.'

Sammy said, 'The two of us, me and Mr Dayan, we should be enough.'

'And what's your cut?'

It was a second before Sammy realised what she was saying. He said, 'Nothing. Nothing at all.'

'Sammy works for the government, Mrs Grodman. They pick up his tab.' Shaul gave the woman a broad smile, purposefully ignoring Sammy and the look he was shooting at him. Shaul Dayan had been told to keep his mouth shut about the government but it was a prohibition he chose to ignore. He didn't see the point of it. He argued, if people know the government are involved, they feel their patriotism is being properly appreciated.

Shaul continued, 'Me, I just work for expenses. You have to understand, these deals take time, Mrs Grodman. I gotta eat, you know.'

Mrs Grodman said, 'We all gotta eat. Me, I gotta eat now. I'm late with a meal, I'm out of synch with my whole regimen. So are we going to meet your Arab guy, Mr Ben Naim?' She shook her head. 'We should break bread with the enemy. I tell you, if my Gerry was alive . . .'

She ended with a heavenward gesture, her eyes and hands following the direction set by her hair. The Grodman Foundation had been set up by her late husband, funded with the money he earned selling Middle America its trousers. Mrs Gertie Grodman was continuing his work, even extending it. The strange thing, for a woman who was buying up so much real estate, she didn't have an apartment in Israel. Whenever she visited, she stayed in the Hyatt. The rest of the time, she lived in Florida.

Shaul Dayan said, 'One second. You'll forgive me. I just have to say another couple of words to these gentlemen.' He pointed to the group of Hasidim. 'Sammy, please.'

Sammy followed Shaul over to the group. He didn't know why Shaul wanted him to speak to the men. He was still perplexed when two of them stepped forward to meet him. He knew them, of course: Klein and Levy, both Americans. The one thing Sammy and Shaul had in common, they were born in Israel, though Shaul was Ashkenazi not Sephardic.

Sammy nodded and said, 'Klein, Levy.'

'Sammy.' They spoke in unison, the big Klein overlapping the diminutive Levy.

Klein said, 'So how are things going with Shin Bet?'

Sammy paused, sucking his teeth. 'You've got me mixed with someone else, *adoni*. I'm not Shin Bet. I work for the Ministry of Housing.'

'Of course you do. Which is why we should talk.'

Of the two, Klein had the reputation. His hat made him seem about seven foot tall but even without it he had to be six four. He covered this giant frame in a black coat so heavy there was nothing he could do to keep from sweating in the Jerusalem heat. All the Hasidim tended to have body odour problems, but Klein's was particularly bad. He probably knew about it but was willing to risk his personal hygiene: he carried two machine-pistols underneath his coat, one under each arm. For some reason, he favoured the Mach-10 over the Uzi.

Levy carried his pistol in a holster over his back pocket. Sammy knew it was a Colt. What else, he was working in the Wild West Bank. Sammy considered Levy to be a moron, but in another sense he was the brains of the operation. He and Klein worked as enforcers in the *yeshivas* that their group set up in the Arab areas of the Old City as well as in Hebron. They were basically paramilitaries in Victorian frock-coats. Klein gave the students weapons training and organised the patrols around the buildings. It was Levy who planned the mass sorties on Friday mornings when the students would march through Arab areas, chanting prayers in Hebrew to disrupt the Muslim Sabbath.

Sammy hadn't known either of the men were involved with Grodman. Either his information was out of date or it was a recent development. He suspected the latter, that they had only just heard about the Grodman Foundation. It looked as if Shaul Dayan was angling to get their group a donation.

Shaul confirmed it. 'Not to mince words. These guys need dollars.'

'They've got a ton of money.'

'They need more, isn't that right?' Shaul turned to Levy.

Though Levy's Hebrew was good, you couldn't call it lively. It came from the Torah, not everyday use.

'We move forwards, we keep on moving. We have a very long way to go.'

Klein spoke up: 'What is anyone else doing? Hey? Nothing is what.'

Levy said, 'What Dan is saying, it would be just to give us all the money because we are the people who have use for it.'

Sammy said, 'You're the only ones doing anything? You've already got the whole machinery of government behind you.'

'Behind us, yes. Ready to stab us in the back. Or ready to turn their backs on us whenever it gets too hot for them.'

'That's the point, Levy. You're deniable — if we were working openly, you think we would deal with people like you?'

Shaul jumped in, a true Mr Fix-It, trying to calm the situation with charm. 'Please. Gentlemen. We're all working towards one cause, the whole of Eretz Israel in Jewish hands. One destination, one vocation. Just different routes, it's all it is.'

Sammy shook his head, 'Not me. And not the government.'

'You think Netanyahu doesn't want Israel to be whole?'

'I'm not a mind-reader. I've no idea what he wants. I know what he's aiming for as Prime Minister, the exact same policy as Rabin: Jerusalem unified. And land for the Palestinians.'

'We give them land? The land God gave us?' This was Klein, shouting.

Sammy shouted back, 'Yes, we give them land. We give

them the smallest possible units consonant with limited autonomy.'

'What does that mean?'

'It means what it says. Isolated townships with a measure of local government.'

Levy said, 'Ghettoes?'

'Whatever.'

Ever since Sammy had got attached to the land deals team, he'd had to liaise with men like these. The term for it was strange bedfellows. It made him shiver. The idea of sharing a bed with Klein and Levy, squashed between the pair of them, both in their overcoats and hats like a whacked-out comedy sketch. Or something like a cartoon in one of the leftist papers: the secret service guy being squeezed between two hardliners. The tag: So who's running the country? No. Probably a line like, if they're fucking each other, who's fucking the country?

Shaul tried again to calm the situation. 'Come on, it's all for the good of Israel. So Messieurs Klein and Levy think they're using you and you think you're using them. So what? We're standing here arguing in Jerusalem, praise be to God that it's so.'

Sammy said, 'We should go.' He turned to Klein and Levy. 'We'll talk soon. Once this deal is through, it's going to be a bridgehead for a big expansion into the Christian Quarter.' He put out his hand. 'You're right, you're doing more than anyone. We're going to need you and your troops.'

They took his hand and shook.

Shaul was collecting Mrs Grodman. He walked with her towards the gates of the house and the car waiting outside. Sammy followed.

Shaul said, 'Me and Mrs Grodman, are we gonna be canoodling in the back?'

Sammy ducked slightly, checking the passenger seat. Salman was sitting even lower than before, almost in the footwell.

'If you don't mind, yeah. Take the back.'

As he pulled out into the afternoon traffic, Sammy mumbled: 'Dr Salman, Mrs Grodman.' He didn't hear either of them say anything in greeting but he wasn't surprised. They would have to speak later, at the meeting. In the meantime, Sammy just kept his eyes on the road. It was school-run time and the traffic was pushing towards insane levels.

In the back, he heard Mrs Grodman ask if Dayan was any relation . . .

Sammy couldn't believe it. Shaul was claiming he was a semi-distant relative of Moshe Dayan. His brazen cheek all the more stunning because Dayan was not even Shaul's real name. His family name was something like Brodetsky and it was Shaul, not his Polish-born father, who decided to take a new Israeli name.

Shaul's reflection was bobbing about in the rear-view mirror. There was no way of telling from his expression that he was lying. Which confirmed for Sammy what he already knew, Shaul was a shady customer. Sammy had always been slightly disturbed by Shaul's files, not by what he found there but what seemed to be missing. Years for which no account existed. Whether the relevant pages ever existed, or whether they were removed by someone higher up the department, Sammy didn't know.

Mrs Grodman listened to Shaul talk about Cousin Moshe. But she was also clutching her stomach – reminding Sammy that she needed to eat. He had planned to take her to an Italian but he was having second thoughts. He just remembered the restaurant wasn't kosher. He didn't know how Mrs Grodman would take the news, whether she would mind or not. It was better that Sammy checked now.

He turned in his seat, saying, 'There's a problem . . .'

A car honked to the side of him, someone trying to cut in while he didn't even have his eyes on the road.

Sammy slammed on the brakes. Edward Salman slid even lower. He seemed to quiver for a moment with only the small of his back touching the edge of the seat, then he crumpled down into the bottom of the car.

Shaul Dayan said, 'What the . . . Don't tell me you had this guy offed?'

Sammy slewed to a stop. The car pulled left across two lanes of traffic. Sammy ignored the curses, the sound of horns. He had a hand underneath Edward Salman's head and was turning it towards the sunlight.

Sammy's fingers felt for a pulse on the man's neck. He didn't expect to find one but he was thinking of Mrs Grodman when he said, 'I think it's a heart attack.'

Mrs Grodman said, 'Yeah? Then why's he bleeding from behind the ear?'

9

The best restaurant in Ramallah, perhaps in Palestine, was al-Bardoni. Sophia knew that her father and Edward Salman planned to travel there together.

She said, 'So how were you thinking of getting there, Uncle Tony?'

'How was I planning to get where?'

It was now twelve midday. Elias Khouri had scheduled the meeting with the lawyer for one o'clock, but by the time Sophia and her mother had persuaded him that he was too shaken to make the journey it was past eleven. Sophia was happy to take his place but it was too late for her to take the desert road to Ramallah.

She said, 'You weren't thinking of driving back to Bethlehem, just to go all the way around to Ramallah?'

'No.'

'And what's Father David doing here with you?'

When she looked over at David, he smiled back at her. It was a warm smile though not exactly spiritual. It was more a kind of cheerful lechery. But he didn't seem to have anything to say.

Tony said, 'He wants to rent the apartment, don't you, Father?'

'Call me David,' said David. 'Please.'

'You want to rent this apartment?'

'Yeah. Really. It's a great place, great location. It's in Jerusalem, which is a definite plus for me.'

Tony said, 'It's exactly what you were looking for, right?'

'Right.' David smiled at Sophia again. The way she looked back at him, she obviously expected more of an explanation. He said, 'I wanted a retreat. I need a place to contemplate.'

Tony said, 'So we're happy? Let's get to Ramallah and get you to sign on the dotted line. One thing, David. Tell me you remembered to bring a driving licence with you?'

David nodded. He had several.

'Then let's hire a car.'

The three of them walked down a hill into the heart of the souk and then climbed back up to Damascus Gate. The car rental place was quite close by, across the carpark where the *sheruts* had their pick-up point, on the far side of a run-down shopping centre in East Jerusalem. It was a Palestinian Arab company but the cars it rented carried the yellow plates of Israeli-registered vehicles rather than the blue plates of those from the occupied territories. David asked if that was all it took to travel in freedom across the West Bank: change the blue Palestinian plates for yellow Israeli ones. Tony nodded.

'Until you get caught, then it's prison.'

The car was parked outside the shop, a mid-sized bottom-range Fiat. After David signed the rental form, he headed for the door, jiggling the keys at Sophia, who was waiting by the roadside. Tony paused for a second. When he joined them outside he was holding a borrowed kaffiyeh.

David said, 'What's that for?'

'For you. A new law. All foreigners have to wear one.'

David looked from Tony to Sophia. She nodded. It was another beat before he was sure they were joking.

Tony said, 'It's in case we run into trouble. If you put the kaffiyeh on the dash, everyone knows you're a Palestinian.'

David took the scarf. 'I don't mind wearing it. Maybe I should try and look like Yasser Arafat, that would really prove my solidarity.'

Sophia said, 'It wouldn't work. Arafat wears his folded into three points at the front, but it's a national secret how he does it. The story is Pierre Cardin designed it specially for him.'

David pushed the kaffiyeh under his seat, between his legs. Tony sat next to him. Sophia spread out in the back. There was no air-conditioning in the car and with the windows down, she had to shout to speak to them. She asked Tony how well he expected Edward Salman to do this afternoon. She knew the lawyer had arranged for a judge to take a deposition. The original idea was that her father would make a statement, now Tony was going to have to do it in his place. But then what?

Tony was too bulky to turn round in his seat. He tried to shout over his shoulder. 'Edward will ask for a court order, binding your neighbours to keep the peace. The judge will rule in our favour and then nothing at all will happen.'

'You think this trip is a waste of time?'

'We're going to eat at al-Bardoni.'

Tony didn't mean to make light of his brother's problems. But in a sense, they were intractable. The Hebronites had everything invested in Palestine, they didn't dream, even occasionally, of getting out and putting all the problems behind them. The thing that linked Bethlehem and Ramallah, everyone had family abroad, most people spoke at least one other language and sometimes two or three languages. Hebron was different, and it was becoming the heartland of Palestine. The problem between Elias Khouri and his neighbours, the Battle of the Chicken Farm, was just another soon-to-be-forgotten incident in the Hebronisation of Palestine.

They were approaching the Ramallah checkpoint. David slowed the car, joining the line of traffic moving through at a smooth crawl. Tony wasn't expecting any problems. As he said, this time of day, the soldiers weren't checking every car. A yellow-plated car would be waved through. But it didn't stop him from tensing slightly.

Perhaps it was the way he was holding his face, his mouth and eyes set grimly ahead. Perhaps it was just the rigidity of his hands, clasped on his knees. Whatever, David must have sensed his nerves because just as the soldiers glanced over the hire car's windows, he leant over and whispered, 'They're looking your way. I think they want a piece of your cherry ass.'

Tony's head jerked back. He hissed *hush* at David as he tried to turn, checking whether Sophia had heard the joke.

She didn't seem to have done. But she was a smart woman. Tony didn't like having to invent a story to explain David's presence in the apartment, not because he was averse to lying but because Sophia was so intelligent. It wasn't a good idea trying to fool her. It didn't help that David seemed to have got into a playful mood all of a sudden. Tony preferred him when he was moaning about insomnia or his suspect flu.

He shot David a resentful look. David shook his head and shrugged as a kind of shallow apology. Then his eyes flicked back to the rear-view mirror and Tony realised that he was watching Sophia. The next moment, David was fumbling in his top shirt pocket and pulling out his packet of cigarettes. He shook one cigarette proud of the packet and held it to his shoulder.

'Cigarette, Sophia?'

She shook her head. But she glanced across to meet David's eyes in the mirror.

'Thanks anyway, David,' she said. 'And thanks for helping with the neighbours.'

'Well, I didn't do anything there.'

'It might have been worse. It looked nasty for a moment before Uncle Tony arrived with the police chief.'

'If I helped . . .' His eyes were still on the rear-view mirror. The smile that split his face in two, Tony knew it was supposed to read as modest.

Al-Bardoni restaurant was in the busiest part of the downtown area, twenty yards from a roundabout with some kind of civic monument at its centre: an obelisk. The obelisk was trussed up in green wires, waiting for dusk when they would sparkle into fairy lights. Above street level, streamers and strings of dinky flags were slung across the buildings, the obelisk marking the centre of a party-coloured web. All of the major events of the National Palestinian Festival of Music and Dance were taking place in Ramallah. There was even an English-language banner advertising the fact. There was already enough music in the air. David didn't know if it had anything to do with the festival but he could hear music coming from inside the restaurant, from all the cars tracking up and down the street, and from the barrows of the falafel sellers by the roundabout. The surprise was that, despite the hard press of city life, you left it all behind once you stepped into the restaurant. Even the racket of different music seemed to find a syncopation as David crossed from the roadside into this urban oasis. The tables were set out on a terrace of white and pink stones. They took their seats in the shade of vines and wistaria. While they were waiting for the lawyer to arrive, Tony asked the waitress to bring lemon tea and a plate of olives. David ordered a bottled beer and accepted the idea of Taybeh, the local brew. Sophia took a beer, too.

The waitress had only taken two paces when Tony called her back. He had decided, Edward Salman wouldn't want them to starve while they waited for him. It was better if they ordered the *maza* now, then, when the lawyer arrived, the appetisers would be there to welcome him. Tony ran through the menu quickly, ordering ten or twelve dishes then asking how they sounded. David nodded. It sounded good, at least in the abstract. But he still wasn't sure his appetite had returned.

Tony turned to Sophia, asking her about Elias. 'Should I have stayed? I didn't think he was so weak when I left.'

'No, Uncle Tony. We thought he was fine then. But the whole affair left him exhausted. About three-quarters of an hour after you left, he almost fainted.'

Tony didn't like the sound of that. 'Fainted?'

'Not fainted fainted. But one minute he was talking, then his face suddenly lost all its colour, and he had to sit down.'

'The bastards really wanted to get him in a cell.' Both Sophia and Tony knew all about Elias's terror of gaol.

The beer had arrived. David was already retopping his glass, simultaneously sucking at the beer frothed along his upper lip. He said, 'What are you talking about?'

In English, Sophia said, 'About my father and prison.'

'Oh my God,' said David. 'Don't tell me about prison.' He stopped quickly, trying to back-pedal into his priest character. 'I was a prison visitor. So I'm not surprised your father has a phobia about them.'

David expected to get a look of praise from Tony: applause for his excellent recovery. Instead, Tony only looked puzzled. And when he turned back to Sophia, her look was pure angst.

Tony said, 'How did you know that Elias has a phobia about prison?'

There was a pause. David's brow wrinkled, blinking once then twice as he tried to bring the picture into focus. Finally he said, 'I have no idea where that came from. Has he got a phobia?'

Sophia said, 'I think I told you.'

'Yes?' David didn't remember. He shook his head but the shaking must have dislodged something – the shadow of a memory. He came up with a summer smell, a little girl . . . the pieces fell into place. Fragments of the girl's confession in the garden behind the church. The girl, of course, being this slender woman, lips resting on the rim of her beer glass. So that was how he knew.

He nodded. 'Oh yes.' As their eyes met, this time a beam pulsed between them, emphasising the shared secret.

Tony just felt bewildered. But he cleared his throat noisily and said, 'Elias was a member of the Communist Party. The Israelis rounded them all up in the 1970s.'

'He was a communist?'

'Well, I don't know how much he cared for dialectical materialism.' Tony looked to Sophia for a clue. She shrugged so he continued. 'Anyway, he joined the party. At the time, the communists were the only ones who wanted to speak directly to Israeli political parties. Which was such a way-out idea, obviously, the Israelis threw them all in prison.'

'How long did he get?'

'More than a year. And since he was also tortured, he's been uncomfortable on his feet. That's why we all worry about him.'

The thought of torture could have been enough to put David off his food. But he didn't have any appetite anyway. The *maza* dishes were arriving in threes and fours and they all looked good. David half expected his appetite to flood back. What was going to stimulate it, if not marinated olives; salads like thick green tabbouleh made almost entirely out of parsley, alongside a simple tomato and cracked wheat salad. The dips: hoummus, tahini and variants – tahini and aubergine, tahini and parsley, tahini with tomatoes and cucumber. Bread and meat, lamb kofta, grilled chicken livers, pitta and spinach bread, which wasn't bread but actually pastry parcels of spinach. Then vine leaves stuffed with meat and rice, falafel and *kibbeh*, lemon-shaped pasties with cracked wheat shells and fillings of perfumed meat and pine nuts.

David always believed, if you were a grazer, or you ever suffered from the munchies, or if you simply wanted to eat and go, or perhaps you were the type who wanted to eat continuously without ever reaching the main course, whatever, you would find food heaven in Lebanon. This was the kind of food he remembered from their days in Beirut, with only a few missing dishes. He ripped up a piece of pitta bread and swiped it through the tahini and aubergine dip. The aubergine tasted darkly smoky, searching out new corners of his mouth, finding new taste buds to saturate. But, somehow, the journey from his mouth to his stomach was creating problems. He could appreciate the food but he couldn't eat it.

Across the table, Tony waved a piece of bread that was already heavy with hoummus over the *maʒa*. It looked as though he was halfway through an invocation, ready to appease the gods of snack food. He was more than halfway through testing the dishes, leaving smeared tracks through them, like tank tracks across rough terrain.

David said, 'Are you sure your lawyer knows this place?'

'Everyone knows al-Bardoni.'

'Better reorder, then, because you're not leaving him anything to eat.'

Sophia was picking her way more delicately through the *maʒa*. She noticed that David wasn't eating. 'What's the matter? Are you still feeling ill?'

'I don't know.'

'You saw the doctor, though? The night you arrived?'

'That was about the smoke grenade, but I'm well over that. It's just lethargy or something. It just came over me now.'

David used to be a lot better at lethargy. It was his speciality. There were times, he had to wait weeks before a deal could go through. The safety of any major consignment always depended on hundreds of smaller components. Every single one had to get into alignment, create a balanced constellation; then when everything augured well, when the entrails read, they would ship out. It might mean weeks in a strange city or a remote village, slumped in the sun, smoking, spending half a day over a meal like the one in front of him now. But then he had been out of the game for so long now, maybe it was just nerves. This deal with Tony's apartment, it might not be drug-smuggling, but it was the closest he'd come to a piece of business in a very long time.

Tony said, 'I wish I could lose my appetite.'

'You've definitely filled out.'

'I thought, what you said, I was a fat bastard.' Tony was eating two-handed; he had a pitta bread scoop in one hand, loaded with tabbouleh, and in the other a well-packed vine leaf. 'You know, I blame the intifada. For five years, we didn't go out, no dancing, no visits to the swimming pool. The restaurants were on strike and the nearest nightclub was in Jordan. If you decided to use your initiative and have a party, word would get out and someone would pay you a visit. And these visitors, maybe you would call them patriots. Some of them were nothing but hooligans. But they warned you to think again. Parties were too frivolous, the intifada was serious.'

'How does that make you fat? It should make you thin.'

'What would you do if you spent five years on your backside? We stayed home, playing cards and eating. That's how I got fat.'

'After the intifada was over, couldn't you go on a diet?'

'Okay. Shut up now.' Tony flung out a hand to show his exasperation and sending a soft lump of hoummus flying into the air. It landed on top of one of the spinach pasties. Tony shrugged. It was a small act of God. He picked up the pasty by one of its three corners and put it in his mouth, saying: 'Have you tried these? No one needs an appetite to eat these.'

'They just leap off the plate – you're an innocent bystander.'

'You know, you're still talking. I thought I told you to shut up.'

David grinned. He might be having a few sleepless nights, whatever. But when he and Tony got like this, bickering with each other, it was like the old days again. David was joking that if the intifada was boring, he should try going on the run for fifteen years, that was boring. Tony looked up and caught the full heat of David's smile. He bounced it right back.

They took a moment, in the sunlight, among the vines and flowers, to stare at each other. Then, in unison, they turned and looked at Sophia. They had only just realised what they'd done – they had betrayed themselves.

Sophia's eyebrows were a dark line across her forehead. It over-scored the severity of her look.

'How do you two know each other?'

Tony gulped, opening and closing his mouth on a semi-chewed wad of spinach.

'Sophia . . .'

He just didn't quite have anything to say.

Sophia said, 'There's something odd going on here.'

'Sophia . . .'

Tony looked to David for help. David was sorry, he had gone blank. There was nothing he could think of saying.

Sophia stood up. 'Whatever it is, I don't want to know. Okay?'

She started walking away from the table.

'Sophia . . .'

She ignored her Uncle Tony, leaving him flapping behind her, the sound of his lips splashing wetly on food that had turned to cotton in his mouth. She quickened her pace and landed on the sidewalk, looking for a taxi to take her to the law courts.

She was dropped close to the steps that led to the courthouse's double doors. She paid the driver and paused. She was breathing so hard, she was practically hyperventilating. Then catching hold of herself, she forced one big last breath and held it before releasing it slowly, to a ten count.

In front of her, a familiar voice said, 'Don't tell me, this is yoga. No, it's a Sufi trance state, you're reaching a higher state of consciousness.'

Shadi Mansur's face swam into focus in front of her eyes. She felt a warm surge, she needed an old friend and one was here.

Shadi was saying, 'Are you all right, Sophia? You look upset.'

With those words, the warm feeling shrank inside her. She had no doubt that Shadi was being genuine, but it was no good. She remembered that he was a government man, a Fatah appointee, and she could hardly tell him her suspicions about her Uncle Tony and his friend. Shadi was better at dealing with suspicions than her, she would only have to tell him a few words about her lunch and he would have the whole picture: he would have it in panoramic widescreen with Dolby Surroundsound.

'What are you doing here, Shadi?'

'Me? I'm putting my nose into things, as usual. I notice your father had some business here today.'

'Had? What's the problem?' Sophia felt there was something Shadi wasn't saying. 'Have you heard something about the case?'

She had this sudden idea the whole case had been cancelled. She could believe the al-Bannas' family contacts stretched all the way to Ramallah and threaded right the way through the court system. She needed to see her lawyer.

She said, 'Have you seen Dr Salman? He was supposed to meet me for lunch.'

Shadi shook his head. 'Not me. Why? Did he not show?'

There was something Shadi wasn't saying, something he knew. He didn't seem surprised about the lawyer's non-appearance.

Sophia looked over his shoulder, into the dim foyer of the courthouse. Then she turned around, squinting into the bright afternoon sunlight, wondering if she would recognise the Salman family car.

There was a man sat across the street, slumped on a bench in the shade of a tree. His head, a bushy mass of grey hair, rested on his chest as he slept.

Sophia said, 'Isn't that him?'

'Where?'

As she pointed towards the sleeping man, she became certain. 'Can you believe the man's sleeping? We were supposed to meet at al-Bardoni.'

Sophia started towards the sleeping man, slowly at first. It was Shadi who started running.

He said, 'It can't be Dr Salman. It's impossible.'

10

Sophia was standing with Tony and his friend, this unlikely priest, at the rear of the ambulance. When the medics wheeled Edward Salman's body towards them, she turned, saw the man's bloodless lips, his skin lifeless, his eyes marbled. Then she turned away and went to join Shadi.

Shadi was making a call, twenty yards away, over by the courthouse. He was turned to the wall, his mobile phone tight to his head and his hand cupped around the flip-down mouthpiece. When he caught sight of Sophia, he coughed and ended the conversation.

She told him what the ambulance driver had just told her. There was a deep wound in the side of Edward Salman's head, just below the ear. Shadi nodded. She didn't see any surprise there. His expression was either sad or blank, she could read it either way.

Shadi said, 'Has anyone spoken to his wife?'

'Uncle Tony did, just now.'

She looked back at the ambulance. Tony was there with his own mobile pressed to his face. He was a horrible colour, both ashen and flushed at the same time. Telling Doris Salman about her husband's death had brought a rash out on his forehead. He was scratching at his hairline as he spoke on the phone.

Shadi said, 'What about Yusuf, who spoke to him?'

'No one's found him. He's supposed to be here, in Ramallah, but his phone is not working.'

A Moroccan band was playing an open-air concert later that night at the old campus of Bir Zeit University. Yusuf would be there, working. Someone would have to go and find him.

Sophia said, 'It can't be you, Shadi.'

She kept her eyes steady, waiting to see if he would falter. He knew something about Salman's death, too much to then go and find his son and tell him the bad news. She was sure that he had been talking to someone about the murder as she walked up. The way he held his phone, that was the clue.

Shadi said, 'Don't blame me. You think about it, you knew what Dr Salman was doing.'

'So, go and tell Yusuf that his father has been executed. You're the spin doctor, you explain official policy to him. It will sound better coming from you.'

'Please.' Shadi held out his hands, pacifying. 'I didn't kill the man. I don't even know for sure why he has been killed. I'm just trying to add two and two. I might have got the numbers wrong.'

She was defiant now, her eyes quietly blazing: 'So are you going to help me find Yusuf?'

'No.' Shadi's expression had suddenly, unexpectedly become frank. 'If you think I know something about it, won't he?'

This was what had happened to the class joker, to little Shadi Mansur. It would take more than a crack on the head with a smoke grenade to alter someone so much. All the other boys from the convent school had changed, of course. Seeing them around Beit Jala, Sophia found it difficult to believe they were the same people. She would have the memory of a fifteen-year-old, nearly always thin, always alive, planning new ways to disrupt classes: throwing rice or eggs or phials of nitrous oxide. Blowing up the toilets with dynamite. Then she would have another picture, the way that same boy looked, twelve years later: sweating fat, double-chinned and heavily moustached. Shadi was physically very much the same, he had grown taller but he was still slim and wiry. He wasn't balding, he didn't have a moustache. And then there was his laugh, that hadn't changed at all. She often forgot that the laugh was no longer natural: these days, it was something he used for *spin*.

Shadi must have seen something in the way she stared at him. He smiled now. 'Look on the bright side. You get to see the band – everyone says it's going to be a great gig.'

David drove her to Bir Zeit for the concert. He would have offered anyway but Tony volunteered him before he even understood what they were talking about. The fact was, no one else could do it. David had the hire car, he could drive Yusuf back to Bethlehem once they found him. Tony lent Sophia his mobile phone and then went looking for a lift for himself.

The traffic was getting heavier. David dropped down into the back streets, following Sophia's directions, but soon ran into a traffic jam. Crawling in the dust, hands off the wheel, using the gas and clutch to inch forward, he decided he could at least try to sustain his cover. He could try a little priestly sympathy. He asked Sophia if she was okay. She only nodded.

Nicholas Blincoe

'I suppose you've known this lawyer guy a long time?'

He was Yusuf's father, it was a safe bet. But Sophia didn't seem ready to talk. David wondered if he should leave it, whether he should keep quiet or whether he should talk about other things: like why he knew her Uncle Tony so well. He and Tony had tried coming up with a story: that they had met at university, old friends, went different ways; Tony opened a second-hand car lot, David got himself priested up.

He said, 'The fact he was murdered. It makes it worse, more frightening. Do you want to talk about it?'

She said, 'If you want to know why I'm upset, it's just selfishness. I'm more upset that we've lost our lawyer. Now I don't know what we're going to do about the neighbours.'

David tried to take an optimistic line. 'Everything went okay today. Tony's got his policeman friend, he looks like he can handle anything. Who needs a lawyer when you've got a policeman in your pocket?'

'Uncle Tony doesn't have much influence with the police.'

Sophia remembered two incidents. One was the skirmish in September 1996 when the Israelis and Palestinians fought at the checkpoint. The chief of the Beit Jala police kept the Israelis pinned to their positions most of the day; in fact, until the orders came to cease fire at nine in the evening. The other was more recent. She told David about a couple of Danish girls who were staying with a Beit Jala family on an exchange programme. It was late, they had come back from the Pink Parasol with the son of the family and another boy and they were fooling around in his father's Renault Espace, saying their *goodnights*. Sophia gave the word a twist; it was a euphemism.

'Then one of the new policemen passed by. I don't

think he had even visited Bethlehem before he got the job. He lives in a village outside Hebron which is famous because everyone has red hair. They say because their ancestors were raped by the Crusaders. In his case, I think the hair affected his mind. When he saw two couples kissing in a car, he had a rush of blood. He decided the girls must be prostitutes, which made the Espace a mobile brothel.'

Sophia took a cigarette off David. He was about to flick open his Zippo but she took the lighter out of his hand. She lit her own cigarette before continuing.

'He arrested both the Danish girls and the boy whose father owned the car and took them to Bethlehem police station. The other boy ran around to Beit Jala station and told the chief there what had happened. The chief couldn't believe it. When he found out that it was true, he attacked the station and freed everyone.'

'He actually attacked another police station?'

'He surrounded it with his men but no one fired a shot. They didn't have to, he has a reputation.'

'But if he's on your side . . .'

'He can't do what he likes. He got away with that because it was so stupid, you can't arrest tourists. But the next time the al-Bannas try and have my father arrested, he might decide there's nothing he can do.'

David sucked on his teeth. 'Your father had been arrested that day I met you in the park, hadn't he?'

'I was telling you that he was scared of prison.'

He remembered that part okay, the part that had surfaced through his cannaboid-clouded memory. He sympathised with Elias: prison was awful. David hated it too. But it seemed that it was worse with Elias Khouri. That his fear was more pathological – a crippling phobia.

Sophia said, 'You're not a priest, are you?'

They were clear of the traffic now, driving through the countryside. He had an excuse to look away from her, he had to keep his eyes on the road.

She said, 'Well, are you?'

There was a man leading a donkey up ahead. David always thought donkeys were sympathetic animals: they made slowness and stupidity into virtues. As he approached it, he slowed the car right down. And he turned to Sophia. She had her eyes on him, framed on one side by a lock of hair and on the other by a tinsel trail of cigarette smoke.

'No. I was just dressed like one,' he said. 'Coincidentally.'

'Listen, then. It's obvious you and Tony are planning to sell his apartment – maybe that's why Edward Salman was killed, maybe it's for another reason. But if Uncle Tony is killed, we have no one. He doesn't have much influence, but he's all we've got. And he can't do anything if he's dead.'

David said, 'It's over. We've abandoned the whole idea.'

'You aren't trying to sell the apartment?'

'Not any more. The scam is over.'

David could hear music halfway down the street. He and Sophia joined the crowds on the hill, following them through the old gateway, into the university. The concert was being held in an open-air auditorium, reached via a courtyard that had been turned into a market for the night. The stalls were vaguely counter-culture. Some sold nuts, *shwarma*, soft drinks. Others were selling handmade clothes, handmade by people who had no real talent for tailoring but hoped their cosmic sympathies would be their guide. There were political stalls for various causes and organisations and one for the local radio station, Ramallah FM. It looked like any festival organised for a university and David had been to a few in his time.

They were early, the stage was set but empty. The music David heard on his way in came from a DJ. The band wouldn't come on until nightfall. There was no sign of Yusuf. David bought two cans of ice tea and handed one to Sophia. Before the band arrived on stage, he drank another three and tried to eat a *shwarma*. When he gave up, he passed it to Sophia but she said she didn't want it either. She did, however, smoke his cigarettes. She went through half a packet as she wore down the battery on Tony's mobile phone, trying to raise Yusuf. There was no sign of him in the auditorium.

As night fell, David saw why the band waited for dark. The stage was built against the walls of a castle-like building lit with spotlights. It was a fantastic backdrop — orange-warm stone, silhouettes of palm trees cast against it. Then the stage, draped with banners, lifting in the night breeze. David followed Sophia down into the seats. The reflected light off the castle walls bathed the whole auditorium in a warm glow. As a rule, any day with a homicide in it is a bad day. But David felt the warmth enter his soul. He had a good idea of the reason. It had nothing to do with the night and the light and the music. Sophia was a pace ahead of him, still scanning the banked seats for Yusuf. As she turned her face upward, the breeze rustled through her hair, exposing a translucent ear, lobe-less but perfect. David sighed.

He took a quick two-step, bringing him level with her. He

said, 'You know, I'm happier now you know I'm not a priest. It wasn't me, it felt like a lie, you know.'

'Okay.'

'I wasn't trying to fool you – I mean, it was your mistake and I got trapped in it. Kind of.'

She looked him over. 'You took my confession.'

'And the worst thing is, I can't remember it. I'm sorry.'

She shrugged, going through the pantomime of being non-committal. He got the feeling that whatever it was, it still mattered to her.

He said *Sorry* again. He thought he should leave it.

A man wandered on to the stage and the applause began. Following on behind, there were another five similar guys, their wiry hair fitted like helmets to their heads. Two carried instruments that looked like pizza paddles but were strung like bass guitars. Another walked over to a pair of upright bongos and started pounding them with the heels of his hand. Another had something like an Irish tambour and the last had an acoustic guitar, but one of those outsize monsters that the unluckiest man in a mariachi band gets to play. Their first number started as a groove but soon hit a melody. The crowd was a mix of Ramallah teenagers, students and the younger professors, about two thousand in all, so the band had to be a major draw. Everyone was stamping and cheering, whistling as the songs were announced. There was no doubting how much they loved the music. But there was a kind of laid-back quality to their enthusiasm: they were there for the band, but they were also up for the night and the party.

David lost Sophia for a moment. She was moving through the bleachers; he had stopped to take in the act. When he caught up with her, it was because she had also paused. The band were starting their second number and her eyes were on the stage rather than the crowd.

'Is something wrong?'

She shook her head. 'I just like this song.'

She wasn't the only one. The whole crowd was moving to the music, but also talking and laughing with each other. There seemed to be something almost ironic in their attitude to the band. David couldn't put his finger on it. The Moroccans were deeply funky. The men with the pizza-paddle basses thumbed the strings like they were on loan from a disco band; one of the classier ones like Chic. The taller of the two swung the neck of his bass backwards and forwards, confident that he gave good strut. All the same, David had a feeling the concert was different from those he was used to. There wasn't that same wall between the audience and the performers – the barrier that lifts and separates, to steal a phrase from a bra ad. The effect that creates superstars.

Throughout the concert, people kept coming to the front and passing pieces of papers to the band. David once saw Steve Earle play, and when someone shouted out a request for *Copperhead Road*, Earle had said: 'The scary thing is, the guy really thinks there's a chance I won't be playing that one.' And you knew from the way he said it, Earle had marked the song for his last encore. As he said later, when another punter shouted out a request, 'Come on, man. I'm a professional. You think I haven't put any thought into what I'm going to play.' Steve Earle wasn't just a professional, he was also an intelligent guy. But he tried to have it both ways with the barrier. David didn't believe it was possible. He laughed at Earle's lines but at the same time felt deflated; he didn't want a rock 'n' roll critique of the live experience.

But here in Ramallah, the barrier wasn't there. The mystique was all different.

The Moroccans had no problem with people making requests. Whether they actually played a song they wouldn't otherwise have played, David didn't know. But they always went to the front, took the piece of paper and read the title, nodding with approval. But then one read a title out loud and Sophia unexpectedly started giggling.

'What's the matter?'

'The request. That song isn't one of theirs.'

The band looked perplexed. Especially when they got the same request again; and then once more, two songs further on.

Sophia was still giggling. At first, David was worried she had cracked: she had wound herself tighter and tighter and now she had snapped, these weren't giggles they were hiccoughs of pain. But as he listened to them, he could feel they were genuine. He accepted them as a miracle or as magic.

He was watching her more than the band now. When she turned and caught him, he didn't know where to put his eyes. He quickly lifted his gaze to the stage and then back to her. He shot her a nervous smile and said, 'They're still asking for that song?'

She said, 'Yes. It's called, *My Beloved Home*. It was a big hit for another Moroccan band.'

The taller pizza-paddle man was shrugging. He didn't know what to think.

David asked, 'Are they asking for the wrong song on purpose?'

Sophia started giggling again. She had her head down but David caught the blush, the dimples, the crackle in her eyes.

She shook the giggles away and answered his question. She thought, the first time, someone had made the request as an honest mistake. Now it had become a joke.

David was beginning to feel sorry for the band. He thought the crowd could give the musicians a little more respect. He looked at the stage, to the tall bassist who was now caught in a *Star Trek* beam, his solo spot. A low melody began, and then a rumble started from behind David, sweeping across the whole auditorium until it erupted into stamps and shouts, even shrill ululations. Two thousand people making some noise. Sophia mouthed up at him, *This is it*. He guessed: the band's big number, their most famous song. The crowd was so wild for it: the first verse was over before they even began to quieten down . . . and then two beats later everyone was joining in with the chorus.

Sophia sang along too. She threw her head back as she sang and there was a ripple in the curve of her throat, the words ripe with laughter.

As the chorus ended, and the wordier verse began again, he nudged her, looking to her for a commentary. She smiled up. 'The reason everyone's singing, the chorus is the same as the song title, it just repeats *Adultery and Wine*.'

'For or against?'

'It's a split decision. The audience is for it and the band are against. In the verses, they sing about what terrible sins they are, but they've got such strong Moroccan dialects, no one can catch the words. But every one knows the chorus and joins in: *Adultery and Wine*.'

The strutting bass player was slamming with his left hand, working with a dervish intensity. The whole stadium was moving. And when the chorus started again, David struggled to try and catch the words. He tried to lip-read off Sophia but couldn't do it; he wanted to see the words there, shaping themselves into a kiss . . . not only *adultery* but also *wine*.

A hand was slapping him on the back but he didn't turn around, he just continued staring at Sophia. Then another hand came down to wrap itself around her shoulders and Yusuf was there, grinning across his face. *What are you guys doing here?* And immediately Sophia lost everything – song, giggles, the light in her eyes.

11

Sophia sat in the front passenger seat, but with her body twisted round so that she always faced Yusuf. The two of them generated the kind of silence that consumes space. David felt left out, hands on the wheel and eyes on the tail-lights of the car ahead. There was a steady flow of traffic running back to Ramallah. David didn't need directions until they hit the centre of town. Sophia told him, take the Jerusalem road.

Driving at night, the difference between Israeli roads and those on Palestinian Authority land was obvious. On the roads between the PA towns, everyone drove on full beam, and even then you hit a pothole every ten yards. In Israel, there was barely a reason to use headlights, the roads were so well lit. It was as though, one side of the Ramallah checkpoint, night was a wholly different commodity: it was the orange night of the West. The two-tier level of civil engineering became even more obvious as they cleared the ring of settlements that marked the new boundaries of Jerusalem and approached Bethlehem.

Sophia told him to take a right. David didn't understand. He knew the road well enough by now to recognise the main checkpoint into Bethlehem. But he did what she told him: a right followed by a left. They entered a tunnel, an orange tube injected into the mountain, and emerged on a bridge that was so far off the valley floor it felt like a high wire, slung between heaven and earth. This was the newly built bypass linking swollen Jerusalem with the settlements to the south. David felt the extravagance of the project like a hard slap, then it was over. The car plunged into another tunnel. On the far side, at the end of the bypass, they were waved through another Israeli checkpoint before taking a right turn to detour back on themselves. David realised they had skirted around Bethlehem and were now sneaking into the city from the eastern, Beit Jala side. The old, unlit road snaked upward and David got another chance to see the Israeli bridge, this time from above. Ahead of them, at eyelevel on the opposing mountain ridge, the settlements formed an unbroken wall. Looking from this side, Bethlehem and Beit Jala seemed shabbily defenceless.

'Where now?'

David could see plastic barriers ahead. They looked harmless but he knew they were filled with concrete. They were placed in the centre of the road so anyone approaching had to slow down and slalom through them. A soldier was leaning against what looked like a bus stop on an English council estate.

He asked, 'Another checkpoint?'

'We're already inside Zone C.'

So that was it. He had already been told that downtown Bethlehem was Zone A and was run entirely by the Palestinian Authority. All the land of Beit Jala, from the old Hebron road to this mountain-top, was Zone B – the Israelis patrolled it but had to have a Palestinian escort shadowing them. Zone

C covered the remaining land of the West Bank and was out of bounds to Palestinian police.

David asked, 'They won't check your documents?'

'We should be fine.'

But David knew he had already blown it. His rhythm was wrong, the car didn't have that confident glide. The soldier read his hesitancy and flagged the car down using the heavy-duty torch he was swinging in his hand. David pulled in beside a plastic barrier. The soldier stepped up to the car, waiting for Sophia to wind her window down. It gave David the few moments he needed to remember how an international smuggling man ought to act.

The soldier was about twenty years old and wore glasses. David smiled at him and said *Hello* straight out. He wanted to let the kid know that he was an English-speaker, hoping that he would then assume everyone in the car was the same, a stranger in these parts.

'Passports.'

David leant across Sophia with a couple of passports in his hand. He slid his thumb over the uppermost passport, a move too basic even to be described as a trick, but it carried enough of a subliminal charge. The soldier took that passport and lifted his torch to shine on the cover. It was Irish. David continued leaning forward, one hand across the back of Sophia's seat, cradling her as he casually flicked the cover of his spare passport between the fingers of his other hand. It was a US passport, but in the dim of the car it looked the same as the Irish one. Just so long as the soldier didn't take it in his hand and shine the flashlight on it.

The torch beam played over the inside of the car. The soldier picked up on the easy way that David was nestling against Sophia, their sense of familiarity and the second passport which must be *hers* because he was already holding *his*. His torch continued across, reaching Yusuf in the back, then moving on.

It was over. They dropped Yusuf at his home in Beit Jala. Sophia walked him to his door and then left him to his mother. David waited in the car. Sophia lived less than two minutes away. As David pulled up outside her house, he recognised Tony's car. Whether he was expressly waiting, David didn't know, but he came down and joined them on the pavement by the Sunday school. David turned his wristwatch towards the light from the house. It looked to be 12.30.

Tony said, 'How is Yusuf?'

Sophia shivered. She didn't know. She thought Yusuf was scared but he was putting on a show for his mother. As she spoke, she looked up at the house. The number of lights must have made her suspicious because she suddenly said, 'Is there a problem?'

'No.' Tony shook his head vigorously. Then he turned slightly towards David as he said in English, 'It's Sister Hilda. She's come to tell tales on you.'

David stared at the house. 'She's in there?'

He remembered the last time he saw her, in the Church of the Holy Sepulchre in Jerusalem. She had refused to leave him, even to pray, until he'd promised that he would visit her soon. She could not stop talking about his voice and how beautiful it was.

'What's she doing here?'

'She followed me.' The way Tony said it, you knew it was not anything he wanted to re-experience any time soon.

David remembered that he and Tony were together when the nun caught him singing.

'How long has she been here?'

'Hours. Samira has already served coffee three times.'

David wondered what to say, whether to give Tony a sleazy leer, like the old days: his lips apart and his tongue flicking between his teeth. Saying, *It's not my fault, man. I'm fatal.* But he only had to look at Tony's face to realise he wasn't in the mood. He was ready to mumble *Sorry* when he heard the wail.

Before they reached the porch steps the wail had turned into a scream. Samira Khouri was standing in the front door, letting go completely. Sophia pushed her mother to the side – there was a body lying on the tiles, crumpled as a suit. Sophia started shouting, 'No, no.'

It was Elias. His mouth was moving slightly but he couldn't find any air. His eyes shivered and lost their focus.

Sister Hilda was at Sophia's shoulder, saying: 'Let the father through, let the father through.'

David was rooted in the doorway. He was staring at Elias's face as it turned grey-purple: the colour of dead lips. Sister Hilda caught hold of his wrist and pulled him over, saying: 'It's a blessing the father is here.'

With a kind of cold clarity, David was the first to realise that she meant him. She was asking him to perform the last rites. He tried to back out of the door but the nun had her hand in the small of his back.

'Father. Please.'

Her eyes were wide open: her whole expression was wide open, transparent even. She was pushing him forward, telling

171

him to seize this chance, he could save a soul and reaffirm his vocation.

'Father.' Her other hand bit into his wrist. All the while Elias was slipping further and further away, like a liquid finding its level on the cold floor.

Sophia saved him. Her elbow struck out, hitting the nun in the hollow of her breastbone and breaking her hold on David.

'Get a doctor. Uncle Tony, get a doctor.'

Tony ran for the door rather than the telephone. David didn't understand what was happening. He could hear Tony shouting a few doors lower down the street. After a moment, David realised the doctor was a neighbour.

Everyone knew it was a heart attack. Samira's screaming had bought the janitor out of the Sunday school. When the doctor arrived, he seemed to bring half the neighbourhood with him, all following where the doctor walked, called on by the wailing. The noise even set off the dog in the yard; maybe it was the dog that actually woke the neighbourhood. And in the thick of the crowd, Sister Hilda was still flailing around, shouting for David.

It was close to three when Sophia found David smoking a cigarette, slumped in his car so low that only the smoke was visible. When she banged at the passenger window he jumped, still jittery from the nun. Then, when he saw her, he thought for a second that she must have lost her mind. She looked so fierce. And there was no reason to search him out: unless she actually *wanted* him to pray over her dead father. He froze in his seat, his eyes locked on hers but his ears closed. Not wanting to have to hear her ask for something so impossible.

Gradually her rising voice got through to him. She wanted him to drive. She had to get away.

He flipped up the door stud.

She swung into her seat. 'Go on. Go on.' Ordering him to move as she slammed her hand against the steering wheel.

'Is your father dead?'

'No. Sleeping. Drugged.'

He still didn't understand. He said, 'Shouldn't you stay.'

But her mother was with Elias and the bedroom was too small for them both to crouch by the bed. She didn't tell David that, she just shook her head. But although her face was set blank and firm, she had somehow become readable: David could look at her and see how scared she was.

'Come on. Drive.'

They took the mountain road back up through Beit Jala, back past the single soldier, swerving through his S-bend of plastic barriers. This time he let them go, he didn't even lift his flashlight. At the Israeli bypass, David was about to go right to Jerusalem but Sophia shook her head.

'No, go the other way.'

After ten minutes on a deserted stretch of road they came to a new checkpoint, this one marking the point where Zone C met the one-time edge of the West Bank: the old Green Line from the days before the war of 1967. This time there were soldiers waiting and the Fiat was flagged down. One soldier came to the window, crouching to speak while two others sat nursing their rifles. Above them, maybe a quarter of a mile away over rough ground, David saw what looked like a wire-bound fortress but was probably a settlement.

The soldier said, 'Shalom.'

David nodded and passed over the car documents.

'Passport?'

He handed over his Irish passport.

'Entry visa.'

David said, 'There's a stamp in there.'

The soldier flicked through, shining his torch on every page. When he found the entry stamp, he pointed to Sophia and said: 'Where's hers?'

David said, 'She's my wife.'

'Where is her passport?'

David hadn't prepared himself this time. He knew the other passport was somewhere in the car but he didn't have it to hand. He wondered, if he said it was in the boot, would they let him pass? He doubted it.

Sophia took the initiative. She leaned over, holding a passport-sized document up to the window. David didn't dare look, not wanting any emotion to register on his face. But he didn't believe this would work, The Israeli-issued travel document that marked her out as a Palestinian came in an orange plastic cover. If she was hoping the soldier would be fooled, she was crazy. She really thought it would look Irish green in the reflected glow of the headlamps off the road, or the lights from the settlement on the brow of the hill?

The soldier leaned in to the window, leading with his torch. He shone it directly on the cover of Sophia's passport. David followed the beam around, staring at the passport himself. It had the American eagle on its cover.

The soldier nodded, passed David's passport back to him and waved them away, into Israel. David waited until he had pulled clear of the cones before he turned to Sophia.

'You've got American citizenship?'

She shook her head. 'No. The passport's one of yours.'

He fumbled on the dashboard, where she'd thrown it. It was his: his US passport, a fake. He said, 'What if they looked?'

'I didn't care.'

David didn't know what to say. He tucked the US passport into the top pocket of his shirt. He should at least keep a closer eye on it now.

The road led them into a thick pine forest, the headlamps carving ghosts out of the spaces between the trees, then took a nosedive. They were in a narrow pass.

David said, 'Where are we going?'

She said, 'I'll tell you.'

After another twenty minutes they reached a village and Sophia told him to park. When David opened his door, he was swept away by the scent of flowers in the night air. It was so strong he almost expected to see a cloud of perfume like a violet haze. Instead, he saw a Crusader church, hovering above the houses in its own halo of spotlights. The lights bled into a warm glow, bright enough to show how pretty the village was.

As they took the steps up to the church, David said, 'Why do you need so many false passports?'

He was trying to anticipate her first question. On any night when her father hadn't almost died, maybe she would be interested in his multiple passports. He continued anyway: 'I'm a friend of your Uncle Tony's, someone out of his shady past. So when you thought I was a priest, we didn't know what to say.'

'Were you with him in Beirut?'

David nodded.

'So you're probably immune to this.'

He didn't know what she meant. Then realised she was talking about death, thinking about her father and, perhaps, the lawyer too.

He wasn't immune. He told her, he had never seen anyone die in Beirut. He had seen corpses stretchered in ones and twos into ambulances after the artillery bombardments. All the same, he tried to stay focused on the issue: how to get the shipment on to a boat. Or maybe that was a defence mechanism, his brain telling him to concentrate on one task. He didn't want to stare at a body in the road, wrapped in plastic sheet, the edge of the sheet weighted with chunks of masonry from the shelled buildings.

He had left Beirut at the beginning of August 1982, after the artillery barrages but before the blanket bombing. He had taken the first half of their consignment with him. Tony had stayed a week longer, trying to plan a route out for the rest of the dope. He had spent the week on shuttle diplomacy, moving between the different factions. By this time, the Israeli army controlled all the countryside around Beirut. At first, Tony had got through their lines with very little difficulty. But then he'd decided, no more. He couldn't trust the people he was bribing. So he had followed David to London just in time for the wedding.

After the incident at the church and their escape, David had flown into Cyprus, on the lookout for a boat to take him to Beirut. Something resembling international diplomacy had finally got going and the Palestinian army, the PLO, were to be evacuated by sea. The second consignment of dope should have been evacuated with them. But when David finally got into Beirut, Tony had told him the bad news: their dope was going nowhere. Not until they found out where it was hidden. They'd had to sit on their hands for another fortnight, David keeping calm by keeping stoned. Tony had preferred to eat. At last, their contact had come through, telling them the dope was safe. It was in Sabra, packed inside polythene and buried in the shallow foundations of a wooden-floored canteen tent.

So far as Tony knew, it was still in Sabra on the night in September when the Israeli army opened the camp up to their allies and the massacre began. David knew that hundreds of unarmed civilians were killed in a few hours, both at Sabra and Shatilla. He had only seen two, both lying on a Red Crescent blanket. One was a woman. David had thought of her as old, although he now realised she had been less than sixty. The other was a boy of about nine. David could tell he had been ugly-tough when he was alive, but his corpse was twisted so awkwardly he looked only helpless in death. Except for this pair, David had never looked at any dead body in the Lebanon. He hadn't looked at them for long, but he had never forgotten what they looked like.

David didn't want to tell Sophia everything. He would have preferred to have told her about the fun parts, about the times he and Tony enjoyed being dope smugglers. But he was finding it more and more difficult to recall those times now. They were long gone, unrepeatable now. So he glossed over most of the details and ended by trying to answer her question: 'So no, I didn't see that many dead bodies. And I didn't like the ones I saw.'

What he wanted to tell her, that he had never been happy since, not in all those years he'd spent on the run. Never as happy as he was now, sitting on this wooden bench, breathing the damp, warm perfume of the heavy flowers, bathed in the lights on the church.

Sophia told him how her father would bring her here when she was a child. He liked to come because it reminded him of his own childhood. As a Palestinian village, before the war of 1947, it was like a holiday resort, or a weekend retreat. When Sophia visited, after the war of 1967, there were no Arabs left – the village had been colonised by Israeli craftsmen and artists: potters, weavers, some watercolourists. Now even these had been squeezed out. They couldn't afford the rising house prices.

She said, 'Maybe the old woman you saw at Sabra came from here.'

'Is that possible?'

'It's possible. Although the people from this village ended up in the camps in Jordan and the West Bank. More likely she was from Haifa or Akka.' She paused. Then said, 'Come on.'

She wanted to get back to her father. David did his best to get her there as quickly as possible. But as they were driving back through the forest they got stuck behind a truck and every time David tried to overtake it, he came upon a curve and the truck would float out. There was no passing. When they reached the checkpoint, they were glued into the truck's slow crawl. Neither his Fiat nor the truck was stopped by the soldiers.

The truck continued for another hundred metres before it pulled over on the verge where another, much older truck was waiting. The two rested, nose to nose. The newer truck with its yellow Israeli plates, the rusting older one with the blue plates of the occupied territories. David was ready to sail on by when Sophia touched his arm.

'Pull up around the next bend.'

'What's the matter?' He wondered if she was going to be sick.

'Pull up.'

He did what he was told, stopping the car behind a shallow hill. These were the outskirts of a hamlet of a half-dozen houses. The night was dark, he could see the silhouettes of goats grazing the hill, but no light except for the glow from the Jewish settlement above the hill's ridge.

'I want to go up there.' Sophia pointed to the hill. 'I want to know what they are doing.'

He could have said something. But he had decided, if he was in love with her, he should just act. And he was in love with her.

He got out of the car and started climbing the hill. The ground slipped beneath his shoes, like gravel over rock, but when David dropped to his stomach at the top he felt the bristle of grass on his face. This was what the goats ate? One of them was stalking in his direction – perhaps it thought he might be more edible. He looked over his shoulder, Sophia was a few yards below him. She was also on her stomach.

They continued crawling forward until the trucks were in view. The Israeli truck was moving off again, but David realised it was only changing its position. A man was standing on the roadside, guiding it around the Arab one so they were now tailgate to tailgate. The same man now started to supervise the unloading of one truck, the loading of the other. David began moving down the hill to find out which way the transfer was going to go: Israeli to Arab or Arab to Israeli.

When he reached the road he waited. He wanted to tell

Sophia to stay where she was, so far back from the vehicles she would be invisible in the dark. She shook her head even before he spoke. She was going with him.

They crossed the road and dropped down into a field on the other side. There was a steep escarpment – the field was almost six feet below the level of the road. David crouched, keeping his head below the blacktop. He could already hear the clanking of the roller doors on the Arab truck. He heard a man speaking American English with an Israeli accent. He was asking what they had: 'Is this grade A produce?'

An Arab voice said, 'It's excellent.'

David lifted up his head. He saw four pairs of feet in the spaces between the wheels. One in dark trousers, two in denims and one in white pyjama bottoms, all working together as they moved between the two trucks, lifting boxes out of the Arab truck and filling the Israeli one.

He heard the Israeli again, telling everyone to be careful. 'Guys, guys. Eggs are fragile, you know.'

The Arab said, 'Kosher.' And he started laughing.

The Israeli said, 'Now they're in my truck they're kosher.'

David turned. He hissed at Sophia, this time she really had to stay put. He was sure the Israeli was armed.

She hissed back, 'They're the al-Bannas.'

David nodded. He thought so too. But he was going to get closer, just to make sure.

He edged forward until he was right below them, his eyes level with the the bolts on the wheels of the Arab truck. The two Arabs in sweat-shirts and jeans were al-Banna's sons. David didn't recognise the one in traditional dress. But it was the Jewish man that interested him. The man was wearing dark trousers and a short-sleeved shirt. A neatly trimmed beard.

A sprightly man, about the same age as David. The reason David recognised him, the man was on the same Interpol lists as David, always a couple of places higher in the most-wanted stakes. As David remembered, his name was Saul Brodetsky, though there were plenty of a.k.a.'s. The man was basically into cons, a swindler. Though it looked as though he had now got into the smuggling game, smuggling eggs into Israel.

12

Today was the first day David had got to share the dawn with someone else. He and Sophia remained hidden behind the escarpment, listening to Brodetsky joke and al-Banna's sons work. It was more than half an hour before Brodetsky's truck was loaded up and driven away. David and Sophia waited for another twenty minutes. By this time, the sky was turning a pink-orange and the grazing goats had picked up a rosy aura around their woolly edges. Sophia didn't seem to notice; she was either tired or lost in thought, David didn't know which. When he finally dropped Sophia at her gate, the al-Bannas' truck was parked on the edge of her father's spare land. It was clear now why the al-Bannas were so keen to get hold of his property – they needed a back route out of their chicken farm, away from the main road. The egg-smuggling business required discretion.

As Sophia climbed out of the car, David asked what she planned to do with the information, whether she could shame them or blackmail them into moving the chicken farm somewhere else. Sophia said she doubted it, she didn't know.

David said, 'What about the Israeli? An international criminal's got to be worth something.'

'Maybe.' But she doubted it. She said, 'The Israelis don't extradite Jews, so he's safe. And we don't have laws against selling produce to Israel. If we didn't do it, we wouldn't have any money.'

'But he's pretending they're kosher.'

'As though anyone here is going to care.' But she said she would think about it. There might be something she could do. Now, she just wanted to get some sleep. It was going to be a long day.

She pointed to a house a little way to the south, where the hill started up to the centre of Beit Jala, and told him it was Yusuf's house. Today was his father's funeral.

Leaving aside the scent of chicken shit, it was too beautiful a day to bury a man. The sun was so bright, David could barely look at the steps to Yusuf's house. Where he put his foot, the shadow was black and the lines were clean and sharp against the glare of the polished stone. He could have worn sunglasses, but even after years of travelling he had the mindset of a man from a dingy country: sunglasses were accessories, they were too frivolous to wear to a funeral. David was wearing a black suit he had bought from a place called Today's World, opposite the *shwarma* store close to his hotel. He didn't want to play the foreign sophisticate and sneer at the local traders, but he could tell the suit was way out of fashion. Leaving his hotel room, he thought he was going to have to turn sideways and edge out of the door, the suit was so padded at the shoulders. Plus, the trousers had five pleats either side of the zipper, giving them room to balloon. David knew he should have asked Sophia where to go for the suit, but he imagined she was immersed in mourning, she wouldn't have the time to dress him. He might be suited up like Kid Creole, but he was going to have to live with it. After his third night with no sleep, he was too tired to shop around.

As he stepped into the shade of the Salmans' house, he realised that the dark suit and the black tie weren't necessary. There were chairs set around the entrance hall and the old men sitting there were wearing suits of different colours. One was even in his shirtsleeves. David was the only man wearing a tie. As he moved into the salon, David passed two agitated men whispering at each other. He didn't know them, but he tried to plug into the fellowship of grief. They looked up and nodded, but were soon back together, talking. It almost seemed as though they were arguing. They had empty coffee cups in their hands. As they spoke, they twisted them around.

The salon had two entrances, David walked in one and out of the other, picking up on the sub-currents of anxiety that disrupted the mourning. It was palpable, and it wasn't as though David was a sensitive man. As he moved from room to room, he realised the anxiety was fuelled by coffee. There were Thermos flasks and trays of coffee cups on every surface: on the mantelpiece, on the small stools that were scattered around like occasional tables, as well as on the dining-room table. The flasks had a pump action, and every so often a man would get out of his chair and go and push the top of the flask a couple of times to get a refill. Then they would sit again and start whispering to their neighbour. There were seats against every wall, pushing right into the edges of the three living rooms and snaking around the corners, through the arch that separated the salon from the dining room and down the short hallway into the TV room. Many seats were empty but there were still around fifty people in the house. David didn't know whether he was supposed to sit, stare silently at the floor as he nursed a coffee cup or try to join in the discussions. He didn't need to understand Arabic to know what they were talking about: whether Edward Salman was a traitor or not, speculating on the circumstances of his death. David hadn't yet seen anyone he recognised. He decided to keep on moving, the kitchen next.

The women were in the kitchen, a long room divided into a space for cooking and a casual dining area, complete with a mini-TV. The TV was covered with a cloth. David looked at the cooking area first; this was the coffee factory. An enormous pot sat stewing on the gas. As the empty flasks were brought in, the coffee woman would scoop a plastic jug into the pot and refill them. She was careful to avoid the debris of coffee beans and cardamom seeds floating on the surface of the oil-slick liquid.

Two women, close to the doorway, were hissing quietly at each other when they suddenly erupted. Another woman pushed between them, separating them as she simultaneously swept them out into the hallway. She moved so quickly their argument didn't spread into the heart of the room. The real mourning took place around the kitchen table, where the women were so intertwined in grief the table looked like the Raft of the Medusa, a picture of horror and misery, carved out of brownish light. David stared for longer than was respectable, and it was still a while before he realised Sophia was sat among them, just off-centre. Her head was resting on another woman's shoulder and one arm was outstretched to touch her mother, who was sitting on the far side. David didn't feel he was tuned to whatever she was feeling so stepped back before she saw him. He pressed up tight to the Frigidaire, he hoped out of everyone's way. He wasn't entirely sure why he had even decided to come to the wake and funeral, except that Sophia suggested it. If she should ever need an older and more stupid stranger for anything, he would be there for her. He might have his uses.

He was holding a coffee cup. A woman had pressed it into his hand. In his other hand, she placed a lozenge-shaped pill. The way she folded his fingers around the pill, it seemed like a Palestinian tradition. David took a look at it and then swallowed it with a mouthful of coffee.

Over the next hour, he pretty much stayed in the one place, except that he took frequent trips to the lavatory and continued pumping the coffee that made him go so often. He noticed that the women were dressed in more traditional mourning clothes than the men, predominantly black, with even a few veils. And he realised that nearly all of them were drugged. There were bottles and plastic-moulded packets of Valium-style downers on a shelf by the door and on top of the fridge. And at least two women were circulating, placing pills into the hand of anyone who opened up a palm.

The hard grief, the coffee and the pills stirred up such intense feelings, it was squeezing him out. He took another couple of pills: they had to help. When Tony walked up and hugged him, David hugged back. At first Tony didn't seem surprised by the firmness of his grip, but after two minutes he broke free.

David said, 'Sorry. But this place. You know.'

Tony nodded. 'There's a group in the salon saying that they don't know what they're doing here, the man was a traitor. Another group asking, so why are you here? There's his brother and a cousin in the dining room and they refuse to even acknowledge he was killed, they want to pretend it was an accident. I'm scared to sit down, in case I find I'm in the wrong camp.'

Tony pulled one of his shrugs. David felt his helplessness and moved in again for another hug. Tony stopped him.

'Are you feeling okay?' He looked into David's eyes. 'Are you stoned?'

David giggled.

Elias Khouri arrived ten mintes later, just ahead of the hearse carrying Edward Salman's body. Sophia ran out to help her father up the steps and into the house. Four men carried Salman's body through to the salon and set it down on two chairs, one at the foot and one at the head. A mound of leafy herbs and lilies was piled on Salman's chest, then his wife stepped forward and placed a large wooden crucifix on top of the greenery. David followed the other mourners as they crowded close to the body, though he was only following the shine of Sophia's hair as she supported her father. When he caught sight of the corpse, it was almost a shock. The only visible part of the body was the face, but it had a strange waxy polish and the mouth was settled into a smile that David didn't recall seeing on the man when he was newly dead in Ramallah.

A queue formed on the right side of Salman's body and the mourners stepped forward to look closely at the face, perhaps kiss its forehead or its lips. David noticed that many of the mourners bent low to the ear and held the position for seconds after the kiss. It was a few moments before he realised that they were looking for the stab wound.

It had been established that Salman had been stabbed with something like a long sharpened needle. The puncture hole was now hidden behind lacquered hair.

Sophia and Elias Khouri were one and two places ahead of David in the queue, and when Elias got his turn at the casket he stood without bending, just gazing at the body. His heart attack had taken him so close to death the previous night that he shouldn't even be here; he should be in bed. But he clearly needed to see Salman, it was obvious from the way he looked at the body. He continued staring, as though he was trying to find something in the face, something death couldn't put its twist on. Then he turned and walked away, Sophia holding him by the elbow. She didn't look at Salman's body. She just helped her father over to the salon door where a grey-faced man was standing. David saw with a shock that it was Yusuf, so altered by grief. Elias and Sophia hugged him but he barely responded.

David dropped out of the body queue – he had only wanted to stand close to Sophia. Now he walked back outside. The pills mixed with the coffee had left him feeling pretty stoned, Tony was right about that. And aside from an empty griping in his stomach, he didn't feel too bad at all. The pills seemed to relieve the symptoms of his flu. If the pH value of his gastric juices hadn't been so unbalanced from the coffee, it would even have been possible to believe that his appetite had returned. David reached into the pocket of his suit and brought out the moulded plastic-and-tinfoil sheet he had taken from the top of the refrigerator. Now he popped another couple of pills out of their cups and swallowed them. His throat felt a little tight, but he didn't need a drink to get them down.

He never had been interested in pills, at least after the age of about twenty-five when he decided that he was a smoker and that was it. His bag, he was sorted. Maybe he'd been missing something. He continued down the steps to sit on the front wall. The hearse was right in front of him. Behind the glass, there were so many ornate and fiddly bits: rollers set in the polished floorboards, a little metal fence marking out the space where the coffin would go. Screws and T-bars and spikes and strewn petals. It was an over-complex affair for such a simple procedure: taking the body from its house to its plot. David decided, when his time came, he would have it all pre-organised. He would arrange to die on a mountain so his last act could be a leap into space. Or, assuming he was sick and incapacitated, he would arrange for friends to steal away his body and burn it, like the singer Gram Parsons' friends did for him. Of course, he was going to have to find some friends first. He hadn't had any for so long. It was a shame because he liked having friends.

He started crying.

Earlier, as he was shopping for his funeral suit, there had been a thought working away at the back of David's mind: the real downside to the man's death. There was no longer any reason to stay in Bethlehem. They could not risk selling the Jerusalem apartment. Unless David thought of a new money-making strategy, he would have to go back to his old travelling life.

David always did his most creative thinking while he was smoking. And for the past week he had been peculiarly straight. Now his head was settling again into that primordial soup from which his best thoughts emerged. He stood as tall as he could; it was time to act. He sniffed the tears back into his eyes. All he got was a nose full of nitrates. The chicken shit trickled through the air like the thin yellow vapour of a cartoon fart.

The hearse climbed the hill up to the Hebron–Jerusalem road at Bab al-Z'kak, followed by the cars carrying the immediate family and closest friends. Sophia travelled with Yusuf, David followed on foot with a group of about twenty mourners. Before they reached the Grand Hotel, the number of walkers had shrunk to ten; perhaps because so few of them could cope with the exercise, more likely because they were beginning to attract hostile stares from the sidewalk as the shoppers realised who was in the coffin. Where the road forked by the Lutheran church, the hearse took the path to the right. The foot mourners opted for the left-hand fork, the most direct route which took them down the old steps by the souk. David stayed with the hearse. He barely noticed he was now a one-man cortège. He was growing light-footed. He was tripping, almost flying down to the square. He needed the hearse in front of him, just to slow down the pace.

As he reached Manger Square, he looked to his left. The other mourners were dribbling in on foot on the far side of the square. All trying to look as though they had arrived there by coincidence. David started giggling again. He knew he was stoned. He slipped into left-side-brain thinking and felt a wash of relaxation come down, swilling away his anxiety. He was going to be fine, he could function at his best. He was perhaps the only mourner neither drowning in grief nor disorientated by the tranquillisers. In fact, he could handle a few more of them.

He popped another pill out of the plastic, just to confirm what he already knew: his metabolism functioned best under constant sedation. A handful of barbiturates, like grade A dope, only set him straight, floating down the left-hand side of the road of life. He hovered where he was, a fraction of a hair's-breadth above the square, until the cortège caught up with him and swept him along. He was the only one who knew he wasn't walking, he was flying one sliver above the tarmac. He spread his wings and flew down to Christ's church.

The service was to be held in the Catholic chapel of the church. The tourists were still forming a bottleneck at the door into the Orthodox chapel. The entrance to the Catholic chapel was far bigger, easily wide enough for both the coffin and its pall-bearers. They passed through a vaulted passage and emerged into a courtyard with a statue of St Jerome at its centre. As the mourners flowed either side of the statue, David stepped back, hiding in the strips of shadow under the colonnade that surrounded the courtyard. He wanted to take a back seat, watch what others did and try to get a handle on the funeral etiquette.

Everyone was inside the chapel. David was about to slip in behind them when he felt a tap on his shoulder. Sister Hilda was smiling up at him, her hand on his elbow. Then, with some kind of superhuman strength, maybe even God-given, she gave him a spin and he found himself encircled by a group of friars, all in brown and black robes. He felt himself passed around the circle, murmured over and parcelled on to the next man. As they shared him around, they whispered their blessings, circling him with sweet candy-floss sentiments until he was wrapped up. Each of their languages like a different flavour: Arabic, French and American English.

He started murmuring back at them, 'Brothers, brothers, thank you. I am touched.'

One of the brown-robed species clasped his hand. 'Won't you come share a meal with us, after you have said your farewell to Dr Salman?'

David was staring at the man, at his carefully trimmed moustache and beard and at the large crucifix that hung in the middle of his chest. 'Are you Tony Iommi?' he asked. 'The guitarist with Black Sabbath?'

They didn't seem to understand the question.

Another, in French-perfumed English. 'Is it true you were ordained in Montreal, Brother?'

'Yes.'

'And how is the bishop?'

David hadn't thought that they might all know each other. But he nodded and said, 'The old twat's well.'

The service was starting. David hoped he could tear himself free of the group but the sticky threads of their good wishes stretched with him. As he took his seat in the three-quarters-empty church, the brothers were still tying him up. He had friars to his left and his right. Sister Hilda perched above him like a magpie at his shoulder.

A priest stood by Edward Salman's open casket, giving a eulogy in Arabic. David stared ahead, as though he was trying to catch a flavour of the man, even if he didn't understand the meaning of the words. All the while he was planning his escape. As the congregation went through their motions, standing up and sitting down, he was always a beat behind, but he tried to act pious.

As the service ended, the few mourners moved into the aisles, walking towards the front. The intention seemed to be to touch the body a final time. David pushed among them until he found himself squeezed between the coffin and Salman's widow. The widow pawed at the breast of the corpse, her hand moving as though she had no conscious control over it. Tears streaked her face, but David couldn't see her eyes behind her sunglasses.

He felt both distraught and ashamed. He couldn't nail the shame; if he could, he would have tried to confront it and make it go away. He rolled around the outside of the crowd, still trying to keep low to avoid his friar friends. Towards the back of the church there was a side entrance into an older chapel. David took a leap sideways, finding himself in the Armenian section, dedicated to the smallest of the three religious groups to have secured a stake in the Church of the Nativity.

He found Sophia there. He was lucky to have even seen her – she was all but sandwiched between a smoke-stained tapestry and the wall, her face turned into the dark. She was wearing a black dress that blended in with the surroundings. David recognised her by the light in her hair and the smell of her perfume, even though the incense vapours and the methylated spirit fumes barely gave her subtle scent house room. He always did have a finely tuned nose. It was coming back to him.

He said, 'Are you all right? I thought you would be out there.'

'No. It's over. Only the men go to the graveyard.'

'It's over.' He thought for a moment. 'Well, would you like to go to the seaside?'

13

David got lost on the highway into Tel Aviv. Not lost exactly – even with all the pills he'd taken, it wasn't easy to get lost on a straight road. But when every exit he passed signposted the city, how could he know which one gave the best route to the seashore? He asked Sophia if she knew. She shook her head and mumbled a few words he couldn't catch.

He leaned across to her, slumped in his passenger seat. 'Huh?'

This time it sounded like *Nancy Ryan*. Then when he grunted again something that sounded a little like *Johnny Say Pa*. David thought she was listing obscure singers or song titles. Then realised she was speaking French. He didn't know why. She seemed pretty dazed, but she had been hammering the tranquillisers as well.

He decided to rely on his own antennae. He cruised on down the highway, passing scarily flimsy skyscrapers all built from prefabricated modules, stacked and glued. He took a left at a building labelled The Diamond Center and realised eighty per cent of the city had to be prefab. He should have checked out a guidebook, found out something worth knowing about the city. But he could tell, just from looking around as he pushed his Fiat against the crosstown traffic, most of the city had been thrown up in a hurry. And you could call it haphazard, flaky, even chaotic – it was still impressive.

He definitely didn't know why the Tel Avivers couldn't be more appreciative. They were honking all around him, unwilling to wait for him while he slowed the car and took his sightseeing looks through his window. If they got level with him at traffic lights or on stretches of two-lane highway, they even started hurling abuse. The way it looked, he was the only chilled guy in the city. And come to think of it, even he was beginning to feel the heat. The weather was untrue, like a sweat-box in a Japanese prison movie. He had got rid of the wide-shouldered funeral jacket but he was still too hot. He rubbed at his chest through the unbuttoned neck of his shirt. His skin had a sheen of sweat; beneath the glaze it felt icky-sticky.

Sophia was still out of it when he reached the corner of Dizengoff and Jabotinsky. It was such a fabulous-sounding address, he decided this was where he had to park. There was even a carpark right there, if he wanted a sign that the stars were smiling down on him. It was a cramped lot between two hostels, and it was only as he was locking his car that he began to think the hostel to the left could be a brothel. He staggered for a moment, blown away by the brazen sign advertising the joint: a hardboard cut-out of a bazooka-titted McCrumbish woman. He could be back in Bangkok, or at least Miami. He stood there, looking from the sign back to the car. Maybe the car was the problem; maybe it was a spaceship, it had whisked him into another dimension. He ran round the car to open Sophia's door.

Wherever he was, Tel Aviv or Planet Freak, he was glad to be here.

It was only now he was beginning to realise how cramped his psyche had got, playing it straight every day. He was ready to get down on his knees and kiss the tarmac, like the Pope did on foreign jaunts. Not that he thought the Pope was a suitable role model in this city. That, too, was one of the attractions.

He leant Sophia against the car and went to speak to the carpark attendant. The man was sat in a wooden shed, equipped with a couple of fold-out chairs, one for himself and one for a much older guy. Despite the age difference, the two of them were talking like friends, just chatting about the heat, this and that. In particular, whether it was possible to blame the heat for the way the older guy's neighbours were fighting. The man was holding up his hands as though he was shaking an invisible melon and saying, 'All day, from morning through the night, he's asking her if she really wants to live in a shitting sewer. There she is floating on turds and she's got a smile on her face. She's telling him, You think I'm smiling? I'm just dreaming, you drowned in the shit, you whore's bastard. There's dog shit steaming off the shitting walls, she says, and when it collapses, I hope it collapses on you, you shithead son of a bitch.'

The younger guy said, 'My God.'

'I don't know whether I should kill myself. The things I hear, I wonder I can go on living. Alternatively, I could go knock on the door and applaud their performance. It may be unbearable, but it's also got a certain artistry.'

David said, 'Excuse me. Do I pay now or later?'

'How long are you staying?'

David had no idea. He thought it might be late already; perhaps they might end up stopping over. Tel Aviv looked like a place that deserved a little effort. If you got to know it, it would make it worth your while.

The attendant said, 'You don't know what time you're returning, then you should pay for the day.'

David paid the day rate. Before he left, he said to the old guy, 'I had neighbours like yours once. You know what I did?'

The man shook his head.

'I seduced the woman. I thought, as long as they're not physically in the same room, at least things will be quieter.'

The man shook his head. 'Let me guess: she started fighting with you? Or – no, worse, she uses the same kind of language when she makes love?' The man shivered. 'Can you imagine that?'

David said, 'You know her too?'

Before he headed off down the street they shook hands and the younger man told him not to worry about his car, he would keep an eye on it.

David said, 'Who's worried? It's a rental.'

Sammy Ben Naim watched from his car as David headed south down Dizengoff with Sophia Khouri. Earlier, when the girl was resting against the car hood, she had looked truly out of it. Now she was striding along the sidewalk, maybe a little robotically, but at least she was moving. David had more of a loose-limbed shuffle: it could have been a very laid-back look but for the ridiculously baggy trousers he was wearing. The two of them together, they were easy to pick out on the street and easy to follow. Sammy turned to his driver and said, 'Take the rest of the day. I'll handle it on my own now.'

The driver said, 'Okay, boss.' The way he said it, it was like a whoosh of relief. Sammy couldn't blame him. They had got on David's tail in Jerusalem, and the way he drove anyone following him really needed to take regular rest breaks. The driver was young and ambitious, though. Before he pulled away, he tried to prove the strain hadn't left him completely catatonic by asking: 'The two men running the parking lot, they his contacts?'

Sammy shrugged. He had never bothered explaining why David was under twenty-four/seven surveillance, or why they tagged his Fiat with a tracking device. Anyone with so many contacts among the Arabs could be considered a security risk. With his longish hair and his slightly spacy manner, David could easily pass as one of the more dangerous Western sympathisers. He was the right age, had the right profile. Back in the seventies, the Palestinians used to have a special cachet for Euro hobby revolutionaries; a leader of the Baader-Meinhof gang tried to send her pre-teen daughters to a PLO camp in Lebanon for weapons training. Sammy guessed his driver was smart enough to recognise that David was not that extreme, but he could be a fellow traveller. One seventies throwback deputising for another, a dope smuggler for a politico, both with their ideas on radical chic. It was natural to look for signs of a conspiracy. He wouldn't imagine that the reason they were putting so much time and effort into the man was because they were desperately trying to salvage a real estate deal.

Sammy said, 'You think it looks suspicious, talking to a carpark attendant.'

The driver didn't know whether he was being asked his opinion or whether he was being teased. He kept it non-committal, saying, 'Could be.'

Sammy nodded. Maybe yes. Maybe no. He was actually thinking himself, there was something strange about the scene. He couldn't quite pinpoint what it was but he was going to find out.

He let the car go without saying goodbye. As he crossed the street, he heard it U-turn, crossing left across the traffic and heading away. Sammy was on his own.

He approached the carpark attendant's hut with his head down, glancing at a piece of paper in his palm as though he was reading an address. The technique here, the routine: he was playing the part of a man who needed directions. He scanned the buildings on either side of the parking lot as though he was *shocked* and *confused* to find the carpark right in this spot: a job-lot of emptiness where he expected to find *something*. Once he was sure the carpark guy had noticed him, Sammy started on his little preparatory speech, picking on a word almost at random to give an extra flavour of confusion. As though he was hacking his way back to the logical beginning from a point midway through a sentence.

'From the baker's, was it the baker's? I don't know if I'm reading the numbers upside down or the right way around . . . Could you help me?'

The old man looked first. He grunted and nudged the attendant, who stared across with a frown between his eyes.

Sammy repeated himself. 'Could you help me?'

'I am sorry. The Hebrew not yet perfect so slower please.'

Sammy felt his jaw slacken. He tightened it quickly. 'Russki?'

The men nodded, *Da, da.*

'*On govorit pa Angliski?*'

They shook their heads; they did not speak English either.

Sammy looked back up the street to where his driver was almost out of sight. Then down the street, at the fast-disappearing figures of David and the Arab girl. He didn't remember anything in the report that said David was fluent in Russian. And Sammy had already used up all of his own Russian, his six-word lexicon.

He grimaced at these two new Russian immigrants, then set off down the road. The way he handled that situation, and the way he now had to run just to maintain visual contact, it was like he'd never gone to secret agent school. He'd just watched a goofball spy film and taken it from there.

He lost David and Sophia before Ben Gurion Boulevard. They crossed the road, a couple of cars passed between them, and they were gone.

Sammy took stock. He decided to stop acting like an asshole. It wasn't as though they were trying to throw him off track. It was just a result of tailing amateurs. If they weren't trying to be evasive, they tended to be so much more unpredictable.

Sammy hated to admit it, but his big mistake was to call off his driver. He had his reasons – he was looking for a chance to talk to David, one to one. It was necessary to choose the exact moment, always a delicate judgment. But maybe there was another reason why he let the driver go: he felt he was playing too hard when his target was so soft. Since the lawyer's death, he knew he had to come up with something special to save the deal. And a good plan had to fit the people involved. Sammy hoped to draw a strategy out of the situation, like a hermeneutic, letting an understanding emerge unforced through dialogue.

Sammy took a look up the block, back down. There were a few fast-food joints selling *shwarma*, a money-changer's, but mostly there were hostels with names like The Back-packer or The Ego Has Landed. The kind of place that would let out a bed in a dormitory for less than ten dollars. Sammy took a guess. If David and this girl were looking for a bed, they wouldn't want to sleep communally.

Then Sammy saw Sophia Khouri sat on her own on a street bench, close to a *shwarma* café. He circled her and walked inside the café. He bought a can of iced tea and then took up a position in the window. As he stood, he felt the heat of the gas burner froth and steam the skin across his back, making his shirt stick. But he had a good view of the back of Sophia's head, and he could try to follow the direction of her gaze. If her head hadn't kept dipping down, nodding sleepily at the road then jerking awake again, he might have spotted David earlier. As it was, it took fifteen minutes before Sammy saw him on the first floor of the Curious Yellow hostel, hidden behind the overflowing window boxes on the balcony.

He watched as David stood and shook the hand of a younger guy. Or to rephrase: he was either shaking hands or making an exchange. However it was going to appear in the final report, the conclusion was the same: the deal was done. David was smiling. In fact, he even looked to be whistling. Then he began fumbling for the buttoned pocket at the back of his chinos.

Up on the balcony, David said, 'Thanks, man. If you don't mind, I'll skin up here. I've been missing it.'

The kid nodded towards the street, sending his big bushy

head of hair wobbling. 'It's fine with me, man, but what about your old lady?'

'That's okay. She's resting.'

As David pulled out his Rizlas, he got a flash of the inclement conditions they must have suffered the past week while they had remained squashed into his back pocket. Chiefly, the sweat damage. The sweat had done its worst on the first twenty or so sheets. Now their individual identities were lost to a gummy wad.

'Here, use mine.' The kid held out a giant pack embossed with the cannabis leaf symbol.

David said, 'Hold on a mo ...'

He carried on scooping the sheets out like a magician doing the scarves-tied-together trick and was rewarded with a run of free papers. It was a joy to behold, the way they slipped out of the letterbox, unfolding and separating one by one. He could have used the kid's skins; they were the extra-large design specifically made for joints. But he preferred not to: and it wasn't just the straw colour of their recycled paper that turned him off. He just liked working with the everyday rolling size. There was something about a Rizla skin and its many myriad attributes. The delicate translucence, the hint of pin-stripes in the paper like a watermark, the centre scored with a perfect crease. The strip of sticky stuff. David rested against the balcony edge and licked a centimetre of one paper to stick it lengthways with another; the third paper went across the top to make an L-shape. He liked his joints long and Biro-thin but needed a little more width for the roach end.

Aside from talking and kissing, no activity calls for so much specialist tongue work as making a joint. David licked down the length of his cigarette so the paper bulged and split along the wet line. He used a fingernail to tear down the wet strip and expose the tobacco and then used the back of his nail to nudge two-thirds of the tobacco into the central crease of his Rizlas. It lay there, holding its shape. David twisted the remains of the cigarette into a disposable parcel and dropped it in the ashtray.

All day, his Zippo had been flopping heavily in the hanky pocket of his shirt. Now he took it out, cracked it alight and began warming the lump of resin the kid had just sold him. As it began to smoke, David held the block to his mouth and sucked in, getting a first taste. It was sweetish and herby with maybe a trace too much of something combustible and petrollish. It reminded him of the blue paraffin he used to see sold in French gas stations but nowhere else, so even that seemed exotic and different. The warmed dope crumbled easily, like a butter-and-flour pastry mix before any water is added. He let what he judged to be a sixteenth fall among the tobacco and then used his fingernail again to fold the mixture into an even blend.

He rolled the joint so it flared only slightly at the end he would light. It was not so much a carrot, more like the leg of a pair of rodeo jeans. David liked to pack a joint quite tight, something he often got into arguments over. His reasoning was that he liked some resistance behind every draw – making him work for his smoke. He twisted the flared end closed and then held the joint up so he could look in the narrow end like a man looking in a small telescope. He couldn't see anything that might obstruct the roach when he slipped it inside. It all looked fine.

He made the roach from a book-match that said *The Grand Hotel, Bethlehem*. He always used book-matches, if there were any to hand. Better than ripping the flap off your Rizlas, or destroying your cigarette packet and risk losing the cigarettes. The flap off a new set of book-matches always had a pleasing stiffness, giving the roach a springiness that, as it unfurled slightly inside the joint, ensured it stayed wedged tightly in place.

He looked it over. 'How's that?'

'It's one way of doing it.' The kid had a smug smile. Like he really could roll a finer number. Then, 'You sure you don't want to ask your chick to step over and admire this major work of art?'

David looked back across the street at Sophia. She was sat upright, yawning and stretching. As she blinked her eyes, David felt her focus and smiled her way.

The kid said, 'Am I tripping, or is there another guy looking our way?'

David said, 'Yeah. He's been following me at least since Jerusalem. Do you think he's secret service or what?'

The kid flipped.

Sammy saw the kid with the wild hair begin waving his arms at David. Even over the traffic on Dizengoff he could hear him shouting in English.

Over the next few moments he only got louder. 'Get off my fucking balcony, man. I don't know you. You hear me, I do not know who you are. So fuck off.'

David was laughing. He ambled down the steel staircase that ran from the balcony to the street. Then when he reached the pavement, he turned sharp left, towards Dizengoff Square. Sammy had to decide: was he was staying with the girl or was he following his man? He stepped on to the street. Sophia

Nicholas Blincoe

Khouri didn't look as though she was going anywhere. Sammy tossed his iced tea into a trash can on the sidewalk and headed south, after David.

He caught up with him outside a café just off the square, on Pinsker. There were tables and fold-out chairs halfway to the street. David had a table all to himself, to the left of the café door. Sammy slowed up, asking himself how the situation looked to the people sat around. It was called *s/r* in the textbooks, or 'self-reflection'; an overly philosophical term for the most basic reflex: trying to imagine how others see you. Everyone sat outside the café looked young – too young even to be in the army, although they probably weren't. A quarter had coloured hair and even more of them had piercings. Sammy was fairly sure that he was the only guy in the area without tattoos – though he couldn't speak for David. Maybe he had some prison tats. The dossier might have missed out on David's Russian proficiency, but it didn't skim over his prison time.

David was grinning. He said, 'You're not really an airport cop, are you?'

Sammy shuffled. He was tired of cataloguing the number of incidents that fucked with his professional stride. From the man's wayward driving to his parking-lot conferences, his detours to buy dope, and now this knowing 'I-made-you-immediately' routine. He told himself, just go with it.

'No. I'm not an airport cop.' He looked at the spare seat at David's table. 'I wondered, do you have five minutes?'

'If you want to help me smoke this, then okay. Otherwise, I'd prefer if you left me alone. I only came here to buy drugs. With you around, I could have blown it. I know I make it look easy, but scoring in a strange town takes some talent.'

Sammy shook his head. 'You were driving so badly. Trying to stick on your tail, we must have looked suspicious.'

David said, 'You think I was driving badly? Maybe you could harass me with some kind of motoring offence.'

David's coffee arrived, interrupting the situation developing between them.

Sammy said, 'Come on, why piss each other off? I'm the one put at a disadvantage, since you made me so quickly.'

'I'm not looking for flattery. Just a quiet place to smoke before I rejoin my girlfriend.'

Sammy decided he was fed up with sitting on the lower side of the seesaw. He was going to take a sudden leap and give the guy a shock. He said, 'I've been wanting to ask you all week, what kind of name is Ramsbottom?'

David's mouth turned a little tighter; there was a bulge in his throat that he swallowed. But you had to be a professional to see any of it. He just said, 'It's a small town in the North of England. What else do you know about me?'

'Just odd snippets. Something I didn't know, you speak Russian.'

'Manchester University, Russian language and literature, 1970 to '74. Where did you learn your English?'

'You noticed the accent? Most people assume English is my first language. American English, that is.'

'I've been around. I've got a sensitivity for accents.'

'Well, you're right. I studied English literature at Yale.'

David kicked back in his chair. 'So, aren't we civilised. Just a couple of intellectuals, talking over their alma maters.'

'That's all. Like the moment in the Mamet plays where they say, What is this?'

'What is this?'

'Yeah, you know. Someone says, What is this? What is it that we have here? It's just two guys talking, that's all. It's all it is. Two guys talking.'

'And then one of them gets fucked over.'

Sammy asked, 'You're a fan of Mamet?'

'I've seen a few things. It seems everyone talks that way these days. Guy talk.'

'It's all it is. All over the world, everyone talking *guy*.'

'Meaning someone's always trying to fuck someone over. So what do you want?'

'I want to help you.'

That was the moment when David realised he'd been mistaken. This man wasn't an ordinary secret policeman, he was political. And because he didn't want to rush into any more mistakes, David decided to slow things down. He reached into his breast pocket and pulled out his Zippo. His eyes remaining locked on the man's, taking in his dark eyes, his dark skin, the boniness of his features. You couldn't call it an honest face, the eyes had way too much depth for that. But this agent, this Shin Bet man, seemed at least to be open in his love of strategy. He wasn't hiding it, he was an operator, that's what gave him his spark. But there was something else there, working to dampen it: a touch of defensiveness. Maybe it was working within an organisation, the pressure of office politics when all your strategies have to be submitted upward. That would flatten the pleasure, wouldn't it?

Or perhaps David was reading too much into a slightly downturned mouth.

He lit his joint.

If David had a strategy, it was to lead with his intuitions.

He'd sparred with the man, tested out his stare and gone through the verbals. They had drily fingered each other's balls to see who had the brassiest pair. And David knew, it could easily be the other guy.

He said, 'You want to help me with what?'

'I want to lend you my professional assistance. Now your lawyer's dead, I'd say you'd reached an impasse.'

David took a long drag on the joint and held it, hoping it would smoke out the remains of the tranquillisers. The way those things felt, they could almost be 'ludes. He hadn't had any of those for twenty years.

He needed a shock move, even if it meant giving up everything he had managed to guess in one throw.

'So you're the one who dumped the lawyer in Ramallah?'

Sammy nodded, yes, that was down to him. He said, 'It was a messy situation. The guy dropped down dead at a particularly sensitive moment, we had to move him somewhere else.'

'I imagine you promised him that he'd be safe, before he ended up dead.'

'I'm not saying it wasn't unfortunate. It was not one of the department's finest moments. But we can offer you security.' He stressed *you* : David really didn't need to worry. 'You know the Palestinian Authority had another lawyer in custody?'

David nodded. 'I saw him being taken out of Bethlehem police station. Is he someone else you gave guarantees to?'

'With him, we delivered. He's safe now, here in Tel Aviv.'

'Well, okay. If my partners decide to go through with the house sale, I know who to call.' David took a final drag on his joint. 'But for now . . .'

He flipped the joint up so it spun end on end. The secret

service guy had secret service reflexes. He managed to snatch it out of mid air. Perhaps he did it without even burning his hand. David couldn't be sure, he only saw it out of the corner of his eye as he ran. He cut across the flow of traffic to where Sophia was waiting in the getaway car. It was a taxi, engine idling, the back door open ready for David to dive inside.

14

Sophia was swaying. She hadn't managed to catch her balance since they had left the taxi. She had an arm wrapped around David's waist, his arm wrapped around hers. She wondered what they looked like, walking together like that, so totally mismatched, so obviously drugged.

David had stolen her pills out of her pocket while they were still in the taxi. She was twisted round in her seat, looking at the shrinking figure of the Israeli secret agent on the street corner. The man was positioned slightly off-centre in the taxi's rear window, as though he were framed for Cinemascope. He grew smaller as the frame pulled back. She imagined him wishing that he owned a hat. He looked like someone who wanted to snatch a hat off his head, screw it into a ball and throw it to the floor. The deathless moment of classic cinema: the hat-throw of exasperation. Or the classic moment of wordless cinema. The dying moment of breathless cinema. Sophia could not decide. Then she felt David's hands in her pocket and the secret agent faded out of the picture.

She asked him what he thought he was doing. *Are you crazy?*

David pulled out the two plastic pod sheets of tranquillisers.

'I need these.'

He had several packets of his own, she didn't know why
he needed hers as well. But she let it go. The same way
that she had hailed the taxi and instructed the driver, who
was an Arab, to *follow that man* down the street. The same
insouciance in both cases: she did it because he asked her to,
because it was his idea to visit the seaside and because she was
straining to be self-effacing. She had an idea, the less she was
aware of herself, the less likely she was to burst into tears.
She had been feeling fragile, at least since the funeral.

Her strategy was working, she had so little self-awareness
that she only realised she wasn't dressed for the seaside when
she saw the beach. She was wearing a black coat and black
dress. Her black pantyhose was laddered on the right leg.
She didn't have any other clothes with her.

She asked, 'Where are we going?'

David said, 'Where the Russians are.'

She should have asked him then, what kind of Russians did
he expect to find when he was using barbiturates as bait?

By three in the morning, Sophia was standing on an eleventh-
floor balcony of a tower block with the man David was
describing as his new best friend, Yuri. Sophia wanted to
know why she couldn't see the sea at all. Yuri explained
that they were looking inland.

'So if you had an apartment on the other side of the
building, then you would have a sea view?'

'No, around the other side there is also no view. Only
another tower block.'

They weren't the only ones on the balcony. When she stepped outside, trying and failing to find any fresh air, she was followed by Misha, Ludmilla, Natasha and Mannie. David was the only one in the whole party who didn't follow her.

Sophia thought the lack of any view was a pity.

Yuri agreed. 'It is a terrible shame.'

He gave a grave nod and the black curtain of his fringe swung across his face and back. He held up the vodka bottle, said *Okay*, and refilled her shot glass, then everyone else's glass and finally his own. Before they were allowed to clink and drink, Yuri had to give the signal. He cleared his throat.

Sophia said, 'What? Now we have to drink to having no view?'

'No. This is another toast. This is for the luck that brought new friends to our door.'

Sophia took the glass of vodka as Yuri offered it and murmured, 'Here's to the luck and to the drink that isn't a drink to the poor view.'

She already knew she didn't need another vodka. She doubted that she could even drink it. Yuri was certainly having problems drinking his, but that was because he had forgotten to remove the joint from his mouth. The glass went up to his lips and met a mysterious obstruction.

He said, 'But there is something wrong.'

Sophia thought, there was surprising little wrong with Yuri. He was slim and wiry, with the musculature of an athlete. A doped athlete, considering the amount of things that were thickening his bloodstream. He had his vodka, his hashish and the pills that David had given him.

They had come across Yuri on what Sophia thought was a street corner. It was a street corner, but it was also right outside a bar. Yuri thought he was still inside the bar: when he stumbled out into the oncoming traffic, he thought he was heading for the lavatory. David saved his life: or at least, Yuri claimed that his life had been saved and David did not contradict him. Soon they were talking Russian together, David doling out the pills and accepting drinks. Sophia could not follow all of the conversation, but then David said: 'Here's to my new best friend.' The first toast not in Russian.

Yuri's toast speeches were medium to long, delivered in a sonorous Russian wah-wah that David obviously enjoyed but which meant nothing to Sophia. She tried to read Yuri's hand signals. It seemed to her she was in the audience of one of those TV game shows of charades. His gestures were so stylised, she thought he was signalling a film or a book or a song: two words, three syllables. Sophia was fairly numb back then; later she was less so. It was only later that she began to have a better idea of what was happening. Plus, once Yuri invited them back to his flat he switched to English.

Yuri explained he spoke English because his flatmate Mannie didn't understand Russian. If he had known that she didn't speak Russian, he would have switched earlier. He was deeply sorry. Sophia believed him.

She looked from the balcony, back through the glass doors into the apartment. She struggled to focus on what she could see of Yuri's living room in the spaces between the other party guests. She was surprised to find the room still so distorted – she had thought she was possibly sober now because for the past half-hour she had seemed fine in her own mind. In fact, if she were a blind woman, she might not even have known that she was drunk. But then she tried closing her eyes and she knew that she was wrong about that.

Yuri had refilled their glasses. His next toast came swelling out of her dizziness; she thought it had to be an aural hallucination. She opened her eyes and knew it was true.

'And for all that . . . here's to Israel.'

She held on tight to the balcony rail. Around her she heard the others chime in: 'To Israel . . . to Israel'

'Pooh.'

She suddenly stopped swaying, she could stand straight. She didn't know if it was adrenalin, if it was fear or fight and flight. She only knew she was ready to be reckless; she didn't care if she started a new Israeli/Palestinian conflict.

There was silence. Then Yuri began giggling. Natasha and Misha were not far behind. Yuri even had a story. He began it as soon as everyone's glasses were refreshed.

'When I first decided to journey to Israel, I was told I must first speak to the officials of the emigration department in Moscow. So I carried myself to the department and for two days I waited in line to speak. Finally, I was sat before this grey-faced personage and he asked me, "Why is it you wish to emigrate to Israel?" I told him, "I wish to follow my wife, she is going to Israel." He looked at me and said, "That is not what I asked. I want to know why *you* wish to emigrate to Israel." I told him, "Well, my wife's sister and her family, they are all heading to Israel." The emigration official is now growing stern. He tells me, "I understand. But you must tell me why you wish to go to Israel." I tell him: "My wife's mother and her husband and also my cousins, they too are all going to go to Israel." The official now is beginning to shout, he says: "Listen, Yuri Edwardovitch, you have told me about your relatives, your friends, your acquaintances, all of them are going to Israel. Okay. But I need to know why *you* wish to go." So I told him, "It is simple. I do not wish to go but I am the only one who is Jewish."'

Yuri looked around the balcony, laughing. 'It is true.'

The sound of laughter seemed to suck the air out of the night like a pair of bellows: sucking it out and blowing it back. Sophia was reeling again. The night was muggy and even on the eleventh storey she could not find a breeze.

She said, 'I need to sit down.'

The whole party followed Sophia back into the apartment. Yuri's sofa, his springless armchair and the three kitchen chairs were arranged in a circle around a kilim. The Russians believed, if you were partying, you were doing it together. You didn't break into particles and form semi-detached constellations, you kept the energy going at the heart. David had explained this to her. Then broke the rule himself. He was squatting on the kilim making yet another joint.

There were four Russians and one English boy, Mannie, besides herself and David. Everyone seemed more than happy to speak English, though. Misha, the other Russian man, and Natasha spoke the language reasonably well, Ludmilla less so. Yuri was still apologising for failing to speak to her in the bar, earlier in the evening. He never meant to exclude her from the interesting conversation and enjoyment, in fact he intended the opposite. He had been worried that she found him too *insistent*, his efforts to communicate repulsed.

David looked up from the floor and said, 'Sophia's a little vacant today.'

Yuri looked across to Sophia for confirmation and she nodded her head. She was so unused to hashish, she hadn't smoked since university and she had forgotten how lethal the alcohol and cannabis combination could be. Not to mention the tranquillisers and, so far, far back, the funeral – the primal event that kick-started this rollercoaster ride. She knew she should not mention the funeral, and not because it was already yesterday's news. It was just too dangerous. Yuri was so pumped full of intoxicants and sentiment that he would try to bowl her over in a hurricane of emotion. The apartment was a fragile pile of concrete, Sophia didn't think it was strong enough to cope with anything like that.

David said, 'How did you and I become best friends, Yuri? Roughly?'

Yuri shrugged. 'You are a friend of Natasha?'

David turned around, smiled at Natasha and passed the lit joint over to her. He watched as she took a drag, then shook his head. 'I don't think so.'

'Oh. Then maybe you are the friend of Ludmilla's sister. I remember.'

'Ludmilla's sister? Was she the woman in that first bar?' He looked from Yuri to Ludmilla, his hand vaguely pointing out through the balcony doors.

Yuri didn't bother looking. 'No. The woman in the first bar was a waitress. Ludmilla's sister is a prostitute.'

'Then I don't think I know her. But you never know, maybe. I just don't have any recollection.'

'I have it, now at last. Mannie. He is an Englishman, so you two are friends.'

That definitely wasn't right.

Mannie said, 'I met David less than an hour ago, right here. You introduced us.'

'That is true.' Yuri nodded. 'Then it is a mystery. Or it is fate. You know what, why should we worry over it? We are here.'

The tower block was one of six or seven, set in a dead straight line parallel to the motorway. From the balcony, Sophia had looked down on to the flat roofs of the lower buildings. Like everywhere in Israel and Palestine, these roofs were prickly with washing lines, water tanks and stray bits of reinforcing rods prodding their way out of the concrete. But there were also people, camped out under the Tel Aviv sky or living in shantytown boxes purpose-built on top of the buildings.

She said, 'Does everyone here live here?'

Mannie grunted sullenly. Yuri shot him a look and said, 'But of course. What can we do? There's too many people and not enough money and we all want to live in Tel Aviv. You know the price of real estate in this city?'

David intoned, 'Worse than London. Worse than New York.'

Sophia remembered the flatmate Mannie saying this earlier. David was parodying him, perhaps consciously.

Yuri spread out his hands. 'The real estate market here is worse than anywhere.'

David said, 'Worse than Jerusalem?'

'Ah, well, that depends. Jerusalem has many differentials. The new settlements are very reasonable, somewhere downtown with a bit of history not so reasonable. But still people choose to live in Tel Aviv. Why?' Yuri looked around. 'Are we crazy? I do not think so. It is possible to find ways to live here, I think.'

David proposed a toast. 'To Tel Aviv.' Then realised he had no drink. He lifted himself from his crouching position, remembering somehow that there was another bottle of vodka on the sideboard.

At an altitude of four feet above the rug, he hit the smoke level. There was a time David could have lived off that smell. Give him a knife and fork, he would cut chunks out of the air and chew on them, even stash a few slices for whenever the air got too thin. But now, this Tel Aviv evening, he staggered as he connected with the thick fug hovering above him. After a week living in Bethlehem, he just wasn't the head he used to be. And there was the vodka, of course, that had to be a factor. *Just factor that fucker in there, put it in the mix.* David clamped his mouth shut, just in case he started babbling out loud.

He steadied himself. His aim, just to maintain and do it at a gentle pace. Then he lost his rhythm entirely by plonking down heavily on the sofa. He caught a glance off Sophia, a look in her eyes asking if he was okay. He gave her a clipped apologetic smile, then looked to his left to see who he could have disturbed with his forced landing. He was lucky, the person sat beside him was the flatmate Mannie. David didn't really care about this miserable bastard. Next to Mannie there was the thin girl with the cheap bleach thatch and, balanced on the arm of the sofa, another guy, a friend of Yuri's. He didn't seem to have disturbed either of them.

The bleached girl, he remembered, was Ludmilla, the one with the prostitute sister. The man was Misha. He was whispering, Ludmilla was listening intently. As far as David could make out, she was trying to grasp a technicality of the Israeli welfare system, but it might have been a point of immigration law. Misha only broke off his explanantion as Yuri leaned over, passing over one of the three joints that were circling the room.

Yuri and Misha were between thirty-two and thirty-seven: David had always found it difficult to tell with Russians. He had spent a year in Moscow while he was at university and it was there that he developed his morphology of the Russian face. It was fairly straightforward. There were only two types: Skins and Bones or Brezhnevs and Nureyevs. The Skins were fleshy, like Misha and Natasha. They could look younger than their age for years until, almost overnight, they didn't any more. The Bones were the opposite. They had tight, translucent skin that never seemed to wrinkle, only go papery until it looked like milky cling film across their skulls. As children they always looked scary, like the spawn of alien invaders, but they aged better. David, at least, wished he had that kind of genetic make-up, a bone structure that could have been thought out by a diamond cutter, every angle and every facet. Ludmilla, with her skull of bleached hair, was a Bone type. While Misha was explaining the *system* to her she listened with a grim concentration. Tiredness and anxiety had turned her face into a death's-head. David had to admit that she didn't look so good. The best Bones were always men.

Yuri was a Bone-man. He had all the bone structure anyone could want, and then some to spare. David looked at him through the swathes of dope smoke. The man's face seemed to twist and bulge, twist and bulge. It was perturbing. David blinked, moved swiftly from perturbation to resentful paranoia. Then immediately felt sick. He headed for the kitchen.

He was throwing water from the sink into his face when he realised the boy Mannie had followed him.

'Can I drink this water?' asked David.

Mannie said, 'I do.' Then, as David took a slurp from the tap, added: 'But I can't afford to buy bottled.'

All night, the kid had annoyed David, either by his silences, his wisecracks or his sulks. When David had first met him, he had tried to squeeze some bonhomie out of the coincidence of them both coming from North Manchester, even if they were twenty years apart. It hadn't worked. Now they were in the kitchen together, David was struck again by the boy's sickly looks. As though he had been a fat boy, his mummy's healthy eater, but had somehow lost his flesh too quickly. There was something hangdog about him, and it didn't help that he had thick dark bags under his eyes.

David said, 'I'm sorry. Am I keeping you up?'

'Me? I'm too scared to sleep here.'

For a split second, David wondered if he understood the boy. Was he trying to give him a coded threat: like, *I'm so scared, why don't you step up and show me how hard you are?* Then he realised that Mannie was actually telling the truth.

'Sorry. I take your point, they are pretty dodgy.'

David wondered why a twenty-five-year-old English boy was sharing an apartment with a Russian criminal like Yuri and whoever else Yuri happened to bring back that night. Mannie admitted, he never knew who he was going to find when he returned from his night job. It was normally a couple of girls from Odessa, new to prostitution. It was rarely fortysomething Englishmen and young Arab girls.

Mannie asked how he and Sophia came to be there.

'I was thinking of getting back into drug-smuggling,' David said. 'Plus we needed somewhere to hide out from the cops.'

David coughed back a laugh as he saw Mannie's face turn. It was obvious the boy had had enough of criminality. David looked down at his hands, noticed there was still a joint trapped between his fingers. He took it and passed it over, asking the kid: 'Why don't you move out?'

When Mannie inhaled on the joint, it sounded like a gasp for help. When he exhaled, he just sounded hopeless. 'I need to scrape the money together for a new deposit.'

Mannie had no money. His mother had always wanted him to visit Israel and when she died suddenly he had decided to make his aliyah. But now he had spent all his money doing half a semester at every university in Israel. He couldn't seem to make any headway as an Israeli and he couldn't see himself moving back to Manchester. He didn't know what to do – he no longer expected to blossom into a pioneer type.

As David listened to the story, he tried to keep an eye on Yuri and Sophia. It was difficult because every time he moved, Mannie would follow him. He caught an image of Sophia bent at the waist, slightly turned towards Yuri. It seemed that Yuri's arm was around her shoulder but then Mannie's head was in the way again.

David asked Mannie, 'But why did you ever move in with a guy like Yuri?'

'It was only going to be a month. Short-term, mutually beneficial.'

Now Sophia was standing. Yuri followed her up. David had to weave to keep them in view. He felt like a dancer in a Hindu film. He could feel his relationship with Yuri deteriorating by the second, matched only by a corresponding improvement in his feelings for this English kid. Even in spite of his big fucking head.

'You must have been able to tell what Yuri was like.'

'It was like a business deal, we were going to make money.'

David didn't like to ask how they were going to make money. He knew Yuri's type: he was a man with ideas. It was what those ideas were, exactly, that was worrying him. Yuri and Sophia were now floating across the room together. David made a move towards the living room himself but Mannie put his hand out to stop him. He had picked up on the slight rise in his personal polls. He wanted to exploit David's goodwill while it lasted.

'Now he's telling me, I've got to wait. He needs to get some more girls lined up first.'

'What?'

'There's Natasha, then Ludmilla and her younger sister, they're new . . .'

Mannie counted off the girls on his fingers. David listened but his eyes were on Yuri and Sophia. They had slipped back on to the balcony, this time on their own, not as part of a group. It was too much.

David launched forward, breaking past Mannie and making the living room in a paranoid blur, scared for Sophia and her virtue. He knew he was moving with a palpable force, if rather slowly. When a man and a woman staggered from a bedroom, he turned his head long enough to take in every part of their appearance. The smile on the man's face like a slow puncture, the purple of the girl's eyeshadow like bruising against her pale skin. And then the plait of semen running from her ear, along the line of her chin and on to her neck. She might have been too stoned to notice it; David wasn't, quite. From what he could guess, if he stripped away the make-up and stray spunk, she was Ludmilla's sister.

He continued towards the balcony.

As David tore away the curtain, he found Yuri with his arm around Sophia. She was leaning over the balcony rail like someone being violently sick, but she was crying rather than vomiting. The tears were pouring out of her eyes and her whole body was shaking.

'What's the idea, man?' David imagined his voice would be cracked with rage, but when it came to the moment he sounded almost relaxed. 'Like, what gives here, really?'

His hands should have been balled into fists; instead they were waving in the air like those springy insect antennae that children used to wear on their heads. They had about as much dramatic punch.

Yuri said, 'Her father has a heart attack, she spends all night at his sickbed then all day at a friend's funeral. So you decide to bring her to a party?'

David tried to comfort Sophia. While he held her on the sofa, Yuri sat on a reversed kitchen chair and ran through a series of idioms, folk sayings, philosophical comments and anything else that pertained to pain and loss. In between, he said, '*It is important to grieve, and grief will always find its expression. It cannot be held back.*' Also, '*We live in sorrow. But when we cry the tears of our grief, we also hope that one day we will be at peace.*'

David never stopped feeling guilty about bringing Sophia on this trip to Tel Aviv. He knew it was a mistake, but perhaps it is true that acts of madness help us to overcome sorrow. Or that every tear is also a prayer for peace. He had to say, though, he was glad that Yuri was speaking Russian. He wouldn't want Sophia actually to hear the nonsense the man was talking.

Yuri was addressing the whole room, using Sophia's situation to illustrate his own views about life. David tuned him out, cradling Sophia's head against his shoulder. She was no longer shaking, it was more of a wobble now. Her fingers were wrapped up in the folds of his shirt. David didn't know how much pleasure he was supposed to take, sitting there feeling like a great protector.

Yuri finally ran out of wise sayings and couldn't invent any more. He turned to David and said, 'You two, you are not man and wife?'

'No.'

'If you were, you would be very lucky, I think. But of course, these days, we should consider what we hope to achieve through marrying.'

David looked across towards the armchair where Ludmilla was sitting, perched on the arm above her sister. The sister's client was long gone and Ludmilla had cleaned her sister's face.

He asked, 'Are you and Yuri married?'

Ludmilla shook her head. 'No, I am married to Misha.'

Yuri said, 'I am married to Natasha at the moment.' He pointed to her, she was sitting dazed in a corner of the room. He continued, 'We have someone lined up ready for Olga already. The women's problem is they are not Jewish, therefore they require a marriage of convenience.'

'Is that what you do? You're a marriage broker?'

'It is one of my occupations,' Yuri said. 'If you are interested, David, I will explain. What I do is organise a beneficial arrangement between you and her. I even work out a contract. It stipulates that she will pay you a percentage of her earnings every week for so many months. Then when she can get her own visa, you get divorced.'

'You enforce the contract?'

'Should it ever prove necessary . . . but I doubt that you

would find it necessary. If you divorce her too soon, then she is in an absolutely problematic scenario. It is true.' Yuri gave a mournful shrug, as though he was chiefly sorry for the girls. 'She finds that she is illegal, she cannot stay.'

He passed David the joint. 'I myself, I have been married many times. And believe me, here in Israel the married life can be very good.'

David nodded over to Mannie. 'How about him, have you got anyone in mind for him?'

Yuri grinned. 'I think so.'

Mannie was looking even sorrier for himself than he had been earlier, if that was possible. Perhaps it was a result of the drink or the dope. He glumly held up a joint; Yuri said, 'Excuse me,' and stepped across the rug to take it from Mannie's hands. Misha was sat on the end of the sofa, rolling a new one.

David remained with Sophia. He noticed she was beginning to unwrap herself and disengage. He loosened his own grip.

'Are you okay?'

'Sorry.'

'I'm sorry I brought you here.'

Yuri's party would only get seedier the longer they stayed. This whole scheme, his vague plan of returning to smuggling, of searching out contacts, was so stupid. The whole of Israel was swimming with dope and it was all home-grown hybrids like chronic, skunk weed, silver leaf, moon weed. What the Israelis could not grow themselves, they could import from Europe. The dope business had changed so much since his day. The Third World growers were being squeezed out by technology, by the First World hydroponic farmers. In the bar, Yuri had mentioned that he had contacts in the ex-Soviet republics, and David knew that there were heroin fields in a couple of the central Asian countries, but it wasn't for him. He was past it, it wasn't his scene anyway.

He tried to take the blame again for bringing Sophia here but she shook him off.

He said, 'Really. It was a stupid idea.'

'No. I wanted to come with you. I wanted to talk to you about my father. I told you things about him and me that I never told anyone else – I had this crazy idea that I should talk to you again, that it would help me think things through.'

David didn't let any surprise show on his face. But he had absolutely no idea what she was talking about. He could not remember a word of her confession. But he felt so close to her, it must come back to him.

She said, 'Come on, we'll go. We can talk in the car.'

He stood first, swaying as he extended a hand for her. Around them, Yuri was giving a fresh toast. David caught the word *Love* but nothing else among the clink of glasses and bottles and the sound of four or five voices singing out their assent. Then the commotion started.

Misha must have been in the bathroom. He returned, reeling drunkenly, and dropped a lighted Zippo on to the carpet, which was already sodden with spilled vodka. The flames shot across the carpet, at first blue and fragile, but soon they took hold and spread. Ludmilla and her sister screamed. Natasha sat upright, gulping as though she was semi-startled, then just as suddenly she slipped back into her stupor.

Yuri was trying to trample out the flames. At the same time, he was shouting, telling Misha to help. *Did they want the whole place to catch alight?* Fleshy Misha got to his feet, but when he started stamping at the flames it was little better than a shuffle.

Mannie appeared from the kitchen swinging a heavy pan full of water. David never expected him to be the resourceful one. But when he slung the water over the flames only Ludmilla thanked him. Misha complained his feet were wet and the other girls said nothing.

Yuri could have swung either way, showing either gratitude or contempt. Mannie was motionless, unable to catch his breath in the thick fug of ambivalence. When Yuri flung himself at Mannie, it was possible he was going for his neck. But he folded him in a hug and planted three sets of kisses before swinging him out like a dance partner.

'The hero of the hour. Quickly. A toast, another toast to the agile wits of our hero.'

The toast never happened.

Everyone was spinning and stamping, trying to find their glasses while Yuri held steady at the centre of the room, shouting as he held a fresh bottle of vodka above his head like a trophy. After the excitement of the fire, they all felt they should make at least as much noise celebrating as they had done when they thought they were going to be killed in an eleventh-storey inferno. And because they were making so much noise, they didn't hear the man on the stairs until he broke through the door.

The man was huge, even in his bare feet. He was another Russian, a similar age to Yuri but built like an old-fashioned Soviet hero, an Olympic hammer-thrower. He held a ragged-edged carving knife in his hand. He stood for a second in the doorway, just to case the room. Then he charged Yuri with his shoulder.

Yuri seemed to lift up, only stopping as he slammed against the balcony window. Then the big man was on him again, pushing the knife under his throat and yelling. Even though it was Russian, David had to pierce through the expletives before he guessed the man's problem. The night was demoniacally hot, his children believed they could be suffocated in their sleep, it had taken him hours to persuade them to close their eyes. His wife was exhausted, she was no help, she could only cry in a room on her own.

Yuri tried apologising. It was a party, he never meant to disturb the man's babies. Yuri kept repeating the word party, blabbing, stupidly forgetting to take the joint out of his mouth. The way he puffed between sentences only seemed to make the big man even more insane.

David didn't know what to do. He didn't want to attack a man whose only thoughts seemed to be for his family. At any other time, using a knife would seem melodramatic but it was an insane night. The knife made some kind of crazy sense.

And there was another reason for David to stay out of it. The man had headed straight for Yuri. Perhaps he knew Yuri well enough to guess he was the ringleader. But David was sure he'd done it because Yuri was the biggest man in the room. You had to respect someone who automatically took out the biggest man.

Misha was either mindlessly drunk or felt he had something to prove. He had started the fire, after all. He brought a vodka bottle down on to the man's shoulder, missing his head by more than the width of a hand. The man let go of Yuri long enough to turn and swipe the air with his knife. Misha only avoided being cut because he was already falling backwards to the floor. The man gave him a kick to the gut before turning back on Yuri.

Yuri had run for the balcony. When the big man charged him again, Yuri managed to hold on to the rail for a moment, then he lost his grip and toppled backwards. Even as he was falling, screaming, there was hardly a breath of disturbance in the night air.

15

The Russians stalled for a moment, all of them freeze-framed in denial. Perhaps Yuri hadn't sailed backwards off the balcony. Then they ran for the rail. David didn't know what they thought they would see, eleven storeys down. He scooped up Sophia and pushed past Mannie, who was shaking alone in the doorway. Sophia found her feet before they made the elevator lobby.

She said, 'No. Take the stairs.'

She was right. The elevator would be snarled up, ferrying cops and neighbours and anyone else who was interested up to the crime scene. David kicked away the black bin-bags that blocked the door to the stairwell and he and Sophia started down, jumping three steps at a time and hopping on the sharp turns. David remembered that the ground floor was set on a kind of piazza, so they continued down another level to the basement. There was a heavy stink of refuse and the opening to the street was barred by Tel Aviv municipal skips. He slowed down, holding Sophia back with a hand.

The skips gave them cover. David peered round and saw the abandoned cars with their doors open and their noses pointing to a circle of people. Yuri had fallen wide of the piazza and ended up in a main street. The crowd around him was already three deep. David was only glad he couldn't see the body.

He said, 'Okay. Let's go.'

The sirens were quite close. As he and Sophia ran on to the sidewalk, David looked to his left. Instead of seeing ambulances he saw police cars. He turned.

'This way.'

They were heading for the crowd now. One of the onlookers was breaking out of the circle, his hand covering his mouth, failing to hold back his vomit. In the gap he left, David saw the silhouette of what could have been a duvet cover abandoned in a pool of dark liquid. He lifted his arms, partly to shield his eyes from the sight, partly to signal to Sophia to head wide of the crowd. He was half tripping, half running like that when a flashlight went off. He looked up and the second flash caught him full in the face. It was a man with a camera, probably press, shooting aimless scene-of-the-disaster shots up and down the roadway.

Sophia said, 'Up there.' She was pointing to the steps that led up to the piazza level.

David followed her, ten feet behind. Her hand was already on the stair rail when the cops appeared at the top of the steps. She looked over her shoulder and David watched her face catch the light, the white of the car headlamps and the revolving blue lights of the emergency services. He caught hold of her wrist to pull her back down. They turned together. Sammy Ben Naim was standing behind them, braced like a goalkeeper, waiting to see which way he had to move.

David let go of Sophia's wrist. He held out his own hands,

palm up, to show he was coming quietly: so what did they want to do – handcuff him? He couldn't believe it when a cop stepped forward and actually snapped on a pair of handcuffs. Sophia was cuffed a moment later, as they were shepherded to a police truck.

Tel Aviv Central Police Station was less than a ten-minute drive. The way the police driver threw the truck round the bends, even ten minutes was too long to suffer. Sophia bounced between the Russian girls on her side of the truck. David was sat on the bench opposite, wedged tight between Misha and the big neighbour. There was no sign of Mannie. David assumed the kid got away but when the truck doors opened inside a walled compound, he saw him being hauled out of a police car.

The other person he recognised in the police compound was Sammy Ben Naim. He stepped out of a car on his own, no partners, no other policemen. When he crossed over to the station building, he passed within yards of David. He didn't look over, he didn't seem interested in anything around him; a man with his private thoughts. But then he had to wait at the door into the station. It was a secure door and could only be opened from the inside. While he paused there, he looked over his shoulder and his eyes locked on David. He shrugged.

David and Sophia were put in separate cells. As the door closed on him, David tried to guess from the sound of footsteps and the clank of the other doors which of the cells in their corridor was hers. He wasn't sure, he thought the one opposite. Over the next forty-eight hours, he finally worked out that she was on the other side of the corridor, the middle cell of five. The reason he knew, he was taken for questioning four times over the two days and by the end of the second day that was the only cell in their corridor that was still occupied. The policemen grunted their assent when he asked them if his girlfriend was still in custody.

He began to look forward to the questioning, only because smoking was forbidden in the cells but not in the interview room. He was asked about the series of events that led to Yuri Aaronofsky's death, about his relationship with the deceased and about his name and nationality. He waited thirty-six hours before he decided to try demanding to see the Irish consul: that raised a laugh. After that he was sure they knew his real identity, if he had any doubts before. But there was still no sign of the secret serviceman. The last time they took him out of his cells, he asked for the man by name. There was no sign the policeman heard him. He just picked him up at his cell door and took him to the same small room where he was asked to go over the details again.

His interrogator was a fleshy-faced pale man in a short-sleeved shirt. He said, 'There were a quantity of drugs in the apartment.'

'I didn't notice.'

'You know Israel has tough laws on drugs?'

'Were there any drugs?'

'We finished the autopsy. The dead man had a reefer actually lodged inside his trachea. Possibly he swallowed it as he was falling.'

David winced. He said, 'I think there was some hashish around.'

'You don't think hashish is a drug?' The man paused, 'Mr Preston?'

'Yes, I think it is a drug. Is that what this is about?'

David looked from the fleshy policeman to his partner, a much younger, athletic man who so far hadn't said a word. He just stood in a corner, pulling at his jockstrap through his tan trousers. It looked like he had a bad fit inside there. 'If this is about drugs, I think I might be able to do a deal. I mentioned earlier, I have a contact called Sammy Ben Naim.'

David lifted up the end of the sentence, making it a question. There was no response. He tried again. 'A secret service guy. I think you call it Shin Bet, yeah?'

The older cop said, 'Ben Naim is in the housing department.'

'Yeah, that would be right.'

The other cop flexed off the wall. David followed him as he walked round the table towards the door.

'Is your colleague getting a message to Ben Naim?'

'No. He's taking you back to your cell.'

The third day, sixty-two hours in custody according to the clock behind a wire-mesh frame in the cell corridor, the same cop with the same trouser problem came to take David out of his cell. David nodded down to the open cell door he believed was Sophia's.

'Where's my friend?'

The cop didn't answer. David realised the man had never yet spoken to him: he either didn't speak English or was pretending not to. Because David didn't know any Hebrew, he tried a sentence in phrase-book Arabic: '*Hal tatakallam Ingilizi?*'

This time the cop at least turned round. The way he did it, responding to the one language but not the other, David was confident the man genuinely spoke no English. But he didn't answer the question.

It was a different interview room, slightly larger and with a much larger table. There were two chairs either side of the table. The cop pulled out a chair on the far side and nodded at it, signalling that David should sit. David walked around and sat. The cop remained standing. After five minutes, David said, '*Sigara?*'

When the cop looked, David mimed smoking. The cop produced a Camel soft pack and flicked out a cigarette. When David took it, he lit it with a Zippo. Not David's Zippo though, that had gone missing. The cigarette was half gone when the fleshy cop led in Sophia and sat her on the chair next to David.

She had rings under her eyes. Her hair was lank – instead of curving in towards her face it curved outwards, and it did that limply. But she didn't let the tiredness overtake her. She sat upright, awake and ready. David whispered, 'How are you? Are you okay?' She nodded.

They were left with just the younger cop for company. David took a few extra drags on the cigarette, trying to create a smokescreen as he asked her more questions.

'Did they let you speak to anyone? Phone your parents?'

'I never asked.'

He nodded. She had probably made the right decision. David had wondered how her father might react – a man who was recovering from a heart attack and was so deeply phobic about prisons. He still remembered that Sophia had wanted to speak to him about her father in the minutes before Yuri tumbled off the tower block.

David said, 'I've spent the past three days having conversations with the wall. You know . . . imagining I was opening up to you, telling you all about myself. Trying to put the best possible spin on it.' He put on a comic American voice. 'I wasn't a dope smuggler: I was an international herbalist.'

Sophia dropped her head. 'Not in front of the policeman.'

David was about to say, don't worry about that joker, he speaks no English. But he took another look at the man and wasn't so sure. He was leaning in the corner of the room, still tugging at his groin area with a bored expression on his face: perhaps too bored to be genuine.

David said, 'Have they questioned you?'

She shook her head. 'Not questioned. Propositioned.'

'A proposition? You've been speaking to the secret service guy?'

'Yes.'

'So ...' David waited. 'What did he want? Can you say?'

'He wants me to get married.'

David didn't get it. 'The guy wants to marry you?'

'He wants me to marry you. And for a wedding present, I ask my Uncle Tony to give me a house in Jerusalem.'

David got it now. 'And we hand it over to him.'

'He mentioned there would be some money involved,' Sophia said. 'At least enough to get my family out of Bethlehem before they are shot as collaborators.'

If there were any details David didn't fully grasp, he only had to wait another two minutes to hear the whole plan from the man himself. Sammy Ben Naim arrived with a fresh pack of cigarettes and a sheaf of offficial-looking documents. David imagined this was how the Devil might come, carrying his contracts up front. But Ben Naim just sat the papers down on the table, his hand resting lightly on the top. The cigarettes beside them, open; anyone who wanted one could take one.

David listened and smoked. Ben Naim spoke in his American-inflected English, part Yale, part *guy*: the combination was making David dizzy, he wasn't sure he didn't have vertigo. Things were moving so fast: in five days David would be married. Sammy Ben Naim spoke almost exclusively to David, seeming to take Sophia's agreement for granted. To David that seemed the most obvious weak spot in the plan, that she would ever get hitched to him. Ahead, even, of the idea that anyone would believe Tony Khouri was so generous, he would give away an apartment in Jerusalem as a wedding present. David took the second point first.

He said, 'You think people will swallow that?'

Sammy smiled. 'For his favourite niece. Maybe he's going to have to work to persuade them – so what? He can do it. At least the profit motive's there. He could clear two million dollars on the deal, say his share is fifty per cent. The rest, you guys split between you.'

Sophia said, 'That's not the problem – we still have to explain why I would even need an apartment in Jerusalem when I'm not allowed to live there.' She turned to David, saying, 'The Israelis only let the Palestinians born in the city live there. Even then, if they go away for a few months, when they come back their identity card is ripped up.'

Sammy tapped his folder. 'But I've got a pass right here. A Jerusalem identity card – so that's perfect.'

It was only now that David realised Sophia was going to go through with it; she and Ben Naim had been through the details already. He had to ask, 'Are you sure? You must want something more out of a marriage than that?'

'I don't want to stay in Palestine any more.'

'But who'll believe you and me?'

Ben Naim answered that one: 'You run off and spend three days together. Don't you think you'd better get married before there's a big scandal?'

The police had picked up David's hire car. It was now parked in the police station compound. David walked round and got in the driver's seat. Sophia paused at her side, talking to Ben Naim in Arabic. David listened through the open passenger window: listened without understanding. The man still had his documents with him, hugging them to his chest. Sophia hadn't yet got her Jerusalem ID.

When Sophia started laughing, it was completely unexpected. Ben Naim smiled back at her and then pulled a single envelope out of the sheaf of papers. Sophia took it and slipped into the car beside David. They were ready to go.

As they pulled out of the gates, he asked what the joke was.

'I wanted to know why he had an Arabic name.'

'What, Ben Naim? Isn't that one of those *nommes de guerres*, like Ben Gurion?'

'No, that's his real name. His father was an Algerian Jew.' Sophia was still smiling. 'I was asking him about his first name.'

David got it now. He used to know a few Sammys in the Lebanon, all Arabs. He said, 'I guess he's called Samuel.'

'No. He's called Sammy. The reason is, there used to be a fashion for American movie-star names in Algiers. He told me his father was a big fan of Sammy Davis Junior.'

She was still smiling as they turned on to Dizengoff. She didn't notice they were heading in the wrong direction. Perhaps she didn't know Tel Aviv well enough to get her bearings. Or perhaps she just wasn't paying attention. She was slitting open the envelope containing her Jerusalem ID card.

David asked, 'So what? Is he trustworthy? Has he double-crossed you?'

Sophia flipped open the orange wallet. The pass was inside. She held it up. 'It expires in three months.'

'After that, they run you out of town?'

She nodded, her mouth in a tight little line. But then she began looking around, her expression slipped. Now it was more like stunned disbelief. As David slowed the car outside a backpackers' hostel, she was shaking her head and saying, 'Oh no. Not again.'

'I'll only be five minutes, I swear.' David held up his hand, showing the number of minutes in fingers, as though that made it better.

As he ran across the sidewalk, he heard her behind him shouting, 'Isn't this where we came in?' He just waved a hand behind his head. He intended to be as good as his word.

It was actually a little over ten minutes when he returned, this time with a quarter key of weed. The kid he bought it off told him it was domestic and called it Tical. When David asked him if that was Hebrew, the kid said no. It was short for Methodical, *like the rapper from the Wu Tang Clan?*

Sophia wasn't impressed with the story. He didn't know how to explain to her that he couldn't get involved in a scam without dope. There was no doubt, he functioned best when he was mellow. Not tightly wound, insomniac, carrying symptoms that felt like flu and believing that he was in love. It definitely wasn't any time for believing he was in love.

He wanted to ask her, *This is just a scam, isn't it?* But there was no point asking when he already knew the answer. So instead he asked her about the mechanics of marriage: 'What happens: do we just run into a registry office, sign the papers, collect the apartment deeds? *Ba bab boom.*'

They were on the Tel Aviv–Jerusalem highway. He was driving one-handed, a jayski poking through his knuckles and filling the car with sweet smoke. Sophia hadn't spoken to him for the best part of an hour. But she did now.

'There are no registry offices here. The nearest we could have a civil wedding is Cyprus, and that would be no good. This is not going to work unless everyone sees for themselves that we are married.' She turned to look at him. 'It has to be a white wedding for a pair of lovebirds like us.'

It was too much. David said, 'Why are we doing this? Do you really want to get out of the country so much?'

'You don't want the money?'

'I want the money, yes. But I'd prefer I wasn't marrying someone who hates me.'

'I don't hate you.'

'Whatever, it's not exactly a dream wedding.'

'It will be a better divorce than most people have.'

He couldn't argue with that. Well, he probably could but he was too stoned for it to make sense. Although he tossed the joint out the window before they hit Jerusalem, he rode on its afterburn all the way through the city and into Bethlehem. Sophia continued talking, her explanations mixing in with the dope fug. He listened to her, more to the rhythm than to the actual words, but he got the argument. Her father would die with nothing if they remained in Palestine. If he didn't lose his land while he was alive, it would only be because the anxiety had killed him first. It was more important to her that

he lived a long and peaceful life. She was thinking of Canada.
Did David know anything about the different cities?

David hummed, maybe. Canada could be nice.

He dropped her at her home and turned the car around, back
towards the Grand Hotel. The entrance to the underground
carpark was on the busiest section of the high street. David
got hung up in the market traffic, right by a stall selling roast
chickpeas. The smell made David realise how hungry he was
– smoking the Israeli grass had brought on the munchies. His
car wasn't going anywhere so he stepped out and bought a
half-shekel bag.

The boy doing the roasting had hung a radio off the front
of his barrow. As David sat back in his car, popping chickpeas
with one hand, he drummed on the steering wheel with his
other. He judged he was only mildly out of time with the
music. It was a good sign, he had to be relaxing.

Someone rapped on the passenger window and said, 'I
think you've got it.'

David looked up and saw Shadi Mansur.

'I'm serious, man. You really have a sense of rhythm. The
way you're drumming there, you make me want to join in.'

Shadi opened the car door.

'Actually, David, I've been waiting for you. There's
something I want to ask.'

David said, 'Well, it's going to have to keep.'

'Don't say that, David. I promise, it won't take long.' Shadi
wiggled in the passenger seat, making a whole performance
out of getting comfortable. David flashed a look at the glove
box. The bag of dope was inside, stuffed in with the hire car's
complimentary kaffiyeh.

'I'm wrecked, Shadi. Why don't you stop by the hotel bar, say seven this evening?'

'Come on, David. A little talk, what will it hurt? Maybe you could even explain this?'

It was a newspaper cutting. Shadi handed it over. David looked at it solemnly. If he didn't already know, it would be difficult to tell where the photo was taken. Clearly at the foot of a tower block – yes, but it could be anywhere. It didn't need to be a Tel Aviv slum. David guessed the Hebrew caption beneath the photograph pretty much gave away the context. The picture showed David running down the street, Sophia clearly visible a step behind him. David continued staring at it, wondering why his legs looked so strange, almost as though he was skipping. With his arms raised and his eyes caught in the flash, there was something unbalanced about him.

David passed the cutting back to Shadi and pulled at the handbrake. As it slipped through its ratchet, he said, 'I was messing around.'

Heading down into the carpark, he had to keep turning to full lock to get around the bends. Every time he hauled on the wheel, he caught a flash of Shadi's toothy smile. The man hadn't stopped grinning since he got into David's car.

'You were messing around? That's good. I always say that, why not enjoy yourself?'

David pulled the car into a space. It was too dark now to see the photograph. Shadi's smile was still too visible.

David shrugged. 'We spent a couple of days in Tel Aviv.'

Shadi nodded. David had the impression he wrinkled his nose, as though he could pick out the smell of David's last smoke. He didn't say anything, but that could be calculation.

There was never a moment when you could forget that Shadi was a politician. He was always playing angles.

'And while you were there, you were a witness to a murder?'

'It says murder?'

Shadi opened the car door, the inner light came on and he studied the writing underneath the photograph. 'Yeah, murder, I think. What did the police say?'

David took a pause. 'The police were cool.'

'What about? Were they cool about Sophia, for instance? She doesn't have a pass to visit to Tel Aviv, does she?'

'I told them she was my fiancée. So she'd strayed into Tel Aviv. Big deal. We were sightseeing.'

'They accepted that?'

'It's the truth.' David picked up his car keys. 'Sophia's going to leave.'

Shadi said, 'She's going to leave the country with you, just because she got caught in Tel Aviv with the wrong papers?'

'No. She's leaving because she's fed up with waiting for things to improve while everything gets worse.' David felt he was turning the tables on Shadi, he had the right pitch in his voice. 'Now she's got Hebron egg smugglers crowding her out of her own town.'

Shadi said, 'I heard about that. I wish there was something that could be done to help her.'

'Yeah, well. What about getting some fucking law and order? It's just an idea.'

'It'll come. But then who knows, things might get even more uncomfortable. Say we signed an extradition treaty with the UK, maybe we'd have to deport you.' Shadi held David's look for a four count. Then he broke into a laugh.

'Don't worry, I'm joking. You know me, it's just what I'm like. You mind if we go back to my little picture?'

Shadi had the cutting back in his hand.

'You can understand I'm curious. How did it happen? How do you feel after seeing someone splattered across the road like that?'

David looked at the photograph again. You could call it an action photo; it wasn't exactly flattering. David didn't know how he'd got into that position, tripping forwards like that with a wild-eyed stare for the camera.

Shadi said, 'You know, you look a little like Ozzy Osbourne.'

David looked again. It was true. Ozzy used to run around like that, flapping across a stage with his hands up as he threw heavy-metal devil signs at the crowd.

16

David met up with Tony at his Ford dealership. It was another hot, airless day. The heat from the welding torches and the revving engines had made the office too stuffy to live with, so Tony was sitting out on his forecourt on an old settee. He heaved himself to his feet when David arrived.

Tony nodded towards the open door of his workshop. 'I've got a car.'

David saw a black Mercedes standing on the pit. A young man was stood underneath, blasting at the exhaust pipe with a welding torch.

'You've got a black car? Isn't that ominous.'

'I'll get a white car, don't worry.' Tony passed a hand across his forehead, leaving a dry streak through the sweat. He said, 'I think we've got more to worry about than cars.'

David had called Tony the day before, telling him about his conversation with Shadi. They decided it wasn't something they could safely discuss between a hotel telephone and a mobile phone. It needed to be done face to face.

Tony said, 'How exactly did you get your face in the newspaper?'

David shrugged. He and Sophia hadn't gone into all the messy details of their stay in Tel Aviv. They'd stuck to a vague story – that Sammy Ben Naim had approached them. That was it: he'd made them an offer.

David said, 'I don't think it has anything to do with the photograph. Shadi knows who I am.'

'How can he?'

David couldn't claim, hand on heart, that he'd been *Mr Discreet* these past ten days. Sophia had noticed the extra passports on the night he drove her and Yusuf back from Bir Zeit University. Yusuf had seemed out of it, sunk in the back seat of the Fiat, but he might have noticed too. Perhaps he already knew more about David than they supposed: maybe Edward Salman was the kind who liked to chat over the dinner table. What was certain, Yusuf wouldn't want to be taken for a fellow collaborator. If he was smart, he would have gone straight from his father's funeral to the government offices and told them everything he knew.

There were other possibilities, though.

David said, 'When we were working out of Beirut, we had contacts in the PLO. Aren't they all back from exile now, running secret services and stuff? Maybe they've got a file on me.'

Tony shrugged. He knew it was more than possible. 'The fact they know who you are, that's not important. They're not going to care about things you did fifteen or twenty years ago. They're only going to care about what you're doing now – and all you're doing is getting married to a local girl.'

'You think they will really believe that?'

'Let's just take it one step at a time. They don't know about the apartment yet. We've just got to make sure, when the time comes, it looks like a genuine wedding gift.'

'What about a new lawyer? Have you got anyone you can trust?'

Tony looked blank. 'Why do I need another lawyer? Wasn't Edward Salman bad enough?'

'You've got to get the deeds squared, man. The apartment has to be signed over to me.'

Tony said, 'I'm not signing the apartment over to you. Why would I do that?'

Now David was confused. The way he understood it, that was the whole plan. It almost sounded as though Tony didn't trust him.

Tony said, 'Get in the car. I've got to explain something.'

Tony's Mercedes was parked at the side of the workshop. It was freshly washed, the chrome was still silver rather than orange-mottled. David tried to check the age of the car from the numbers on the blue licence plate but they meant nothing to him. When he sat down, he noticed how worn the seats were. Then, as they pulled out of the forecourt, he felt the drop off the sidewalk as a jolt up his spine. Tony only shivered. His fat absorbed the impact, acting as suspension now the Mercedes' shocks were too worn to cope. When they pulled off the main road, the jolts got worse. They were on a track, better suited to the donkey that was setting the pace up ahead than the rust-coated cars they passed. Tony took turns with the oncoming traffic, pulling on to the verge by the olive trees as they squeezed by.

They arrived at the back of Sophia's house. The al-Banna truck was parked on the Khouris' spare land. It was midday; David knew they only used the truck at night. The only members of the al-Banna clan out today were the youngest children, a boy and a girl, swinging on a rope hung from a cedar tree. As Tony parked, he pointed over to the children. He asked, did David see them.

David caught a bruise-like shadow flicker beneath Tony's eyes. It was the only way to tell that Tony was exasperated, he was holding it in so well. But they were only kids, playing out in the sun. David could hear their laughter travel across the land. True, it wasn't their land.

Tony said, 'Elias could die any time, we all know that.'

David nodded. 'It's always possible, but you know, if he takes it easy . . .' He trailed off, realising there wasn't much chance of that, given the situation in Bethlehem. He asked, 'How does Elias feel about it? Is he happy about leaving?'

Tony turned on him. The bruise under his eye was flickering on and off, as fast as a strobe. His exasperation was turning to anger. David didn't know why it was directed at him.

'It doesn't matter whether he's happy. What matters is that he's not stupid,' Tony said. 'There's been no law in Palestine for almost a generation. Anyone in their twenties, like al-Banna's sons, has no idea what it means and it doesn't look as though the new government is going to show them. But that doesn't mean we have no code whatsoever. We got through the intifada, we had to make things work. There were the clan councils, it was always possible to negotiate. Things were never smooth but it worked at a basic level. If you stepped on another man, you knew you would never be allowed to forget what you'd done. Maybe no one tried to stop you. It's often the way. But every time you tried to deal with the guy's friends, you knew they were thinking, next time, it could be me. If you tried to rip someone off, you knew it would keep on coming back to you.'

It didn't sound a perfect system. But David knew, with the situation in the West Bank, there was no one to trade with except for the people around you. And if you were always going to be dealing with the same people, you couldn't afford a bad reputation. He asked, 'So it's still the same now?'

Tony nodded. 'Just the same. But the way it works, people will only hold back when there's a man involved. When there is no man, it's as if there's no victim. Once Elias dies, the al-Bannas will move in, they will think they can do what they like.'

David said, 'But you'll still be around.'

He realised immediately, this wasn't the right thing to say. Or rather, it was too right. It went straight to the heart of the matter. Tony might not do anything.

Tony was pursing and unpursing his lips, his cheeks puffing out and collapsing. He knew ahead of time there was every chance that he wouldn't do anything. Like he said, it was often the way. And if he started pointing his finger at al-Banna later, maybe it would curb the man's behaviour but it would be too late for Sophia and her mother.

'So Elias prefers to go now, when there's the chance of a big pay-off from the apartment in Jerusalem?'

'He doesn't prefer it. But Sophia's persuaded him to do it. Sophia and Samira both, agreeing on something for almost the first time in their lives. They will leave with about a million dollars, plus whatever change I can pick up selling this house for him. It's a lot of money.'

Tony restarted the car and drove the next twenty yards to park at the side of the Khouri house. He banged on the horn and Samira Khouri appeared at the window, waving. A moment later and Sophia was at the door, walking towards them.

David said, 'Wasn't there another point to all this? You were explaining why you aren't going to sign the apartment over to me.'

'You didn't get it?' Tony turned to look at him as though he was embarrassed to explain something so basic. 'Mr International Man. How the hell can I sign it over to you when no one knows you? You don't live anywhere, you've got no family and no roots, who's going to stop you from walking off with the money?'

'You know me. I'm not going to rip you off.'

'It's business, David, like they say in the gangster films. I trust you. I'm just not going to trust you over this, okay.'

'But it was always the plan, how does it work otherwise? You sign the apartment to me, I sell it. What's changed?'

'What's changed is that you were not the last person in the chain before, it was always going to be the lawyer who would do the deal. Now that you're the one with the Israeli contact, it all ends with you.'

David felt a tightening in his stomach. It was a flicker of outrage: he had been insulted, what was he going to do about it? He couldn't believe Tony would trust a man like Edward Salman over him. Even his own son seemed to think Salman was a scumbag. Tony's eyes held his without wavering, though: he was only being straight. There were complex reasons for trusting Salman. In this instance, there was no good reason to trust his oldest friend.

Sophia was almost at the car.

David said, 'So you'll sign it over to Sophia.'

Tony nodded. 'That's right. I'm getting it seen to.'

Tony dropped them outside the Catholic church in Beit Jala. Sophia pointed to a smaller doorway in the shadows of the columns around the main entrance. David looked and saw the frail old priest standing there, waiting with a smile. It didn't seem like the weather for heavy belted robes but it hadn't stopped the priest from coming to the door to welcome them in.

The office was high-ceilinged but short on square footage, like a scaled-up telephone box. David sat on one side of the little table, Sophia sat on the other. Father George looked as though he should be asleep or dead, but he hadn't stopped talking in half an hour. He was giving his instruction in English, in deference to David. One of his special concerns was contraception.

'You know the Vatican has a particular directive on this matter but I ask you to consider also, aside from religious considerations, these practices are not in themselves healthful. Many medical experts have raised doubts over the contraceptive pill. As, too, they have expressed concerns about the so-called *Inter Uterine Devices*. And the condom, there are now also numerous questions. Is it healthful? Perhaps not. It is an unnatural substance, that is beyond dispute. So it is not just God's directives but it is also a matter of your personal health. I ask you to think about these things.'

David giggled. Sophia was staring at the floor but now her head shot up, giving David a look. It didn't help that she was having to bite back the laughter too. She was just doing a better job at suppressing it. David mouthed *Sorry*. He knew there was no alternative, they had to cram all four classes of religious instruction into one session. But he didn't know how he was going to cope for the remaining three hours and thirty minutes.

Father George was the Catholic priest in Beit Jala. They were lucky that he had agreed to take the ceremony at such short notice. Something else in his favour, he was too short-sighted to read the papers David handed him: his baptism certificate and proof of his confirmation, both written the night before.

Father George checked his cup of coffee. It was empty, just the bitter dregs at the bottom. He sighed and then remembered his place.

'Consider also, I suggest, this scenario. You are the parents of a beautiful child. But he is an only child. And the time comes, he is cut down before adulthood by a traffic accident. He is . . .' He let his voice rise, gathering momentum before he threw his weight on to the last word: '. . . dead.'

He paused and looked back at his coffee cup. It was still empty. He resumed his catechism.

'How would you feel? It is a catastrophe. Your life is as nothing, destroyed. But consider now, you have five children and one dies. It too is very sad. But it is not so destructive, you have other children. No?'

David shook his head, mumbling, '*I guess.*'

'And consider, Verdi was the last child of thirteen and none of the others were geniuses.'

'I heard it was Vivaldi.'

The priest sucked at his teeth. 'Perhaps. But the principle remains unaltered. It will always be the case, your last child could be the one blessed with genius.'

They left the church in a good mood. Sophia had her

arm hooked through David's. He felt they looked like genuine lovers – and they weren't even trying too hard. Sophia could remember more of the priest's logic than he, but he could do a better impersonation. She was laughing at David's high-pitched and nasal quaver as they passed through the church gates. Then the beep of a car horn cut his routine short.

They looked across the road to where a taxi was standing at the opposite kerb. Sammy Ben Naim was sitting in the driver's seat. He looked relaxed, giving them a short wave. If he knew he was parked right outside Beit Jala police station, he wasn't showing any signs of anxiety.

Sophia said, 'Does he want us to get killed?'

David said, 'Maybe he's here for my stag party.'

As they crossed towards his car, Sophia tightened her hold on David's arm. He was touched. As Tony had said when he dropped them off, it might be a fake marriage but David still wasn't exactly a catch.

David put a hand on the roof of Sammy's car and leant over his window. 'You couldn't be more subtle? What happens to your plan if you scare us to death first?'

'You aren't nervous, are you? I understood you were back on the spliffs.' Sammy smiled, letting them know they'd been under surveillance from the moment they left Tel Aviv Central Police Station. Then he nodded at Sophia. 'She looks cool.'

David would say she looked beautiful. Even as she mouthed *fuck you* at Sammy.

Sammy said, 'Okay, I'm intruding. But there's a problem. I've got this sweet little old lady back in Jerusalem. She wants to see who we're dealing with before she provides the money for the apartment.'

*   *   *

The more David saw of Sammy Ben Naim, the better he understood his style. Somehow, Sammy seemed both preppy and chippy. He had this force field of confidence, letting you know you were safe so long as you were with him. It was the side of his personality he used when he pulled David and Sophia out of Tel Aviv police station, after they cut their deal and agreed to marry. Sammy just wafted them out of the police station, past all the layers of police officials like he had *carte blanche* or *droit de seigneur* or something classy and French. But there was also something mean about the man: a deep bitterness. It was clear, you shouldn't piss him off. That side of him was just as effective as the other but together they made an unstable combination.

David said, 'You know, I don't have the deeds to the apartment. I thought I should warn you.'

Sammy nodded. 'They're going to sign them over to the girl, yeah?' He didn't seem bothered by the news, as though it was something he had anticipated and already incorporated in his plans.

They sailed through the checkpoint at the top of Beit Jala and swung down on to the new Bethlehem bypass. At the checkpoint just before the first tunnel, there was a bottleneck where the road slimmed down to two lanes. Sammy flashed David a grin, just to show he could wait patiently. Then, as if it was an afterthought, he lifted a stiff brown envelope off the dash and handed it to David. David slipped two fingers into the top and scissored them open. He only needed to peek in the envelope to recognise the photograph: it was his Ozzy Osbourne picture, running wild in the back streets of Tel Aviv.

'I've seen it.'

'Yeah? I wish you were the only one,' Sammy said. 'There's a note in there as well.'

David turned the envelope upside down. A piece of paper fell out. It was a print-out of an e-mail, addressed to a tzvi@jpost.com. The first sentence said *Can you confirm: this is dope smuggler David Ramsbottom?* David checked the sender, joreilly@theguardian.co.uk.

Sammy said, 'The newspapers are on to you. You're a celebrity.'

David scanned the rest of the e-mail as they drove into West Jerusalem. The only hard information the Guardian journalist had was the word of a contact, clearly someone inside the Tel Aviv police force. The journalist wasn't even sure that David was still in Israel.

Sammy continued, 'I haven't tracked down the guy's contact, yet. Someone shooting his mouth off.' He gave a rueful smile, he was still in ironic mode. 'We also have this.'

He was holding a photograph. David took it, saw a picture of himself looking fifteen years younger and a long way smarter, dressed in a morning suit and top hat. It had been taken at his first wedding – it must have been confiscated from his own photographer. David wished he'd paid the man now.

'From a contact in the British MI6. They're also asking if it's true, we've found the elusive David Ramsbottom. That's a very MI6 word, *elusive*. What do you think?'

Sammy paused, waiting for David to chew and swallow, then he reached into his inside pocket and came up with his final surprise, another envelope. As he passed it over, he said, 'Don't worry. It's not a disaster. You are going to be protected. I told you about the guy that the Bethlehem police had locked up. We've moved him to Haifa now. He's got a new identity. He's safe.'

'I've got nothing to worry about?'

'Nothing. Just, please, make sure this wedding goes through.'

What could go wrong? The church was booked, the priest was senile, everything was fine. David opened up the new envelope, expecting more bad news. He found a a cardboard square of faux leatherware: a brand new passport to add to his collection. David turned it over, admired the candelabra insignia on the front. Inside was his photograph, looking dazed and unhappy. It was the mugshot the Tel Aviv police had taken, and they hadn't cared if it was flattering or not.

Mrs Grodman was waiting for them in the lobby of the Hyatt Regency. She was with a younger man, someone in his forties. The pair of them were examining a photograph hung on the lobby wall. As Sammy and David stepped through the hotel doors, Sammy said, 'No surprise, Shaul Dayan's already here, trying to charm the money out of Grodman before anyone else shows.'

David stared at the small, energetic man with his trimmed beard. It was Saul Brodetsky, swindler and, now, egg smuggler. He said, 'What's he doing here?'

'Shaul is the middleman, he works directly with the charities.'

'Saul Brodetsky? He's the last person you let near old ladies or charities.'

Sammy knew the surname was right, *Brodetsky*. He said, 'You know him?'

'I know *of* him. He's the con man's con man. The ten

years he lived in Canada, he swindled the government out of something close to the national debt. Don't you read the Interpol wanted lists?'

Sammy believed David was telling the truth. He had already guessed that someone inside the service was protecting Shaul. There should be bigger files on the man than there were. But now he shrugged. 'Well, he's working for us now, we've licensed him to get money out of old ladies. About four million dollars.'

'I heard three million.'

Sammy said, 'We have overheads at our end.' The truth was, Shaul Dayan was the overhead but Sammy chose not to tell David that.

He started off across the lobby. David pulled on his arm. 'I'm not working with him.'

'What's that?'

'I'm not working with a crook like Brodetsky. I'd rather walk away.' David was serious. This was the man who was making the Khouris' life a misery. He was practically responsible for Elias's heart attack. David remembered Brodetsky cracking jokes as he supervised al-Banna's sons loading their eggs on to his truck. Even a man like Sammy Ben Naim, an *operator* like him, he wouldn't want to deal with someone who laughed at the kosher laws. He told Sammy the story.

'Shaul's smuggling eggs?' Sammy was open-mouthed.

'Off a Muslim family, then he's having them stamped by the inspectors in Israel, claiming he got them from a kibbutz.'

Sammy burst out laughing. 'What's this? You've been Israeli for ten minutes, you're already worried about the state of kosher food?'

David didn't appreciate Sammy's attitude. He said, 'I'm

not. But I'm not dealing with Brodetsky. If he's part of your team, then count me out.'

Sammy lost the smile. Only the mean streak was left. He was nose to nose with David as he said, 'Listen, you piece of hippie shit. This isn't the kind of deal you opt in and out of. You think we spent this amount of time, money and potential fucking embarrassment just to let you walk away? This is binding, it's for the rest of your fucking life. You're in Israel now.'

'Like I give a fuck about your politics.'

'You don't get it: you're in the middle of it.' Sammy got his hand under David's elbow, he steered him around a corner, out of the hotel lobby into a TV lounge. He pointed at the blank screen.

'Turn that on to CNN, you'll find out you're the news of the day. Mr International Dope-Smuggling Man, finally run to ground in Israel. And now we've given you an Israeli passport, you won't ever leave. This is the only place in the world you're safe. Why do you think characters like Brodetsky turn up here? He knows we never extradite Jews.'

David knew this was the end of something: at least of his life on the run. But it didn't mean he had to play it the way it was given. He never liked running anyway. From now on, he had a choice: he could go for dignity. Stop letting circumstances push him around.

He said, 'You know what? Fuck you. I'll just go public, tell the story of the hypocrites running the Israeli secret settlement programmes: giving citizenship to any crook who'll help out.' David had his new passport in his hand. He held it open so the mugshot picture was right in Sammy's eyes. 'I've never seen a shittier-looking fake – it stinks. A fucking police photograph. I mean, I even look like a scumbag.' He prodded at the page. 'And my name there, who's ever heard of a Jew called David fucking Ramsbottom?'

Sammy said, 'It's not a fake.'

David paused. He felt the stiff board of the passport between his fingers. But just because it felt real . . .

Sammy shook his head. 'We don't do that. It's a genuine passport.'

It took a moment for David to work it through. 'You mean I really am Jewish?'

'It's the only way it works. The rabbinate take these things seriously. If they ever fucked up their research, they might lose the right to decide who gets to be an Israeli and who doesn't. You're the real deal, your grandmother, her grandmother, all the way back to Pinsk, all of them Jewish. We've got a complete genealogy.'

David had been slow.

'You mean I really am stuck in this fucking country? I can't ever leave?'

'What it means is, we can protect you. You've been gathered up.'

'I'm safe just as long as I don't try anything clever. Otherwise I'm wearing a ball and fucking chain, sat on the next El Al flight to London.'

'Like I said, we don't extradite Jews. Though we could make an exception in your case, just to prove the general rule.'

They joined Mrs Grodman and Brodetsky in the lobby. David had been warned, call the man Shaul Dayan. They were moving around an exhibition of historical photographs, framed around the lobby walls. Mrs Grodman was looking at a photograph from the sixties that seemed to include just about every past Labour leader, save Golda Meir. Ben Gurion was at the front with a young-looking Rabin to his side and Peres at the back. The thing that interested Mrs Grodman, though, they were all wearing the same shirt.

'Look at that, I remember Mr Grodman retailed that shirt at fifteen dollars. That's fifteen dollars six years back, don't ask me what it cost thirty years ago. I don't know. Look at it, short sleeves, open collar, and I tell you now it's square cut, there ain't a lot of extra material hanging at the back. The most simple shirt you ever saw and every single one of these guys is wearing it. I don't know whether to cry because I'm so impressed by the brass-tacks attitude or cry because it's such a cheapskate shirt. And not one of them wearing a necktie.'

Saul Brodetsky alias Dayan said, 'Different times, Mrs Grodman. They wanted to show they were dead straight. Just practical men doing what was necessary.'

'It's what I'm saying. It was PR. They were sending out a message . . . we're in our shirtsleeves because it's a hot country and we're going to work. They're saying, We're not stupid and we're not interested in what we look like. Read it like a book. Like now, what is it Mr Bibi Netanyahu's wearing all the time, a nylon flight jacket with a fur collar. What do you think he's trying to say, running round dressed like a traffic cop? He's interested in security, even if he has to go out himself, swinging a nightstick. As long as you overlook the fact he looks like a soft toy, padded up like that.'

Again, Brodetsky got in first: 'That's an interesting observation, Mrs Grodman.'

'Yeah, well, clothes make the man. It doesn't matter if

he's buying from K Mart or Grodman's or Calvin Klein, everyone is trying to send some kind of message. As long as you remember that, you're always going to beat the guy who believes in just piling it high and selling it cheap. Clothes talk ... and so does money. And every other thing in between, too.'

Sammy said, 'Everything's a sign, Mrs Grodman. You just have to learn to read it.'

Mrs Grodman said, 'I don't need to tell you. You're the guy with the Ivy League education.'

Sammy decided to move things along. If she appreciated a brass-tacks attitude, she wouldn't mind.

'The real estate in Jerusalem, it's all tied up. In three days, we'll have the deeds.'

'So I can go and see it? Take a look at what I'm donating to Israel?'

'In three days. Otherwise, there's the slightest chance the deal might ...' He tried to choose a word and remembered another from his Ivy League days. '... deconstruct.'

Grodman said, 'I'm always hearing that. Have you got any good news?'

'Well, this is David, our man on the ground. You wanted to meet him?'

David was following Sammy's lead in everything. He had been told his main role was to stay silent. He guessed this was one of the moments he was supposed to speak.

Sammy continued, 'David's something of an adventurer, Mrs Grodman.'

'An adventurer. I got to say, that sounds sleazy.'

'Sometimes it is, Mrs Grodman,' David said, backing it up by pulling a hangdog expression that would win

anyone's sympathy. Even the widow of a Florida mens-
wear mogul.

'Sleazy, but he's cooked up a deal with these people, he's
going to get us the house by marrying into their family and
then selling it to us himself.'

Mrs Grodman whistled. 'I don't know what to say, boys.'

Sammy said, 'The way things have been spinning, this is
the most pain-free route. Believe me, Mrs Grodman.'

'Marrying a Muslim?'

David said, 'A Catholic.'

Grodman looked from David to Sammy to Brodetsky:
'A *shiksa?*'

Sammy nodded.

'Well, I guess you're not the first Jewish boy to marry a
shiksa. But how did a Christian girl get her hands on a piece
of Arab real estate?'

David was going to say, because she is an Arab. But
Brodetsky headed him off, saying, 'It's a bizarre, bizarre
country, Mrs Grodman. I got to say, it's half of the charm.'

Mrs Grodman insisted on taking them down to the coffee
shop by the pool. After the third cup of coffee, Sammy
tried to excuse himself by telling Mrs Grodman there were
some details that still needed working out. The old woman
nodded, she only had one last thing to say. She wanted to
tell David that she understood that the secret agent business
was a dirty business. But she wanted to make him promise to
watch out, no one ever got anywhere in the long run unless
they straightened out at the last.

'My late husband, he was in the toughest business in the
world, you can take my word for it. But what he always said,
when you come to closing a deal, you got to look the other

guy in the eye. I don't care how many times you've bluffed up until then, it doesn't matter. Because, I'm telling you, no one wants to do a deal with a sleaze. It doesn't mean they won't. But they prefer that they don't and they're gonna resent the fact if they do. And you get more deals done when people actually want to deal with you. That's true in my game, your game, shirts and ties or secret agents. You understand me?'

David looked the old woman in the eye. 'Yes, ma'am. No matter how shady the business, I've always been honest with my partners.'

Sammy said, 'This is David's last piece of undercover work. From now on, he can be who he is.'

For the past forty-five minutes, David had been thinking: *I'm Jewish?* He didn't even have to consciously think, it just kept popping back in there. There were a few strange things about his grandmother's cousins, he thought. Like they bought new furniture every time they had their house decorated. On the other hand, there were his own parents. They liked to go to church more than they liked anything.

But it was watching Mrs Grodman that brought it home to him. The way she leant forward and made her point by waving a bony finger. She was so much like his own grandmother. Now that he'd promised to be honest, at least at the end of the day, Mrs Grodman was nodding in the same smug way his grandmother always did when she was satisfied she'd made her point.

He knew he'd said the right thing. The old woman had heard enough to walk away, semi-pacified. Her four million dollars were in the best hands available, given the circumstances. Maybe it helped that David stood up straight when she rose to go. Through most of her speech, he'd slouched in his chair, his mouth open. It really was unbelievable how much the old woman reminded him of his grandmother.

Sammy was shaking Mrs Grodman's hand, bidding her goodbye. David waited his turn, his eyes drifting across the pool. A couple of joiners were building a makeshift bridge across the shallow end. They were all but finished, and a couple of women had arrived to decorate the handrail with garlands of flowers. The women had already set up another of those candelabras at the side of the pool. The candelabra called a menorah. It was about time he started using the jargon.

The pool was going to be used for an outdoor wedding ceremony. He could tell because he'd seen a woman who could only be a bride's mother. And she was talking to a rabbi. All these new things he could discover.

Mrs Grodman was shouting at him. 'I said, goodbye, dear.'

He bent down and kissed her on both cheeks. 'Yeah, see you, Mrs Grodman.'

17

It was the afternoon of the wedding. David was dressed in the same suit he wore for Edward Salman's funeral, sitting outside Tony's Ford dealership and scooping seeds from a bowl resting on the settee's arm. He had already eaten too much, his stomach felt full of pulpy gravel. He tried to throw a sharp look at Tony, who was across the forecourt, supervising one of his mechanics over the final polish of the Mercedes. He was bending low over the hood, hands clasped behind his back so that he wouldn't leave finger smudges on the bodywork. Standing like that, he looked like Prince Philip; only fatter and with a better tan.

David shouted, 'If I knew the other car was going to take so long arriving, I would have gone looking for a better suit.'

Tony straightened and looked over at him. 'You had two days to find a better suit. Now will you please relax.' He walked over and lowered himself down next to David on the settee, saying: 'You know, the last time you were like this, it was your wedding day. You were nervous and you were half-stoned, you were slow getting anything ready.'

'Well, it was subconscious. I didn't want to get married.'

'You know, you were lucky the police came. If they hadn't, I think I might have tipped them off. At least this time you're marrying someone wonderful.'

'Except it's not real.'

Tony dropped his voice as he said, 'Whatever happens, it has to look real.'

He pulled back the lapel of his jacket, inviting David to look inside. 'I've got your wedding present ready.'

David saw a brown envelope, realised what it was and said, 'You haven't given Sophia the deeds yet?'

'What's the rush? You're not married yet.' It came out sounding abrupt, even testy. Tony modified his voice, saying: 'Your job is handling the Israelis, concentrate on that. If you take your eyes off them, you think they won't try and rip you off?'

David hadn't yet told anyone he was also an Israeli now. He said, 'I might be staying around a while after this is over. They're promising to look after me.'

'Like they did for the guy in the Bethlehem police station?'

The way Tony snorted, it set off alarms. David said, 'Yeah, like him. What's wrong? I hear he's safe, he's living on the coast somewhere.'

'You didn't hear how they got him out of prison?' Tony paused: it was clear David didn't have a clue. 'His son was killed in a car crash outside Tel Aviv. The Palestinian cops allowed him to go to the funeral on compassionate grounds. That's where the Israelis snatched him, at the funeral of his only son.'

David was appalled, but maybe there was more to it. He said, 'Maybe the son wasn't really dead?'

'That's what everyone thought. That's why the police went and dug up the body. But it was definitely his boy. The only mystery is whether the crash was a real accident. And if it wasn't, who was responsible.'

This was turning into a real Monkey's Paw Scenario; whichever way you turned, you could end up shafted. David couldn't hope to outsmart anyone, but like Tony said, he could stay relaxed. He had a pocket full of ready-rolled joints.

Tony's other mechanic arrived, driving a white Cadillac. The car was strung with ribbons, from the hood mascot to the side windows. The mechanic got out; he was dressed in a grey suit. Tony got to his feet, saying, *One second*. He trotted up the forecourt towards his office.

The Cadillac came from East Jerusalem. Tony had done a deal with a guy he knew there. David didn't know enough about Cadillacs to guess the car's age: it didn't look too bad, maybe a little slanted from left to right but that might be the cement on Tony's lot. David walked over and nodded at his driver. Tony was out of his office now, holding a grey cap in his hand. As he slapped it on the driver's head he said, 'Now it looks plausible.'

David had to admit, Tony had really tried with this wedding. He said, 'And this time, at least I've got a decent best man.'

Tony said, 'My time has come. Hallelulah.'

They hugged, then David got into the car. The driver needed a seven-point turn to get off the lot. Tony stood there, waving through the whole manouevre. As the Cadillac pulled on to the hill that led to Beit Jala's church, there was another hold-up while a tourist coach pulled out of a local hotel. David stared up at the coach windows; each one was filled with an elderly Christian woman in an elderly Christian hat. Take any one of them, it could be his own grandmother. Granny from Pinsk, as he now thought of her. She always liked to lecture him about the importance of being a good boy. She probably did more than anyone to instil a love of criminality in him. He had no idea what made her hide the fact that she was Jewish. Perhaps his sweet, rather stiff grandfather was secretly anti-Jew. He couldn't really believe it. In his experience, if a Lancashire Protestant had any secret feelings for Jews, it was envy. No matter how primitive they tried to make their religion, the Jews were always one step back: they had the edge in anachronism.

He turned away. The sidewalk outside the tourist party's hotel doubled as a terrace. It was paved with marble, slightly raised and fronted with a row of columns. And flashing in and out of the columns was Sister Hilda, a ghost figure seen in nun monochrome. She was trying to get to David's Cadillac and only the back end of the coach stood in her way.

It only took her a few seconds to hoist her skirts and leap up the steps at the front of the terrace, running for the gap between the coach and the Cadillac. When she got to the car, she started slapping on the window. Her meaty hand was making circular motions; it wasn't a blessing, she wanted him to unwind the window.

The driver turned. 'She wants to speak.'

If she had only been a little slower, they would have been clear of the coach. Even now, David was tempted to tell the driver to step on it. But he knew he couldn't. The nun was out to cause trouble. He had to deal with her.

He opened his door. The first thing she said as she sat on

the seat beside him was, 'You cannot do this terrible thing, Father David.'

'It's too late. I've made my decision.' He caught the driver's eye in the mirror and signalled to him to keep moving.

Sister Hilda pressed against him. 'It's not too late. Never. You should pray.'

'I've prayed already. And I think God is with me on this one.'

They were approaching the church. There was a trail of cars leading up to the church gates and the police had come out of the station opposite to try to deal with the traffic problem. David's driver went wide, on to the wrong side of the road, intending to jump the queue. David leaned forward, and told him to drive on.

'What?'

He couldn't hear over the sound of the nun, who had begun by mumbling but was now getting louder and more dogmatic.

David turned on her. 'Will you shut up.'

'No, Father. Sophia Khouri has bewitched you, but it won't last. Do not forget your vows.'

She was clinging on to his arm. David shrugged violently and managed to pull free. He almost thought he had lost it to her, her grip was so tight. He leant right in the driver's ear. 'Go on, up to the checkpoint.'

'What?'

David said, 'Oh, please.' The driver didn't seem to have much English. At least he wouldn't know what Sister Hilda was saying about Sophia. David waved his hand. 'Zone C, Zone C.'

Just past the church, the road grew even steeper as it twisted up to the place where the soldier had stopped them, on their way back from the concert at Bir Zeit University.

'She has provoked you sexually, but sex is nothing. Your chastity belongs to God.'

'Please, Sister Hilda. This isn't about sex.'

'It's all Sophia has. I am a nun, not an idiot. She has already given herself to you – I understand. But it's not too late to confess.'

They were drawing close to the checkpoint. David hammered a hand on the back of the driver's seat. 'Stop here.'

When he jumped out of the car, she tried to follow him out. He turned and said, 'It's okay. I'm not going to run away.'

He pulled open the driver's door. 'Get out. I'll take it from here.'

'What?'

David hauled him out by the shoulder. He was lucky that the boy was so slight, he weighed nothing. 'I need the car. I need to talk to the nun.'

The boy was a Muslim, he wouldn't know why David needed privacy with a nun just before he got married. If he looked unhappy, he was more worried about the safety of the car than about the nun.

'You will look after the Cadillac importantly?'

David nodded. He promised.

Sister Hilda would not stay in the back seat. She insisted on riding up front with him. As David drove past the soldier in his concrete shelter, she began to get serious. The way she spoke, it was like a hard insistent pecking. 'You made a promise. You presented the Lord with your chastity and you fell. That doesn't matter. If you repent, you can renew your vows. '

David followed the line of the hill above the new bypass, past the curve in the road where he had spied on Brodetsky's smuggling operation. He had his Israeli passport in his hand when he reached the next checkpoint at the old Green Line. The soldier said *Shalom* and glanced at the cover. He waved him through without asking why David had a nun with him.

David planned to dump Sister Hilda in the forest, well inside Israel. He was worried that she must be getting suspicious by now. He was hoping he wouldn't have to get too violent. When he parked the Cadillac in a picnic spot, he just strode out into the trees. He left it to her to decide, was she going to follow him. As he walked, he started to sing. He didn't know many hymns; he decided to sing *My Sweet Lord*.

David always tended to slip a little of the Elvis reverb on to his voice when he sang. It was a way of protecting himself from ridicule, he would prove he could send himself up. But his voice was quite good, he only needed to exert himself. As he reached the Krishna lines, *Hare Rama*, even he couldn't tell that he was stretching for the notes, he just seemed to pluck them out of the air. Walking beneath the pines, his voice was as warm and rich as the scent around him. He was swinging in and out of the perfumed shadows. Finally, he was beginning to find his centre and relax. He remembered now, as a dope-smuggling man, the trick was to stay calm. Let the madness escalate, never let it worry you. And always have a supply at home.

He sat down on the stump of an old tree and took one of his ready-rolled numbers out of his pocket. *My Sweet Lord*.

Sister Hilda came out of the trees. He asked her, did she smoke?

She shook her head.

'Do you want to try?'

He could tell she was wavering. He lit the joint and got it going. Breathing out a mouthful of smoke, he said, 'Please. It would make me happy.'

She reached out her hand. He passed the glowing joint over, holding it upright between his fingers. She took a puff and coughed. David nodded at her, encouraging her to take another.

She sucked again, staggering slightly.

David said, 'I have to tell you about this priest thing, Sister. Something I need to confess. Is a nun allowed to take confession if a priest is unavailable? I think I read somewhere that they are.'

Sister Hilda looked blankly at him. She still had the joint in her fingers but she wasn't smoking. Her face seemed a little green but that could have been the reflection of the trees on her pale skin.

'I want to confess that I never was a priest. It was all a silly mistake. And the funny thing is, it started through a confession.' He felt as though he should begin again. He wanted to say: *Once upon a time, there was a little girl and she was running through a beautiful garden. But the little girl was very sad.*

It was coming back to him now. How tiny Sophia seemed as she tugged at the back of his robes. Her face screwed up with tears as she asked him to hear her confession. The more he tried to hurry on, pulling free of her grip, the more determined she became. She would not let go. Whatever happened, he was going to hear her out. He dragged her halfway across the garden and she just kept repeating that she had sinned.

So he said, *Go on, my child.*

She told him that she had lost her father. He stared down at her, her face like a prune, so clenched that it had a thousand different creases going in every direction and all of them were filled with tears. Seeing someone so upset, he began to think that he had misheard her. *She had lost her father?* It didn't sound like something she should confess to a priest. If she needed help, there were enough policemen around for her to talk to. David could see them collecting at the park gates ahead of him, forming a cordon.

But Sophia didn't say that she had lost her father, she said that she had left him. He remembered it all now. She was saying that her father was so trusting, he thought she was a little angel. But she wasn't.

David dropped his head and turned away from the gates. He didn't want the police to see his face. Sophia turned with him, her fist wrapped in his robes so he couldn't get away from her. But there was nowhere to go, the other gates on Carlos Place were now manned by policemen. David could only look around, see if there was another possibility. There was a slim alleyway to his right, leading between the church and a mansion block on to Farm Street. He turned for that but, already, he could see the blue, orange and white of a police car.

He said, 'Let's sit on this bench.'

He wondered, where was the girl's mother? Sophia only sniffled and shook her head when he asked. She couldn't face her mother now, not after what she had done.

David was still working out the odds. There was a moment when he even considered taking the girl as a hostage but he immediately dismissed it as stupid. The best he could hope for was that she might act as camouflage. He told her, maybe she should start from the beginning. But then her story dripped out so slowly between her tears that he had to tell her to cut to the chase. This was confession, she wasn't pitching a biopic. David was slow to realise why Sophia had started so far back, at her birth. She told him that when she was born, her father was in prison and the men hurt him so much there, he thought he would never see his baby daughter. And now, look. Look at her. What a nasty person she was.

David put his hand around Sophia's shoulder and told her she wasn't nasty. He could tell she was a very nice young lady, and he was sure her dad thought so too. In fact, if she ran home now, her father would probably be waiting to tell her that.

That only made Sophia cry more. Her father wasn't at home. He had been arrested. She had been watching, hiding on the far side of the road, when the police came for him and took him away. David asked her where this was exactly, it had to be somewhere close by. She told him *Selfridges*. David guessed that her father had been caught shoplifting but immediately revised it: Sophia had been shoplifting, but it was her father who took the fall.

Her mother had sent them shopping for a wedding present – David's wedding present, though he didn't know that. Elias Khouri had arthritis and walked so slowly, Sophia was always racing ahead. There were less than twenty minutes left now and she desperately wanted to find some jewellery for herself. She had been told that the man getting married was rich and there was going to be a big banquet. She knew she needed something special, she just wasn't sure what. As she ran between the counters, Elias plodded behind, swinging the carrier bag that held David's cruet set. When Sophia saw a pearl-beaded headband, like a mini-tiara, she thought she'd found the perfect thing. She waited for her father to catch up and then slipped the headband off the tree on the counter and dropped it into the carrier bag along with David's present. Her father didn't see a thing. He was looking at his watch and saying that it was time to meet her mother at the church.

As they were leaving, Sophia began to get worried. She told her father to wait for her. She just needed to go to the bathroom, she would meet him by the exit. She was having second thoughts about the headband. She wondered if she didn't prefer the beaded choker she had seen earlier, on a different counter.

Sophia was pushing back through the shopping crowds, the choker stuck in the back of her skirt, when she saw the security guards surround her father, just the other side of the exit on Oxford Street. He was shaking, trying to make himself heavy so they couldn't drag him back across the threshold of the store. He was shouting her name.

David said, 'After they took him away, you waited outside for him. That's when you saw the cops arrive?'

Sophia nodded. She was trembling less now that she had finished her story.

'And the problem is, your father won't grass you up?'

He had to explain *grass*. When she understood, she nodded. She was sure her father would take the blame.

David told her, 'Come on.' He pulled her to her feet. 'I need to think this through and I think better walking.'

As they went down the alleyway, four policemen pushed past them in the opposite direction. David shouted at them to be careful, what was the almighty rush.

On the street, there was a semicircle of armed police standing by a minibus. David paused and looked down at Sophia. He wondered if he should give her a Hail Mary, but he wasn't sure what one was, whether it was too big or too small for the crime. Instead, he said: 'Forget about the stealing, you'll probably grow out of that. If you want forgiveness for the rest, that's up to your father – so be nice to him.'

He pointed her towards the armed police.

'Ask them where the nearest police station is, they'll probably give you a lift.'

Sophia distracted the police and David slipped away, hurrying in the direction of Piccadilly.

He didn't give Sister Hilda the story. He had to respect the secrecy of the confession. Anyway, he was sure she would never be able to take it in. The green in her face was spreading. It wasn't the fault of the light through the trees, she was feeling sick.

David said, 'I can't be a Catholic priest because I'm Jewish.'

He had his hand on his flies.

'Look.'

As he pulled down the zipper, Sister Hilda screamed, '*Nein.*' She spun round and slapped straight into a tree. As far as David could tell, she was out cold.

David parked in the courtyard of the church. Looking through the open doors, he could see it was almost full. But it was still only five to three; his wedding was scheduled for three o'clock so he had a few minutes. He slipped into the church through the small door and headed for Father George's den. He wanted to make sure that Sister Hilda hadn't come round earlier and warned the old man off the ceremony. As he ran down the corridor, he heard footsteps behind him, then Tony's voice calling his name.

He hissed back, 'Wait.'

David held his finger to his lips. He was outside the door now. He pushed it open a crack and saw Father George slumped in a chair. He was either asleep or in a stupor. As far as David could see, the priest was his usual self. So that was one less problem to worry about.

'What is it, Tony?'

'Elias is sick, so I've promised to give Sophia away.'

'You can't do that – you're the best man.' David stared through the gap in the curtain that separated the corridor from the nave. It gave him a view of the whole congregation. He said, 'Look around the church. It's not like I've got any choice. I don't know anyone but you.'

'Sophia said she'll get Yusuf to do it.' Tony gave a helpless look. 'I have to go, she's outside now.'

David watched as Tony flapped through the curtain and headed up a side aisle, around the congregation. The row of seats facing the altar rail was empty, both the bride's side and the groom's. David wondered if he should take his own seat. It had to be time. The sun shining through the church doors turned into a solid block of daylight, cutting the church in half. Anyone standing inside the beam was a silhouette. When a figure came wandering down and slipped on to the second chair at the front, David assumed it was Yusuf. He'd taken the traditional best man's seat, right by David's empty chair. Then the figure turned, picking out David behind the curtain. It was Shadi. As David stared back, Shadi patted his breast pocket, going into a pantomime of checking that the ring was safe. He did the whole performance: shock, horror, *it's gone*. Then broke into his trademark grin as he held the ring up in his other hand.

A voice behind him said, 'Where have you been?'

David spun round. Sammy Ben Naim was standing behind him, beckoning from the shadows of the corridor.

David hissed, 'Everything's on track.'

'It had better be. The rest of your life is going to depend on it.'

'Come on. Aren't you taking this too personally? What are you on, fifty per cent of Brodetsky's commission or something?'

Sammy jabbed David in the ribs. 'Listen, shithead. Maybe this is a joke to you, you don't know what you're doing, you're just happy staying stoned. But this is serious. There's no politics, no negotiating and no peace deals until we've taken back Jerusalem. You don't think peace is important? There is no more important fucking work, you shitbag. It's all down to me. Until I'm through, no one gets to do anything.'

'Okay. Sorry.' David rubbed at his ribs. The way Sammy had fingered him, he could have done internal damage.

'Has Sophia got the title to the apartment?'

'It's with Tony, she's with him. Everything is cool.'

'Well, make sure the marriage goes through, and it's all yours.'

David took that figuratively. Once they were married, he guessed the apartment would be legally defined as common property. He said, 'Don't worry. She will definitely sell, there's no doubt about it. All she wants is to get the cash, get the divorce and get out of the country.'

'She won't be getting divorced.'

David gave him a thin smile. 'I appreciate that, I really do. But I'm not fooling myself. She can do a lot better than me.'

Sammy sneered. 'I'm not talking about that, you idiot. I'm saying she cannot get divorced from an Israeli. The rabbis make the laws – so only a man can get a divorce.'

David was ready to say, *Look around: this is a Catholic church, for Christ's sake*. He said, 'This is not a Jewish wedding, in case you didn't notice. No one here cares about rabbis.'

'It doesn't matter. So long as it's a legal wedding, that's good enough for the state. You two will be married.'

'So if it counts as a civil wedding, she can get a civil divorce anywhere in the world.'

'She can. But we won't recognise it. Not until Grodman's charity has the title to the apartment, then you have my personal permission to grant her a divorce. If you want to, that is.'

'You had this all worked out.'

Sammy was right in his face now. 'This is a government job, I'm a trained official. What do you think we do? We leave half of it to chance? It's not some kind of comedy caper. We don't gamble with the future of our country.'

When Sammy finally took a step back, it was almost as though he had been holding David up, just through this terrific force of presence. Now David had a little space in which to breathe, he sagged.

'I'll be watching. Just make sure you get your lines right. Anything the priest asks, you answer *I do*.'

The organ rumbled and groaned, gathering itself together before a few true notes filtered out. David looked back into the heart of the church. Tony was there in the doorway. The veiled figure in white had to be Sophia. David thought he would be able to recognise her anywhere, just from the way she held herself.

He said, 'One moment, you fucking smartarse. I've got fresh demands.'

Sammy turned back. 'Yeah?'

'I'm serious. You don't do what I want, you can either shoot me here or I turn myself in to the British embassy. Either way.'

Sammy didn't sound alarmed. 'So what are these demands?'

'I want Sophia's neighbours stopped. You have to go for Brodetsky and smash his whole racket.'

Sammy said, 'Smash his eggs? It's funny, you didn't try to get me to do that before now. Once someone has sorted out her neighbours, there's no longer any pressure on the Khouris – so there's no reason for Sophia to marry you.'

David felt about an inch high. Sammy was right. His voice came out like a whisper. 'But will you do it anyway, please?'

'Why not?'

Sammy watched the service from the back of the church. He rarely spoke Arabic and he was far from fluent. But hearing the Catholic liturgy, spoken in classical Arabic with all its priestly gravity, it sounded very different to the street language he was used to hearing around him. It reminded him of the way his father spoke at times. In the souk, when he went shopping with his father as a child, Simon Ben Naim spoke in the Palestinian dialect he had swapped for his native Algerian Arabic. But when he got the chance, say he met an educated Arab, he liked to speak the classical language. There were other times, too, he would read a piece of poetry out loud, or a phrase from a book review in the newspaper, and then the house would ring with his voice. It was weird to be so powerfully reminded of his father by this old priest. But Sammy found himself being drawn into the service. Minutes went by when he lost his wits and had to jerk his head back to keep lookout.

He sat at the open doors to the church because it gave him the best view: he could see down the aisle to check on David and, also, across the church's carpark to the gate and the road beyond. This was Zone B and the Israeli Defence Force could only patrol if they had a Palestinian escort. Sammy had arranged for them to circle round the church at exactly this time, but not be too obvious. The sound of the heavy wheels on the road brought him out of his reverie. He looked over and saw the patrol pass by, shadowed by a single PA vehicle. As that last truck disappeared, a procession of monks came into view. The leading figures were just about to enter the church gates.

Sammy had an agent stationed just the other side of the doors; another Sephardic Jew like him, dressed in cheap clothes and wearing a moustache like an Arab. Sammy beckoned him over and told him to try to find out what the monks wanted. 'But be subtle. There are a lot of Palestinian cops around.'

The Beit Jala police were lounging against the church gates, looking as though they were simply on a cigarette break from the station. As the monks swished by, they stared at them, bemused.

Sammy waited inside the doors for the report. He suddenly became aware that his foot was tapping automatically against the stone floor. He was more keyed up by this whole affair than he realised. He forced his foot flat to the floor, keeping his focus on the figures at the bottom of the aisle. The still white clouds of Sophia's veil, David's shaggy head, turned sideways to his young bride. Then Sophia's Uncle Tony, who seemed to be playing the part of the father. That only left the best man.

Sammy squinted. He could be wrong but the best man looked a lot like Shadi Mansur, a coming man in the Palestinian administration. He was a fairly minor character but Sammy knew that he would be worth watching. From this angle, Sammy couldn't make a definite ID.

The priest was getting to the section with the vows. The service slowed right down as he began translating everything he said: a line of Arabic and then a line of English as he asked if you, David Samuel Ramsbottom, take Sophia Elias Ramzi Khouri to be your wife lawfully wedded . . .

The other agent came back with information on the monks. He whispered, 'Someone has told them that a brother is about to commit a terrible sin.'

'Where?'

'Here.' He pointed down the aisle. 'They think your man is a priest. They're going to stop the wedding.'

Sammy looked at the wrecking party: a group of elderly types, led by a young Arab man, but they looked determined. And they were almost inside the church. Sammy made a snap decision – he was going to shut the monks out. There couldn't be more than a few minutes of the service left, he was certain about that. He said to his assistant, 'Get the other door.'

The doors were heavy wood with studs of metal reinforcing every strut. The monks would need a battering ram to get through and they clearly didn't have one. If they had, they wouldn't be able to lift it. Sammy found the catch for the rod that held his side of the door open. He uprooted it from its hole. A woman touched his arm and asked him in Arabic what he was doing. He tried to ignore her.

She pulled harder, telling him that it was forbidden. Her fingers were tightening on his elbow. He shook her off but she came straight back at him.

'The doors must be open during a wedding.'

The procession of monks was getting closer. The young Arab at their front was urging them on in both French and English. Sammy's assistant had got his door closed but Sammy was still struggling with his old woman. When he shook her off again, she fell to the stones with a cry.

Father George was almost at the part where Sophia had to say *I do*. He was deaf, if not senile, and he was the only person in the church still unaware of the struggle at the door. When the old woman cried out, even David tore his eyes away from Sophia and looked at the door. He saw the brown and black figures in their robes. He recognised the monk that looked like Tony Iommi, surrounded by all the other brothers he'd met at Edward Salman's funeral. He just wasn't sure why they were here, or why Yusuf Salman was urging them on.

Yusuf was standing with his body wedged between the church doors, standing his ground while Sammy Ben Naim tried to crush him.

David turned back to Father George. The priest was speaking English, saying . . . 'to cherish and to obey for the length that you both shall live.'

Sophia was silent. She turned to David, smiling.

He said, 'Your line. And please hurry.'

She looked over her shoulder. Yusuf had forced the doors open. The last of the monks had joined the procession and was now pottering down the aisle.

David said again, 'Please, Sophia . . .'

For the past twenty minutes he had turned this moment over and over in his mind. He was almost convinced, if they were married he would find a way to be so wonderful and so loving and whatever else it took that she wouldn't even want to divorce him.

She shook her head. 'Sorry. But I'm going to take my time over this.'

And he realised that neither Sister Hilda nor Yusuf had tipped off the monks. It was Sophia. She really was an amazing catch . . . she was so far and away too good for him.

Shadi nudged David. 'Okay, here's the new plan.'

Shadi patted his pocket again, as though he was looking for the ring. He couldn't be, though, Father George was holding that on a neatly embroidered cushion, still going on with the marriage ceremony as though nothing strange was happening.

'Here.' Shadi pulled a heavy-looking automatic pistol out of his jacket. 'I'm arresting you.'

He pushed the gun to the side of David's head, saying: 'Nice and easy.' He used his other hand to twist David's arm behind his back.

It was an uncomfortable way to walk, but they made it up the aisle. The whole congregation turned to look at them. They passed the group of fifteen or more monks, then Sammy Ben Naim at the doorway and Yusuf, who was grinning for the first time since his father's death. Shadi led him on, through the carpark and past the Palestinian cops who were grouped around the church gates. Shadi didn't even slacken off as they crossed the main road. Beit Jala police station was right ahead of them, its doors open and waiting.

18

David was eating and sleeping normally at last. There were still external pressures but the business of being recognised everywhere he went, that was beginning to stop. The news-papers had moved on, they hadn't printed his photograph in almost a fortnight. And without his picture constantly in front of them, the Israeli public were finally losing interest. It helped that he had grown a beard and changed his name again. He was now called David Cohen.

He slipped off a shoe and let the sand inside fall out on to the pavement. It was Tel Aviv sand, accidentally carried to Jerusalem. Tel Aviv was now his home town.

There had been a period when he could read his story every day. The famous drug smuggler who had been captured by the Palestinians and who now owed his freedom to the bravery and intelligence of the Israeli Secret Service. Who else could have broken him out of a Palestinian police cell and spirited him into Israel? The Americans had been giving anonymous briefings, pointing the finger directly at Mossad.

The newspapers described him as the Jewish Howard Marks. He had read it so often, he had begun to think of himself as mildly Jewish, or was that mellowly Jewish? That morning, as he was spitting out his mouthwash, he'd caught sight of himself in the mirror and said, '*Oy vey*.' He still had no idea what it meant, but it felt like the right response. Then he'd boiled up a good pot of coffee, eaten a breakfast bagel and decided to catch the Egged bus to Jerusalem and visit Sophia. He hadn't seen her in a little over two and a half months. He calculated that she only had ten days left in Jerusalem before her permit expired and she would be evicted from the apartment in the Old City.

David crossed the road from Jaffa Street at an angle, walking towards New Gate. He was sure he could remember where the apartment was. He had the address, although addresses didn't much matter in the Old City. The Palestinians didn't seem to use street names, they just described what was on a particular street instead. It worked for them, confused everyone else.

Back when he was a celebrity, the previous month, David had found there were definite advantages. For instance, when the British and Americans demanded for him to be extradited, he was approached by a big law firm who asked if they could handle his case for free. The other good news was that his family found out where he was and even took an interest. Now his sister was due to fly in for a visit and, the real surprise, he was actually looking forward to it. When he told her he had changed his name, she laughed. She had changed hers, too, it was why she got married. She told him, if she'd been born a man, she would have gone on the run just so she could travel under an assumed name.

Strange to say, the name Cohen wasn't such a big leap. He'd always been happy with the name Preston. It was a corruption of *Priest Town* and the Cohens, so he'd been told, were once the Jewish priests. So there was a pleasing bit of inter-translation there.

He buzzed Sophia on the intercom she'd had fitted below the old bell-pull. She recognised his voice immediately. He loved hers, the faint French in her English, the wisp of Arabic carried on her breath.

She said, 'Wait there.'

He waited.

His escape from a Palestinian police cell was a much more amateurish operation than the Americans suspected. The Chief of the Beit Jala police let him out of the back door; Sophia was waiting there for him. When she returned his Fiat hire car to the firm in East Jerusalem, he was hiding in the trunk. They said goodbye to each other at Damascus Gate. He headed to the new offices of the *Jerusalem Post* to tell the world a version of his story, Sophia went to supervise the builders working on her new apartment. She had the title deeds with her when she left him. David asked her if Tony minded that she'd stolen his apartment? She told him that there wasn't much he could do about it. Anyway, she planned to pay him rent.

Sophia opened the door. David looked at her. She was stood on the second step so her face was level with his. She looked too young for him; he wondered why he hadn't seen that before.

He said, 'So how's business?'

'Come up and see.'

Sophia's plan to turn the apartment into a cybercafé must have worked. As he climbed the stairs, David could hear the tap of keyboards and the squeal of phone lines connecting to the Web. He could also smell coffee.

Ahead of him, Sophia said, 'I knew it would work. E-mail could have been designed for Palestinians.'

'Because they all live abroad,' he said. 'Except for you. How are you doing?'

'I'm still here. Though it's not easy.'

There were seven people in the apartment: one boy behind the food counter and six people working on Sophia's four computers. She was full to capacity.

'Do you like living in Jerusalem?'

She nodded. 'It's fine. How do you like Tel Aviv?'

He actually did. Although his lawyer wanted him to move somewhere quieter, like Netanya. Or maybe the middle of the Negev Desert. He believed there was too much scope to get into trouble in Tel Aviv and was advising David to find somewhere else to live until all his appeals were over. The lawyer said, *It's a small country but it's big enough*. David nodded. He was determined to make the best of it, he was there for life.

Sophia said, 'You'll definitely win your appeal.'

'Not a doubt,' David said. The coalition of groups backing him sounded unlikely but they made his position impregnable. Even his lawyer was surprised when a settlers' group got two separate religious parties to swing behind him. It made them look good, fighting for the rights of a Jewish man who had been convicted *in absentia* in three different countries. But maybe they had other reasons. Saul Brodetsky was making himself useful, helping David in order to spite Sammy and the Housing Department. Since the Grodman deal fell through and his egg racket was rumbled, Brodetsky had been running a vendetta against Ben Naim.

David said, 'What are you going to do?'

'When they come for me?'

He nodded.

'I don't know,' she said. 'But I'm going to do something. You have to keep pushing back.'

BETHLEHEM–LONDON 1997–1999

Acknowledgments

I would like to thank the Sansour family for their help and their hospitality during the writing of this novel.

I would also like to thank Nicholas Guyatt and recommend his book, *The Absence of Peace* (Zed Books), an authoritative account of the Oslo peace deal and its death.

DAVID MITCHELL

GHOSTWRITTEN

'David Mitchell's first novel is a firework display, shooting off in a dozen different narrative directions . . . the assurance and panache is truly remarkable . . . A remarkable novel by a young writer of remarkable talent. Sit back and soak up the voices' *Observer*

'Every one of these pages deserves and demands to be read and re-read . . . an astonishing debut' *Independent*

'This is one of the best first novels I've read for a long time . . . I couldn't put it down . . . And it's even better the second time' *Mail on Sunday*

'A remarkable first novel . . . Eastern, ethereal, yet flecked with flashes of commando grit, this multi-faceted novel is full of surprises' *Time Out*

'Mitchell pulls off an extraordinarily assured novel of global reach and millennial ambition' *Esquire*

'David Mitchell's *Ghostwritten* is a boundless, fully imagined novel . . . This is the best modern novel I've read for some time' *Express*

∫

SCEPTRE

JAKE ARNOTT

THE LONG FIRM

'This gangster novel set (mainly) in sixties London is one of the smartest, funniest and original novels you will read all year. It is a gloriously accomplished re-creation of the city in the era of the Kray Twins when aristocratic politicians mixed freely with gangsters, rent boys and actresses of dubious repute in a decadent demi-monde. Arnott is quite brilliant at excavating the cultural minutiae of the time to bring the period vividly to life' *Independent on Sunday*

'Truly fascinating . . . Arnott's ability to powerfully resurrect an era is astonishing' *Guardian*

'This is pulp fiction so polished as to be immaculate' *New Statesman*

'*The Long Firm* manages to hook you from the first. It is compulsive reading, powerful writing with an evocative feel for the bleaker side of the Swinging Sixties' *The Times*

'Gripping . . . slumming it doesn't get much better than this' *Time Out*

∫

SCEPTRE

A selection of other books from Sceptre

Ghostwritten	David Mitchell	0 340 73975 4	£6.99	☐
The Long Firm	Jake Arnott	0 340 74878 8	£6.99	☐
Eating Cake	Stella Duffy	0 340 71563 4	£6.99	☐
One Good Thing	Rebecca Stowe	0 340 67191 2	£6.99	☐
Daytrippers	Hugh Brune	0 340 71875 7	£6.99	☐

All Sceptre books are available from your local bookshop or newsagent, or can be ordered direct from the publisher. Just tick the titles you want and fill in the form below. Prices and availability subject to change without notice.

Hodder & Stoughton Books, Cash Sales Department, Bookpoint, 39 Milton Park, Abingdon, OXON, OX14 4TD, UK. E-mail address: order@bookpoint.co.uk. If you have a credit card you may order by telephone – (01235) 400414.

Please enclose a cheque or postal order made payable to Bookpoint Ltd to the value of the cover price and allow the following for postage and packing:
UK & BFPO – £1.00 for the first book, 50p for the second book, and 30p for each additional book ordered up to a maximum charge of £3.00.
OVERSEAS & EIRE – £2.00 for the first book, £1.00 for the second book, and 50p for each additional book.

Name _____

Address_____

_____

_____

If you would prefer to pay by credit card, please complete:
Please debit my Visa/Access/Diner's Card/American Express (delete as applicable) card no:

Signature _____

Expiry Date_____

If you would NOT like to receive further information on our products please tick the box. ☐